GLADLY THE CROSS-EYED BEAR

GLADLY THE CROSS-EYED BEAR

Ed McBain

1926-

G.K. Hall & Co. • Chivers Press
Thorndike, Maine USA   Bath, Avon, England

This Large Print edition is published by G.K. Hall & Co., USA and by Chivers Press, England.

Published in 1996 in the U.S. by arrangement with Warner Books, Inc.

Published in 1997 in the U.K. by arrangement with Hodder & Stoughton Ltd.

U.S.   Hardcover   0-7838-1899-8   (Core Collection Edition)
U.S.   Softcover   0-7838-1900-5
U.K.   Hardcover   0-7451-5395-X   (Windsor Large Print)
U.K.   Softcover   0-7451-3852-7   (Paragon Large Print)

The text of this Large Print edition is unabridged.
Other aspects of the book may vary from the original edition.

Set in 16 pt. Bookman Old Style by Minnie B. Raven.

Printed in the United States on permanent paper.

British Library Cataloguing in Publication Data available

Library of Congress Cataloging in Publication Data

McBain, Ed, 1926–
    Gladly the cross-eyed bear / Ed McBain.
        p.   cm.
    ISBN 0-7838-1899-8 (lg. print : hc)
    ISBN 0-7838-1900-5 (lg. print : sc)
    1. Large type books. I. Title.
    [PS3515.U585G59   1996b]
    813'.54—dc20   96-21105

This is for
Richard Dannay

1

In the state of Florida, it doesn't matter if it's day or night as concerns the burglary statutes. You can go in at any hour, it doesn't affect the punishment. What matters is if you're armed or if you assault someone, that's Burglary One, and they can put you away for as long as the rest of your natural life. If the structure you enter happens to be a dwelling or if somebody's on the premises when you go in, why that's a Burg Two, and they can lock you up for fifteen years.

Warren was going in during the daytime — if she ever got the hell out of there — and he wasn't armed, though he did own a license to carry. The condo was a dwelling, so if he got caught in there he was looking at a max of fifteen because in the state of Florida, if you stealthily entered any structure or conveyance without consent of the owner or occupant, that was considered prima facie evidence of entering with intent to commit an offense.

But he had to get in there, anyway.

If only she would hurry up and go about her business.

He turned on the car radio.

I had filed my complaint in Calusa's federal court for the Middle District of Florida, asking for an order to show cause. Judge Anthony Santos had signed a temporary restraining order and had set a hearing for the twelfth day of September. A U.S. marshal had then served papers on Brett and Etta Toland, the owners of Toyland, Toyland, ordering their appearance at the hearing. It was now nine o'clock on the morning of the twelfth, a blistering hot Tuesday in Calusa, Florida.

The first thing Santos said to me was, "How are you feeling, Matthew?"

I wished people would stop asking me how I was feeling.

Or what it had felt like.

It had felt like all the lights suddenly coming on after a power failure. One moment there was utter darkness below, while above a raging electrical storm flashed intermittent white tendrils of lightning and boomed ugly blue thunder. I was standing in a deep black pit slowly filling with oily black water that rose inexorably to my waist, and then my chest, and then my throat. I was chained to the walls of this fathomless black pit while above lightning crackled and thunder roared and the fetid black water inched up toward my mouth

8

and then my nostrils. And all at once there was a crashing bolt of lightning and a shattering thunderclap so close they seemed to be inside the pit itself, shaking its wet stone walls, filling my eyes and my head with bursting sound and blinding incandescence and . . .

With a mighty leap, I sprang out of the pit.

That's what it had felt like for me.

Maybe if you came out of a coma five months ago, it was different for you.

"I'm fine, Your Honor," I said.

"Are both sides ready?" Santos asked.

"Matthew Hope, representing the plaintiff, Elaine Commins."

"Sidney Brackett, representing the defendant, Toyland, Toyland."

Brackett was Calusa's best man for legal matters pertaining to copyright or trademark, famous for having successfully defended the landmark Opal Oranges infringement suit. I was Calusa's best man for all seasons, famous for having got shot twice — once in the shoulder and once in the chest — last April. I'm fine now. Really. I'm *fine,* goddamn it!

"I've reviewed the complaint, the affidavits, and the legal briefs from both sides," Santos said, "so I think we can do without any lengthy opening statements. I hope you've explained to your respective clients . . ."

9

"Yes, Your Honor . . ."

"Yes, Your . . ."

". . . that the purpose of this hearing is to determine whether Toyland, Toyland — hereinafter referred to as Toyland — should be enjoined on a preliminary basis from further production, distribution or sale of a teddy bear they call Gladys the Cross-Eyed Bear, for which Ms. Commins is claiming copyright, trademark, and trade dress infringement. It is your burden, Ms. Commins, to prove ownership of a valid copyright and trademark for the bear you call *Gladly*, and — as to Count I — to further prove unlawful copying of protected components. As for Counts II and III, it is your burden to prove infringement of the trademark and trade dress. Does everyone understand this?"

"Yes, Your Honor, this was all explained to my client."

"My clients as well, Your Honor."

"As I'm sure counsel has further explained," Santos said, "*ideas* cannot be copyrighted. Protection is afforded only to the *expression* of ideas. For example, it's not enough to show that both plaintiff and defendant used the *idea* of a cross-eyed bear whose vision is corrected by eyeglasses. In order to prove copyright infringement, it must be shown that the *expression* of this idea was copied. The essence of copyright infringement lies not in the defendant's taking of the general idea or theme of the plaintiff's work, but in the taking of the particular *manner* in which the plaintiff has expressed those ideas in the copyrighted work.

"Similarly, in order to prove trademark and trade dress infringement, it must be shown that a similar use of names and design features would be likely to cause confusion in the marketplace. The design features of a product may be given trade dress protection, but only if they are inherently distinctive or have achieved secondary meaning in the marketplace. Is all of that clearly understood?"

"Yes, Your Honor."

"Yes, Your Honor."

"Has it also been explained that a *permanent* injunction cannot be granted until after a trial on the merits?"

"Yes, Your Honor."

"Yes, Your . . ."

"Before we proceed, then, I should mention that the Court fully recognizes the exigencies of the case, Christmas being right around the corner, so to speak, in terms of getting one of these bears into the stores, whichever party may prevail. At the same time, and exactly *because* of the very real and pressing commercial considerations for both sides, the Court does not intend to be rushed into any decision."

On the other side of the courtroom, seated at the defense table with his clients, Sidney Brackett sat stone-faced. Or bored. Or both. A squat chubby little man who bore an unfortunate resemblance to Newt Gingrich, he sat flanked by two of the more attractive people on this planet, Mr. and Mrs. Brett Toland, accused teddy-bear thieves.

"I should also mention that the rules of procedure in a hearing are identical to those in a trial," Santos said. "There is no jury, but everything else is the same. The plaintiff presents *his* . . ."

I was thinking that everyone in the world already *knew* all this, at least insofar as it bore similarities to *criminal* law. Everyone in the world had watched the Simpson trial for the past twenty-two years, six months, three weeks and twelve days and knew all this procedure stuff even better than I myself did. I was thinking it was too bad there wasn't a jury here because then ordinary citizens who weren't lawyers could catch any mistakes I made, and maybe write to tell me all about what a lousy lawyer I was, I just *loved* getting "Gotcha!" mail. When I woke up at Good Samaritan Hospital, in fact, I'd found a pile of letters from strangers who felt I was somehow responsible for having got myself shot, and somehow derelict in not coming out of the coma soon enough to suit them. Actually, I'd have enjoyed popping off that table in ten minutes flat, but medical problems prevented me from doing so. Better yet, I would have preferred not having the medical problems to begin with. Even better, I would have preferred not getting shot at all. *You* try getting shot sometime, and I'll write *you* a letter when you refuse to come out of a goddamn coma.

Then again, people keep telling me I seem a bit crotchety since I woke up.

". . . a *direct* examination of each witness," Santos was saying, "followed by the defense's *cross*-examination. The plaintiff is then allowed a *re*direct, and the defense a *re*cross. After the plaintiff has rested its case, the defense then calls *its* witnesses, and the same rules of questioning and requestioning apply. If there are any questions from either of the contesting parties, please let me hear them now. I want everyone to understand exactly what's about to transpire."

There were no questions.

"In that case, Mr. Hope," Santos said, "if you're ready with your first witness, we'll begin."

Hurry up and come out of there, Warren thought.

He usually drove a beat-up old grayish

13

Ford, which was a very good car for some-one in his profession to drive unless he wanted everyone in the state of Florida to know just what he was up to. Trouble was, she *knew* the Ford, had in fact been *in* the car more times than he could count, so he couldn't very easily park it up the street from her condo without her making it in a minute. Black man parked in a dilapidated gray Ford, who else could it be but good ole Warren Chambers?

So he'd parked here on the corner in a borrowed red Subaru with a dented left fender, and was hulking down now under the shadow of a big banyan tree dropping leaves all over the hood the way pigeons dropped shit. From where he was parked he could see the exit driveway from the parking lot in front of her condo. He knew her car. He'd be able to spot her the minute she left. If she left.

A fly buzzed his head.

Trouble with sitting here all the windows open.

Hated Florida and its goddamn bugs.

Kept watching the exit drive. It was on this end of the lot, big white arrow painted on the cement, pointing in. Big white arrow on the other end of the lot, pointing out. So come on, he thought. You got an arrow showing you the way, let's do it.

He looked at his watch.

Nine thirty-seven.

Time to get out and get hustling, he thought.

Elaine Commins — or Lainie, as she preferred calling herself — was thirty-three years old, tall and spare with an elegantly casual look that spelled native Floridian, but she had come here from Alabama only five years ago, and she still spoke with a marked Southern accent. She was wearing for this morning's hearing a long pleated silk skirt with a tunic-length cotton pullover. No panty hose or stockings, just bare suntanned legs in a sling-back shoe with a low heel and a sort of openwork macramé toe. On the pinky finger of her right hand was the same gold ring she'd been wearing when first she came to my office. She'd described it then as a Victorian seal ring, its face in the shape of a heart, its band decorated with florets. The gold of the ring and the wheat tones of her outfit complemented her long sand-colored hair, pulled back and away from her face in a ponytail fastened with a ribbon the color of her green eyes. Those eyes seemed wary and intent and — well, not to be unkind, but merely for the sake of accuracy — a trifle cockeyed.

In America, the word "cockeyed" means "cross-eyed," what the British call a "squint," although in America someone

15

"squinting" is not looking at you "cockeyed," he is merely narrowing his eyes at you, looking at you with his eyes only partly open, the way he might look while *squinting* at the sun, for example, hmm? A funny language these colonials have, wot? Lainie wasn't truly cross-eyed. That is to say, neither of her eyes turned inward toward her nose. But she *was* cockeyed in that her left eye looked directly at you while her right eye turned outward. The defect was vital to her claim — in fact, I hoped it would win the day for us — but it nonetheless gave her an oddly vulnerable and exceedingly sexy look. Placing her hand on the Bible extended by the clerk of the court, she swore to tell the truth, the whole truth and nothing but the truth, so help her God.

"Would you tell me your name, please?" I said.

"Elaine Commins."

Her voice as soft as a hot summer wind blowing in off the Tennessee River. Cock-eyed green eyes wide and expectant in a face kissed by sunshine, left eye staring straight at me, right eye wandering to the American flag in the corner behind the judge's bench. Bee-stung lips, slightly parted, as though she were breathlessly anticipating my next question.

"And your address, please?"

"1312 North Apple."

"Is this also the address of your place of business?"

"It is. I work from a small studio in my home."

"What's the name of your business?"

"Just Kidding."

"What sort of business is that, Ms. Commins?"

"I design children's toys."

"How long have you been doing this kind of work?"

"Ever since I graduated from the Rhode Island School of Design ten years ago."

"So for ten years you've been designing children's toys."

"Yes."

"Have you had your own business for all of those ten years?"

"No, I've worked for other people in the past."

"Did you once work for Toyland, the defendant in this case?"

"I did."

"In what capacity?"

"As a member of the design staff."

"Designing toys?"

"Yes. Children's toys."

"Did you design Gladly the Cross-Eyed Bear while you were in the employ of Toyland?"

"I certainly did *not!*"

"When *did* you design the bear?"

"In April of this year."

"And you left your job at Toyland when?"

"This past January."

I walked to the plaintiff's table, and picked up from its top one of two seemingly identical teddy bears. The one I held in my hand as I walked back to the witness stand was some nineteen inches tall. The one still on the table was an inch shorter. Both were made of mohair. Each had hanging around its neck a pair of spectacles on a gold chain.

"Your Honor," I said, "may we mark this as exhibit one for the plaintiff?"

"So marked."

"Ms. Commins," I said, "do you recognize this?"

"I do."

"What is it?"

"It's a stuffed toy called Gladly the Cross-Eyed Bear, which I designed and had copyrighted and trademarked."

"I offer the bear in evidence, Your Honor."

"Any objections?"

"None," Brackett said. "Subject to our argument that the bear was *not* designed by Ms. Commins."

"Duly noted."

"Ms. Commins, was the design of this bear original with you?"

"It was."

"To your knowledge, before you designed

and named this bear, was there any other teddy bear in the world called Gladly the Cross-Eyed Bear?"

"To my knowledge, there *was* not and *is* not."

"Have you registered the trademark Gladly the Cross-Eyed Bear?"

"I have."

"Your Honor, may we mark this document as plaintiff's exhibit number two?"

"So marked."

"Ms. Commins, I show you this document and ask if you can identify it for me."

"It's the original certificate of trademark registration for Gladly."

"You mean Gladly the *bear,* of course."

"I mean Gladly the *Cross*-Eyed Bear. The crossed eyes are a unique part of her design. As are the correcting eyeglasses. They are integral parts of the trade dress."

"Your Honor, I offer the certificate in evidence."

"Any objections?"

"None."

"Your Honor, may we also mark *this* document?"

"Mark it plaintiff's exhibit number three."

"Ms. Commins, I now show you another document. Can you tell me what it is?"

"Yes, it's the original copyright registration certificate for Gladly."

"Did any drawings accompany the application for copyright?"

"They did."

"And do they accurately depict the design of your bear?"

"*And* the bear's eyeglasses."

"Your Honor, I offer the copyright certificate and the accompanying drawings in evidence."

"Objections?"

"None."

"Ms. Commins," I said, "how would you describe Gladly?"

"She's a cross-eyed bear with big ears, a goofy smile, and eyeglasses that she can wear."

"Are all these design elements original with you?"

"Yes."

"Well, aren't there other teddy bears in the world with big ears?"

"There are. But not like Gladly's."

"And goofy smiles?"

"Oh *boy* are there goofy smiles!" she said, and smiled in goofy imitation, which caused Santos to smile a bit goofily himself. "But not like Gladly's."

"Are there other *cross*-eyed teddy bears in the world?"

"None that I know of."

"Then the copyrighted crossed eyes on Gladly are unique to your bear."

"Yes."

"As is the trademarked name."

"Yes."

"How about the eyeglasses? Aren't there teddy bears who wear eyeglasses?"

"Not eyeglasses like these."

"What's different about these glasses?"

"They uncross her eyes."

"No glasses like that on any other teddy bear in the world?"

"None that I know of."

"When did the idea for this bear first come to you?"

There she was at last.

Or rather, there was her *car*, a faded green Chevy not unlike Warren's own faded gray Ford, nondescript and unremarkable, nosing its way out of the parking lot like a sand shark. She looked both ways and then made a right turn and drove on up the block. Warren waited till the Chevy was out of sight. He checked his watch. Ten minutes to ten.

Give her another five minutes, he thought.

Make sure she didn't forget something, decide to come back for it.

As Lainie Commins tells it, there are cul-de-sac streets in Calusa that make you think you've stepped into a time warp. Her house with its attached studio is on one of

21

those streets. This is Calusa — this is, in fact, *Florida* — as it must have looked in the forties and fifties.

I have never thought of Calusa as a tropical paradise. Even in the springtime, when everything is in bloom, nothing really looks as lush or as bursting with color as it does in the Caribbean. As a matter of fact, to me, Calusa usually looks more brown than it does green, as if the grass, and the leaves on the trees and bushes, have been overlaid with a fine dust. Even the bougainvillea and hibiscus seem somehow limp and lacking in luster when compared to the extravagant display of these plants in truly tropical climates.

But in April . . .

Which is when the idea for Gladly first came to Lainie and which, coincidentally, was when I was flat on my ass in the Intensive Care Unit at Good Samaritan Hospital in a coma as deep as — but that's another story.

In April, then, as Lainie tells it, the street on which she lives and works resembles a jungle through which a narrow asphalt road has been laid and left to deteriorate. The entrance to North Apple Street — there *is* no South Apple Street, by the way — is a mile and a half from the mainland side of the Whisper Key bridge. A sign at the street's opening reads DEAD END, appropriate in that North Apple runs for two blocks before it becomes an oval that turns the street back upon itself in the opposite direction.

Lining these two short blocks are twelve shingled houses with the sort of glass-louvered windows you could find all over Calusa in the good old days before it became a tourist destination for folks from the Middle West and Canada. The houses here are virtually hidden from view by a dense growth of dusty cabbage palm and palmetto, red bougainvillea, purple bougainvillea, white bougainvillea growing in dense profusion, sloppy pepper trees hung with curling Spanish moss, yellow-clustered gold trees, pink oleander, golden allamanda, trailing lavender lantana, rust-colored shrimp plants, yellow hibiscus, pink hibiscus, red hibiscus, eponymous bottlebrush trees with long red flowers — and here and there, the one true floral splendor of Calusa, the bird-of-paradise with its spectacular orange and bluish-purple crest.

People say about this street, "It's still very Florida."

Meaning it's sun-down and overgrown and wild and fetid and hidden and somehow secret and silent. You expect to see alligators waddling out of the bushes on this street. You expect to see bare-breasted, bare-chested Calusa Indians. What you do see are suntanned young sun-worshippers — some of them bare-chested or bare-breasted, true enough — living six or seven in each small house, performing any service that will keep them outdoors most week-days and on the beaches every weekend. There are more gardeners, pool-cleaning people, house painters, window washers, tree trimmers, road maintenance workers, lifeguards and boatyard personnel living on the two blocks that form Apple Street than there are in the entire state of Nebraska.

In at least three of the houses here, there are people with artistic pretensions, but that is not unusual for the state of Florida in general and the city of Calusa in particular. Calusa calls itself the Athens of South-west Florida, a sobriquet that causes my partner Frank — a transplanted native New Yorker — to snort and scoff. Four people on Apple Street call themselves painters. Another calls himself a sculptor. A sixth calls herself a writer. Lainie Commins is the only true professional on the street. She is, after all, a trained designer with a track record of production, though none of the toys or dolls, or even a *game* in one in-stance, ever took off the way the companies for which she'd worked had anticipated.

The walls of her tiny studio are hung with actually *manufactured* toys she designed first for a company named Toyworks in Providence, where she worked for a year after her graduation from Risdee, and then for a company named Kid Stuff in Birmingham, Alabama, not far from her birthplace, and next for Toyland, Toyland right here in Calusa, where she worked for three years before setting out on her own in January.

The idea for Gladly comes to her at the beginning of April sometime, she can't recall the exact date, and she tells that honestly to the Court now. The studio in which she works is so shadowed by the plants growing outside that it is dark even in the daytime. She works with a huge fluorescent light over her table, sketching ideas, developing them, refining them. She wears glasses when she works. In fact, she wears them *all* the time, except here in this courtroom today, where Matthew wants Judge Santos to notice that wandering right eye and forge a connection between Lainie's condition and that of the bear she created. The strabismus, as her visual defect is called, commenced when she was three years old. At least, that was when her mother first detected what was then merely a slight turning-out of the right eye. Glasses failed to correct the condition. Two operations to shorten the muscle also proved fruitless. The right eye continued to wander. (When Lainie was sixteen, her mother confided to a friend that her daughter had "a wandering eye," but she wasn't talking about the strabismus.)

Lainie explains her condition to the Court now, gratuitously contributing the fact that the word "strabismus" comes from the Greek word *strabos,* which means "squinting" — there you are, lads. A cockeyed squint, after all!

Gladly comes to her out of the blue.

She's been working since early this morning, constructing a model for a fire engine with a girl doll at its wheel and several other girl dolls, all with flowing red hair the color of the truck, hanging from its sides. Casting each delicate doll from individual wax models, hanging them on the deliberately macho prototype truck she's constructed of wire and wood, she finds herself humming as she works, and oddly —

Ideas sometimes come this way, she tells the Court.

——one of the tunes she initially hums and then actually begins singing is a hymn called "Keep Thou My Way," which she learned when she was a little girl growing up in Winfield, Alabama, and attending a Bible-reading class taught by a woman named Helen Lattimer.

> *Keep Thou my way, O Lord*
> *Hide my life in Thine;*
> *O let Thy sacred light*

O'er my pathway shine.
Kept by Thy tender care,
Gladly the cross I'll bear
Hear Thou and grant . . .

. . . and she remembers all at once that in all the children's minds "Gladly the cross I'll bear" became "Gladly the cross-eyed bear," in much the same way that "Round yon virgin" in "Silent Night" became a chubby little man whose name was John Virgin, or "Lead on, O king eternal" in yet another hymn became "Lead on, O Kinky Turtle." And suddenly she thinks Oh, God, a whole *line* of stuffed toys, starting with the Cross-Eyed Bear and going from there to the Kinky Turtle and Round John and who knows *what* other characters I might find in the malaprop depths of rural America!

She rolls the fire truck to one side of the table, opens a pad, and begins sketching, starting with the outline of the bear's head, tilted to one side, and then filling in the crossed eyes and the silly little grin under its black triangular nose —

And here she shows the original drawing to the Court:

"I would like to offer Ms. Commins's drawing in evidence, Your Honor."

"Any objections?"

"None."

27

Lainie makes some twenty drawings of the bear that night, working feverishly from the moment of inspiration to one in the morning, and she goes to sleep exhausted but content until she wakes up in the middle of the night with her eyes burning, and goes into the bathroom to put some Visine drops into them, and recalls how devastated she'd felt when the ophthalmologist in Birmingham reported that the second operation had not helped her condition, and standing there in the bathroom with the eyedropper in her hand, she thinks I'll fix *Gladly's* eyes! and runs out into the studio again, and puts on her own glasses and begins sketching *Gladly* wearing eyeglasses.

"I offer the following eighteen drawings in evidence, Your Honor."

"Objections?"

"None."

"All right to offer them all as a single piece of evidence, Mr. Hope?"

"If it please the Court."

"That's five for the plaintiff," Santos said.

"As I understand this," I said, "when the eyeglasses are placed on Gladly's nose, covering her eyes . . ."

"Yes."

". . . the eyes look perfectly normal."

"Yes. Facing her and looking at her eyes through the glasses . . ."

"Could you show us, please?" I said, and

handed her the prototype bear with the eyeglasses hanging on a chain around her neck. While Gladly watched in glassy cross-eyed expectation, smiling goofily, Lainie opened the glasses, perched them on the bear's snout and little black triangular nose, and hooked them behind her ears. Instantly and magically, the previously crossed eyes appeared normal.

"You put on the glasses," Lainie said, "and the eyes aren't crossed anymore."

"How do you achieve that effect, Ms. Commins?"

"I had an optometrist design the glasses for me."

"Do you have specifications for these glasses?"

"I do."

"I refer you to exhibit three, the certificate of copyright registration for your bear, and ask you to look at the deposit copies accompanying it. Are these the specifications to which you just made reference?"

"They are."

"And did these specifications accompany your application for copyright registration?"

"They were a part of the application, yes."

"And became a part of the copyright protection, didn't they?"

"Objection!"

"Sustained."

"Your Honor, if I may . . ."

"Yes, Mr. Brackett?"

"Your Honor," Brackett said, "it is not Ms. Commins's business to know or to comment upon copyright law."

"I sustained your objection, didn't I?"

"Yes, and thank you, Your Honor. But, moreover, Your Honor, *eyeglasses* in themselves are not copyrightable, they are not subject matter for copyright. Copyright does not protect ideas or systems, it protects only the expression of ideas."

"Yes, I know that," Santos said. "I'm quite familiar with the 'idea/expression' distinction."

"I'm sure, Your Honor. But for counsel to suggest that copyright protection of the *bear* extends to the bear's *eyeglasses* . . ."

"Your Honor," I said, "the eyeglasses are part of the bear's trade dress. As such . . ."

"All of which is a matter of law for the Court to decide. Meanwhile, let's hear the rest of the testimony."

"Thank you, Your Honor," Brackett said.

"Ms. Commins," I said, "do you *own* these specifications?"

"I paid for their design, yes, in return for all rights to the drawings and the unrestricted use of the design."

"Has anyone else, to your knowledge, ever used such a design in this manner before?"

"Not to my knowledge."

"To your knowledge, has anyone ever

31

used such a design in the form of eye-glasses for a stuffed teddy bear?"

"Not to my knowledge."

"Eyeglasses which, when covering the bear's crossed eyes, seem to *correct* the abnormality? Anyone ever use this design in this fashion before?"

"Not to my knowledge."

"Is this use original with you?"

"It is."

"Did you conceive of this use independently?"

"I did."

"Which goes to the heart of copyright law," I said. "An original *manner* of expression, independently cre—"

"Which goes to the heart of a lawyer addressing the Court directly," Brackett said, "rather than . . ."

"Sustained," Santos said. "Careful, Mr. Hope."

There was the fetid smell of mildew and rot, what you found in a lot of these condos built back in the forties and fifties. Place was constructed of cinder block painted white, streaks of greenish gray all over it where the mildew had been having its way for too long a time. Wooden posts rotted clear through, probably infested with termites, too, supporting a rippled green plastic overhang running past the entrance doors to the units, twelve on each floor by Warren's count. He came down the long open corridor cautiously because the one thing he couldn't change was his color.

Could borrow a dented red Subaru from a friend of his, could dress in tropical beige threads made him look like a visiting real estate salesman or a banker come to call, he *still* looked out of place in this shitty run-down condo where the only tenants were white. So he came cautiously down that long second-floor corridor with the sun hitting the rippled overhang at an angle that cast the plastic's sickly green color onto the corridor floor and the lower part of the white wall, and he prayed none of the doors along that wall would open, prayed no one would step out to challenge him. He was a black man about to stealthily break and enter a structure or conveyance without consent of the owner or occupant, but he wasn't a burglar, and he didn't choose to be mistaken for one.

Warren was carrying in his wallet a laminated card that had been issued in accordance with Chapter 493 of the Florida Statutes, and which gave its recipient the right to investigate and gather information on a great many criminal and noncriminal matters listed in detail in the statute. He took that card from his wallet now, and used it to loid the lock on the door to unit

24, *her* unit, sliding it deftly between door-jamb and Mickey Mouse spring latch, forcing the latch back until he felt the door give, and then easing himself into the unit and closing the door behind him at once.

His heart was pounding hard.

Sidney Brackett was asking Lainie if it wasn't true that she had developed the idea for her so-called original bear Gladly while, in fact, she was still working at Toyland, Toyland. Lainie was vehemently denying this. Sitting at the defense table, Brett and Etta Toland sat calmly watching the proceedings, secure in the knowledge that Brackett would impeach my first witness and get this whole damned thing kicked summarily out of court.

Brett was forty-four years old, elegantly tailored in a blue blazer and gray slacks, white shirt open at the throat, no tie, shoes invisible under the table — but I guessed they were tasseled loafers — suntanned face exploiting eyes as blue as glare ice, thick blond hair casually styled. He sat holding his wife's left hand in his own right hand. Together, they presented the very image of solidarity against this impostor named Lainie Commins.

In Calusa society, such as it was, they were familiarly known as Lord and Lady Toland, though neither was either British or aristocratic. Host and hostess supreme — I remembered an outdoor party where Japanese lanterns festooned the lawn of their multimillion-dollar beachfront home, and goldfish swam in tiny bowls at the more than fifty outdoor tables, and the then governor of the state of Florida was in attendance — invitations to their extravaganzas were sought like tickets to the Super Bowl, though I'd personally felt somewhat uncomfortable in such resplendent digs, perhaps because I'd grown up poor in Chicago; maybe a person can *never* put poverty behind him.

Etta Toland . . .

Ett and Brett, they were called by close friends who cherished the Tolands, *and* their Fatback Key mansion, *and* their parties, *and* their tennis court and swimming pool, *and* their ninety-four-foot yawl named *Toy Boat*, *and* their private jet that didn't have a name though both jet and yacht had painted respectively on fuselage and transom the logo of their toy company, two dolls sitting with legs extended and heads together, the boy with blond hair, the girl with black hair, each smiling radiantly. This same logo was on the little round tag attached to the second teddy bear on Matthew's table, little boy and girl with TOYLAND in a semicircle above their heads, and another TOYLAND in a semicircle below their legs, TOYLAND, TOYLAND, for Toland, Toland, here now to defend themselves against Lainie Commins's charges of copyright and trademark infringement.

Thirty-seven-year-old Etta had hair as black as that on the little grinning girl-doll in the company logo, worn straight and sleek and to the shoulders. High sculpted cheekbones, very dark almond-shaped eyes, and a generous mouth glossed with blood-red lipstick collaborated with the straight, lustrous, jet-black hair to give her a somewhat Oriental appearance, although her maiden name was Henrietta Becherer, and her forebears were German — a fact that didn't stop competitors and/or detractors from labeling her "The Dragon Lady." Rumor had it that Brett had met her at a toy fair in Frankfurt, where she'd been pitching at the Gebrüder Hermann booth. On this hot Tuesday morning in September, she looked cool, self-possessed, businesslike and yet utterly feminine in a glen-plaid silk suit the color of twilight, worn with a dusky blue silk shirt open at the throat over a medallion print scarf. Above the left hand clutched in her husband's right, a gold cuff link showed where her jacket sleeve ended.

"Do you remember which toys you were working on during your employment?" Brackett asked.

"Do you mean at Toyland?"

"Yes. That was . . . how long did you say you'd worked there, Miss Commins?"

"I left them in January. I'd been working there for three years by then."

"This past January?"

"Yes."

"Worked for them for three years."

"Yes."

"Do you remember which toys you designed for them during those three years?"

"I remember all of them."

"Wasn't the idea for Gladly suggested to you . . . ?"

"No, it was not."

"Your Honor, may I finish my question?"

"Yes, go ahead. Please listen to the complete question before answering, Miss Commins."

"I thought he *was* finished, Your Honor."

"Let's just get on with it," Santos said impatiently.

"Isn't it true that the *idea* for Gladly was suggested to you by Mr. Toland . . . ?"

"No, that isn't true."

"Miss Commins, let him *finish*, please."

"Suggested to you by Mr. Toland at a meeting one afternoon during the month of September last year?"

"No."

"While you were still in the employ of . . . ?"

"No."

". . . Toyland, Toyland, isn't that true, Miss Commins?"

"No, it is not true."

"Isn't it true that this *original* idea of yours was, in fact, Mr. Toland's?"

"No."

"Didn't Mr. Toland ask you to work up some sketches on the idea?"

"No."

"Aren't the sketches you showed to the court identical to the sketches you made and delivered to Mr. Toland several weeks after that September meeting?"

"No. I made those sketches this past April. In my studio on North Apple Street."

"Oh yes, I'm sure you did."

"Objection," I said.

"Sustained. We can do without the editorials, Mr. Brackett."

"No further questions," Brackett said.

Warren debated opening the door again, ramming a toothpick into the keyway, snapping it off close to the lock. Anyone trying to unlock the door from the outside would try to shove a key in, meet resistance, make a hell of a clicking racket pushing against the broken-off wood. Great little burglar alarm for anybody inside who shouldn't be in there. Trouble was, *she* knew the toothpick trick as well as he did, she'd know immediately there was somebody in her digs. He'd be lucky she didn't pull a piece, blow off the lock, and then shoot at anything that moved, blowing off his *head* in the bargain.

He locked the door.

Looked around.

The place was dim. White metal blinds drawn against the sun at the far end of the room. Sofa against what was apparently a window wall, sunlight seeping around the edges of the blinds. Sofa upholstered in a white fabric with great big red what looked like hibiscus blossoms printed on it. His eyes were getting accustomed to the gloom. The place looked a mess. Clothes strewn all over the floor, empty soda pop bottles and cans, cigarette butts brimming in ashtrays — he hadn't known she'd started smoking again, a bad sign. He wondered if the place always looked like a shithouse, or was it just now? On the street outside, he heard a passing automobile. And another. He waited in the semidark stillness of the one room. Just that single window in the entire place, at the far end, the only source of light, and it covered with a blind. Figured the sofa had to open into a bed, else where was she sleeping?

Door frame, no door on it, led to what he could see was a kitchen. Fridge, stove, countertop, no window, just a little cubicle the size of a phone booth laid on end, well, he was exaggerating. Still, he wouldn't like to try holding a dinner party in there. He stepped into the room, saw a little round wooden table on the wall to his right, two chairs tucked under it. Kitchen was a bit bigger than he'd thought at first, but he still wouldn't want to wine and dine the governor here.

Pile of dirty dishes in the sink, another bad sign.

Food already crusted on them, meant they'd been there a while, an even worse sign.

He opened a door under the sink, found a lidded trash can, lifted the lid, peered into it. Three empty quart-sized ice cream containers, no other garbage. Things looking worse by the minute. He replaced the lid, closed the door, went to the fridge and opened it. Wilting head of lettuce, bar of margarine going lardy around the edges, container of milk smelling sour, half an orange shriveling, three unopened cans of Coca-Cola. He checked the ice cube trays. Hadn't been refilled in a while, the cubes were shrinking away from the sides. He nearly jumped a mile in the air when he spotted the roach sitting like a spy on the countertop alongside the fridge.

They called them palmetto bugs down here. Damn things could fly, he'd swear to God. Come right up into your face, you weren't careful. Two, three inches long some of them, disgusting. There were roaches back in St. Louis, when he lived there, but nothing like what they had down here, man. He closed the refrigerator door. Bug didn't move a muscle. Just sat there on the countertop watching him.

Another car passed by outside.

Real busy street here, oh yes, cars going by at least every hour or so, a virtual metropolitan thoroughfare. He just hoped one of them wouldn't be *her* car, pulling into the parking lot, home from market, surprise!

He figured that's where she'd be, ten-thirty in the morning, probably down in Newtown, doing her marketing. He hoped to hell he was wrong. The roach — palmetto bug, my ass! — was still on the countertop, motionless, watching Warren as he went back into the main room of the unit, the living room/bedroom/dining room, he guessed you would call it. Red hibiscus sofa against the far wall, he walked to it, and leaned over it and opened the blinds, letting in sunlight.

I had only one other witness, an optometrist named Dr. Oscar Nettleton, who defined himself as a professional engaged in the practice of examining the eye for defects and faults of refraction and prescribing

41

corrective lenses or exercises but not drugs or surgery. He modestly asserted that he was Chairman of, and Distinguished Professor in, Calusa University's Department of Vision Sciences. I elicited from him the information that Lainie Commins had seemed elated . . .

"Objection, Your Honor."

"Overruled."

. . . and glowing with pride . . .

"Objection."

"Overruled."

. . . and confident and very up . . .

"Objection."

"Sustained. One or two commonsense impressions are quite enough for me, Mr. Hope."

. . . when she'd come to him this past April with her original drawings for Gladly and her requirements for the eyeglasses the bear would wear.

"She kept calling them the specs for the specs," Nettleton said, and smiled.

He testified that his design for the eyeglasses was original with him, that he'd received a flat fee of three thousand dollars for the drawings, and had signed a document releasing all claim, title and interest to them and to the use or uses to which they might be put.

Brackett approached the witness stand.

"Tell me, Dr. Nettleton, you're not an

ophthalmologist, are you?"

"No, I'm not."

"Then you're not a physician, are you?"

"No, I'm not."

"You just make eyeglasses, isn't that so?"

"No, an *optician* makes eyeglasses. I prescribe correctional lenses. I'm a doctor of optometrics, and also a Ph.D."

"Thank you for explaining the vast differences, Doctor," Brackett said, his tone implying that he saw no real differences at all between an optician and an optometrist. "But, tell me, when you say the design for these eyeglasses is original with you, what exactly do you mean?"

"I mean Miss Commins came to me with a problem, and I solved that problem without relying upon any other design that may have preceded it."

"Oh? *Were* there previous designs that had solved this problem?"

"I have no idea. I didn't look for any. I addressed the problem and solved it. The specifications I gave her were entirely original with me."

"Would you consider them original if you knew lenses identical to yours had been designed *prior* to yours?"

"My design does not make use of lenses."

"Oh? Then what are eyeglasses if not corrective lenses?"

"The lenses in these glasses are plano

43

lenses. That is, without power. They are merely clear plastic. If you put your hand behind them, you would see it without distortion. They are not corrective lenses."

"Then how do they correct the bear's vision?"

"They don't, actually. They merely *seem* to. What I've done is create an illusion. The teddy bear has bilaterally crossed eyes. That is to say, the brown iris and white pupil are displaced nasalward with respect to the surrounding white scleral-conjunctival tissue of the eye. As in the drawing Ms. Commins first brought to me. What I did . . ."

"What you did was design a pair of eyeglasses you say are original with you."

"They are *not* eyeglasses, but they *are* original with me."

"When you say they're original, are you also saying you didn't copy them from anyone else's eyeglasses?"

"That's what I'm saying. And they're *not* eyeglasses."

"Your Honor," Brackett said, "if the witness keeps insisting that what are patently eyeglasses . . ."

"Perhaps he'd care to explain why he's making such a distinction," Santos said.

"Perhaps he's making such a distinction because he knows full well that his design is copied from a pair of eye—"

"Objection, Your . . ."

"I'll ignore that, Mr. Brackett. I, for one, certainly *would* like to know why Dr. Nettleton doesn't consider these eyeglasses. Dr. Nettleton? Could you please explain?"

"If I may make use of my drawings, Your Honor . . ."

"Already admitted in evidence, Your Honor," I said.

"Any objections, Mr. Brackett?"

"If the Court has the time . . ."

"I do have the time, Mr. Brackett."

"Then I have no objections."

I carried Nettleton's drawings to where he was sitting in the witness chair. He riffled through the stapled pages and then folded back several pages to show his first drawing.

"These are the plastic crossed eyes that are attached to the teddy bear's face. As you can see, the iris and pupil are displaced nasalward."

"And this is a drawing of the plastic *straight* eyes as they're reflected within the spectacles I designed."

"May I see it, please?"

Nettleton handed the drawing to him.

"By reflected . . ."

"With mirrors, Your Honor."

"Mirrors?"

"Yes, Your Honor. If I may show you my other drawings."

"Please."

Nettleton turned some more pages, folded them back, and displayed another drawing to Santos.

"This is the teddy-bear optical schematic," he said. "It illustrates the manner in which I expressed the optical principles of my system for producing apparently straight eyes. A and D are button eyes that will be seen by reflection from the right and left mirrors. Their images only *appear* to be at R and L respectively."

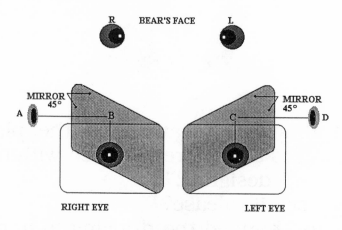

"For the right eye, the distance from A to B equals the distance from B to R at the plane of the bear's face. Similarly, for the left eye, the distance from C to D equals the distance from C to L. The lenses, as I mentioned earlier, are plano lenses."

"I'm not sure I understand," Santos said.

"The next drawing will make it entirely clear," Nettleton said, and began leafing through the specs again.

"Your Honor," Brackett said, "this is all enormously fascinating . . ."

"Actually, I do find it fascinating," Santos said.

"But it has nothing to do with whether the design was copied or . . ."

"It may have *everything* to do with differences between the two bears, Mr. Brackett."

"Your Honor, in order to show originality, *substantial* diff—"

"Well, let's see the drawing, shall we?" Santos said. "Have you found it, Dr. Nettleton?"

"Yes, I have it right here," Nettleton said, and handed the pages back to Santos.

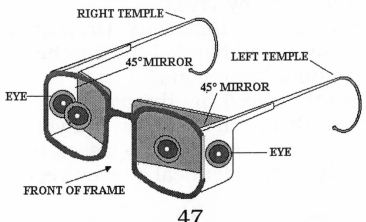

"This drawing illustrates the implementation of the optical system in the manner in which I expressed it. As you see, the wraparound frame allows attachment of the button eyes A and D to the inside surface of the broad temples. The forty-five-degree mirrors are attached to the inside of the front frame and extend back to the temples. The depth of the frame conceals the mirrors. Thus, when the uncrossed plastic eyes and surrounding fur — integrated into the temples — are reflected into the fully silvered mirrors, they appear to be originating from the facial plane of the actual teddy bear."

"That is ingenious," Santos said.

"Thank you."

"Ingenious, Dr. Nettleton."

"Thank you very much."

"Don't you think that's ingenious, Mr. Brackett?"

"If you're using the word to mean marked by originality in conception, I must take exception, Your Honor. In fact, if I may continue with my cross . . ."

"Yes, please do. Ingenious, Dr. Nettleton," Santos said, and handed the specifications back to him. "Ingenious."

Brackett cleared his throat.

"Dr. Nettleton," he said, "would you know whether there are any eyeglasses in existence which are identical or even very similar to the ones you designed for Miss Commins?"

"I have no knowledge of any device which *appears* to be a pair of eyeglasses but which is in reality merely a *carrier,* if you will, for reflective mirrors. If designs for any such device exist, I had no access to them."

"Ah, access. Did Mr. Hope ask you to mention access?"

"No, he did not."

"Do you understand the meaning of the word 'access' as it pertains to copyright matters?"

"I don't know anything about copyright. I'm an optometrist. I examine the eye for defects and faults of refraction . . ."

"Yes, yes."

". . . and prescribe corrective lenses or exercises . . ."

"Yes, but not drugs or surgery. Thank you, we already have that, Doctor. What does access mean to you?"

"It means I saw something. I had *access* to it. I knew about it."

"As pertains to copyright matters, it can also mean you had reasonable *opportunity* to have seen it."

"I never saw any device like the one I designed for Miss Commins."

"What if I told you that eyeglasses similar to yours . . ."

"They are *not* eyeglasses!"

"Your Honor," I said, getting to my feet, "do you think we might stipulate that Dr. Nettleton's design is *not* for eyeglasses, but only for a device made to *look* like eyeglasses?"

"I'll make no such stipulation," Brackett said.

"Then might Mr. Brackett refrain from *calling* them eyeglasses, when clearly . . ."

"What should I call eyeglasses but eyeglasses?"

"Let him call them what he chooses, Mr. Hope. Let's just get on with this, shall we?"

"Thank you, Your Honor," Brackett said, and turned back to the witness. "Dr. Nettleton, are you aware that a design for eyeglasses remarkably similar to yours appeared in an industry technical journal many years ago? Would you *still* say you had no access?"

"I never saw my device anywhere."

"Do you *read* trade journals?"

"I do."

"Do you read *Optics and Lenses*?"

"I've read it on occasion."

"Have you read the March 1987 issue of that magazine?"

"No."

"Your Honor, I ask the Court to take judicial notice that this magazine I hold in my hand is the March 1987 issue of *Optics and Lenses*."

"Mr. Hope? Do you dispute this?"

"No, Your Honor."

"Judicial notice taken. Move it into evidence as exhibit A for the defense."

"Dr. Nettleton, I ask you to turn to page twenty-one of the magazine, would you do that for me, please?"

Nettleton leafed through the magazine, found the page, and looked up.

"Do you see the title of the article on that page?"

"I do."

"Would you read it to the Court, please?"

"The whole article?"

"Just the title, please."

"The title is 'The Use of Corrective Lenses in the Treatment of Strabismus.' "

"Thank you. Dr. Nettleton, would you call your eyeglasses a way of using corrective lenses in the treatment of strabismus?"

"No, I would not."

"Well, isn't Ms. Commins's bear cross-eyed?"

"It is."

"And isn't 'strabismus' the proper medical term for this condition?"

"Yes, but . . ."

"And don't your eyeglasses *correct* this condition?"

"Yes, but . . ."

"Then wouldn't you agree that your design

makes use of corrective lenses in the treatment of . . ."

"Mirrors. It makes use of mirrors."

"Lenses, mirrors, all have to do with optics."

"A mirror isn't a lens. A mirror is a surface that forms an image by *reflection*. A lens forms an image by *focusing* rays of light. They are two separate and distinct . . ."

"Doesn't your design demonstrate one way of treating the condition known as strabismus?"

"Only in the very loosest possible sense. We're not talking about *real* strabismus here, we're . . ."

"Yes or no, please."

"Given the widest possible interpretation . . ."

"Your Honor?"

"Yes or no, Dr. Nettleton."

"All right, yes."

"Would you please turn to page twenty-five?"

Nettleton turned several pages, and again looked up.

"Do you see the drawings on that page?"

"I do."

"Would you describe those drawings as specifications for lenses designed to correct the condition of strabismus?"

Nettleton studied the drawings.

"Yes, I would."

"Would you say they're identical to the drawings you made for Miss Commins?"

"Absolutely not."

"Would you say they're remarkably similar?"

"No, not at all. These are *lenses* designed to correct strabismus. My *mirrors* were designed to create an optical illusion."

"These specifications were published in an industry journal in March of 1987. Would you agree that you had a reasonable opportunity to have seen them?"

"Yes, but I *didn't* see them. And even if I had . . ."

"By comparison, would you say that *your* design adds more than a trivial amount of creativity to the design in this magazine?"

"I would say they're entirely different."

"Oh? In what way?"

"To begin with, the design in the magazine is for *eyeglasses*."

"Well, isn't *your* design for eyeglasses?"

Nettleton rolled his eyes.

"Your Honor," Brackett said.

"Your Honor," I said.

"Answer the question, please."

"My design is for reflecting mirrors," Nettleton said wearily.

"Well, those are eyeglasses hanging around the bear's neck, aren't they?"

"No. They couldn't possibly serve as a tool

53

for correcting or improving vision."

"They look like glasses to me."

"Your Honor, *please*," I said.

"Sustained."

"Would you agree that they *look* like eye-glasses?"

"Yes, but they're *not* eyeglasses. That is not their purpose."

"But the basic design is similar to the one in the magazine, isn't it?"

"No, the designs are not at all similar."

"You know, of course, that Miss Commins submitted your specifications together with her application for copyright?"

He's trying to invalidate the copyright, I thought.

"Yes, I know that."

"How did you come by this information?"

"She told me."

"Did *you* tell *her* that the eyeglasses for which she was seeking copyright as part of her design were not entirely original with you?"

"They *were* original!"

"Did you tell her that a design for similar eyeglasses had been published in 1987?"

"I didn't know that. And besides, they're *not* similar."

"But a few minutes ago you described those published drawings as specifications for the use of corrective lenses in the treatment of strabismus, didn't you?"

"You asked me to read the title of the article . . ."

"But you agreed, didn't you, that the glasses were designed to do exactly that?"

"Yes, I did."

"And you also agreed that *your* glasses were also designed to . . ."

"In the loosest possible *sense,* is what I . . ."

"In *whatever* sense, you agreed . . ."

"Objection, Your Honor."

"Sustained. Get off it, Mr. Brackett."

"Tell me, Dr. Nettleton, you said earlier that Miss Commins came to you in April to show you her *original* drawings for a bear she'd designed."

"Yes."

"How do you know they were original?"

First the eyeglasses, I thought, now the bear itself.

"Well, they were signed by her," Nettleton said.

"Yes, but how do you know they weren't drawings premised on some *other* person's idea?"

"Objection, Your Honor!"

"I'll allow it, Mr. Hope. He earlier described the drawings as original. Answer the question, please."

"Well, I didn't know where her *idea* came from," Nettleton said. "She told me it was *her* idea, I had to assume . . ."

"The same way you told her . . ."

"Objection!"

". . . that the eyeglasses were *your* idea, when in fact . . ."

"Objection, Your Honor!"

"When in fact the design for them . . ."

"Objection!"

". . . had already been published as far back as . . ."

"Your Honor, I *object!*"

"Sustained," Santos said.

"Your witness."

The windows, three of them, were on the far side of the building, facing east, away from the parking lot. There was a view of a strip mall across the way, minimarket in it, video shop, Laundromat, dry cleaners, and bar. Two blond bronzed gods looking like beach bums in tank top shirts and baggy shorts were standing outside the bar, maybe waiting for it to open. A woman in a bathing suit and sandals walked into the Laundromat carrying a bundle of wash. It was still sunny and glaring bright outside.

Warren looked at his watch.

All right, let's get to work here, he thought.

He took the cushions off the sofa, opened the bed — so simple a child of five could do it — hoping to find it neatly made, finding instead a tangled mare's nest of sheets, pillow and a single blanket. The bed gave off a faint whiff of sweat and something else, he didn't know what. He pulled back the sheets, looking for whatever might tell him he was right or wrong about what she was doing here in this apartment, but there was nothing he could see, so he closed the bed, and put the cushions back in place and turned to look around the room again.

Bright sunlight streamed through the windows behind him.

The air conditioner was off, the place was pitilessly hot. A pink baby-doll nightgown trimmed with lace at the hem was lying on the floor near the sofa, well, now he knew what she slept in. He picked it up, held it in his big brown hands, studying it. Put it down on the sofa, thought No, she'll remember, and tossed it on the floor again, where he'd found it. Searched the floor, saw nothing that told him anything. Checked the cabinet on the right-hand wall as you came in the room, opening doors and drawers, found nothing. Checked a standing combination bookcase/bar/entertainment center — actually a series of black wooden shelves resting on a black iron frame — CD and tape player on one of the shelves, but no TV set, another bad sign, he kept hoping against hope he was wrong. Another round table, wooden, larger than the one in the kitchen, with two chairs that matched those in the kitchen, was tucked into the corner just to the left of the entrance door as you came in. A phone was on the table, its cord leading to a jack near the floor. An open address book was resting beside the phone. He pulled out a chair and sat.

What it all got down to in the closing arguments was a simple case of She Said/He Said.

On Lainie's behalf, I argued that Gladly the Cross-Eyed Bear was her wholly original work, that she had designed the stuffed animal early in April, had consulted an optometrist shortly thereafter, and had copyrighted bear and accessories in May, at which time she had also trademarked the name of the bear. I argued that the crossed eyes and the correcting eyeglasses were part and parcel of the bear's distinctive trade dress. I further argued that the notion for the bear had come to her through memories of her own affliction — and here I asked her to look directly into Judge Santos's face so that he could see for himself the similarity of the bear's eyes to hers — and a hymn she had learned when she was a little girl in Winfield, Alabama.

Brackett argued that Brett Toland — himself originally a Southerner from Tennessee — had been inspired by the same hymn and had suggested the idea for a cross-eyed bear to Lainie while she was still working for Toyland under an employment agreement that specified any fruits of her labor would become the sole and exclusive property of the company. Brackett contended that it was Toland himself who'd requested Lainie to sketch a cross-eyed bear for him, and she had delivered those sketches in September of last year, three months before she'd given the company notice. The bear he planned to test-market this Christmas was called *Gladys* the Cross-Eyed Bear because he hoped to capture a market not exclusively limited to Christians familiar with the hymn. The glasses on *his* bear made use of neither corrective lenses nor mirrors but were instead clear plastic lenses behind which uncrossed eyes had been painted. It was Brackett's argument that Lainie had also designed these glasses for Toland, and that the more sophisticated design she'd later purchased from Nettleton was merely an improvement on Toland's original idea.

He Stole It.

She Stole It.

That's what it got down to.

Warren knew the names of most people in Newtown she would have to contact, but he didn't see any of them in her address book. Maybe she was going someplace other than Newtown, maybe she figured she'd be too conspicuous down there, pretty white blond woman in the black section of Calusa. Maybe she knew someplace else to go for what she needed, if she needed it, but maybe he was wrong. He kept leafing through the book leisurely, didn't want to miss any familiar name, but there was nobody there he could identify, so far she looked clean as a newborn babe. He closed the book. Looked around the room again.

She wasn't expecting anybody to come in here and toss the place, so she'd have had no need to go stashing anything in ridiculous places like the inside of a lampshade or the underside of a toilet tank lid. Just her and her secret, if there was a secret, maybe he was wrong, maybe there was nothing here at all. He'd be the first to admit it, run out and buy them both a big dinner at the best restaurant in town. But he knew the signs.

Only place he hadn't yet checked was the bathroom.

Santos was telling us that it was not the Court's obligation to determine whether Dr. Nettleton had stolen his eyeglass design from the *Optics and Lenses* article. Which, by the way, he didn't think had happened.

"In fact, I find that argument entirely specious," he said, "and I'm rejecting it

60

summarily. Rather, the duty of this Court is to determine whether the bear Toyland calls 'Gladys' is a copy of the bear Commins calls 'Gladly,' and therefore an infringement of copyright. The Court must further determine whether the similar though not identical names of the two bears might cause confusion in the marketplace and therefore be an infringement of trademark. And last, as to the third count, the Court must consider whether the design features of the Commins bear are inherently distinctive or at least have secondary meaning among purchasers, in which case the bear may be granted trade dress protection. This is not a simple case," he said, and sighed heavily. "I know, I know. This is already the middle of September, and Christmas is right around the corner. Ms. Commins has had feelers from two major toy companies, and Mr. and Mrs. Toland are eager to put *their* bear into production at once.

"But . . ."

And here he sighed again, and clasped his hands together as if building with his fingers a Here's-the-Church-and-Here's-the-Steeple edifice, resting his chin on the entrance door formed by his thumbs, peering out over them.

"I must give this serious thought," he said. "Before I enjoin Mr. and Mrs. Toland from producing and selling their bear, I need to be certain in my own mind that what Ms. Commins charges in her complaint is absolutely unassailable. I ask you all to be patient. I'll try to give you my decision by the end of next week. That would be . . ." He looked down at his open calendar. "The twenty-second. Failing that, and in accordance with federal law, I could extend another ten days. I can certainly promise a decision before then. In fact, let's say no later than the twenty-ninth. Until then, the TRO will remain in effect. Are there any questions? Then let's adjourn."

Had to be a bathroom behind that closed door across the room. Warren left her address book open to the page it had been turned to, got up, pushed the chair back under the table again, and went to the closed door.

No surprises, no dead body in the bathtub or hanging from the shower head or sitting on the toilet bowl with a knife in his heart. Nothing like that. Thong panties drying over the shower rod, two of them white, the third one yellow, now he knew what she wore under her skirt. No bras in evidence. Twisted tube of toothpaste on the sink, at least she was still brushing her teeth and rinsing out her smalls. Force of habit, he took the box of Kleenex off the toilet tank lid, placed it on the sink to his right, lifted the lid, peeked into the tank, turned the lid over to see if anything was taped to it, put it back in place again, and put the box of Kleenex back onto it.

He opened the medicine cabinet.

Usual array of headache remedies ranging from aspirin to Advil to Tylenol to Bufferin. Bottles and tubes of sunscreen and lotion. Some prescription drugs in little brown plastic bottles with white lids. Several packages of tampons and maxi-pads. A few boxes of cold tablets and allergy tablets. A toothbrush in an unopened cardboard and cellophane container. A bottle of Pepto-Bismol. An empty Dial•Pak dispenser. A toenail clipper. An open packet of dental floss. Several jars of moisturizers and mud. Nothing he was looking for. He closed the mirrored door. Opened the wooden door on the cabinet under the sink. Toilet-bowl brush. Wrapped bars of Palmolive soap; he visualized her showering. Wrapped rolls of toilet paper. An unopened box of Kleenex. A can of Lysol. He closed the door.

Pale blue shag rug in front of the toilet bowl. Matching blue plastic trash basket wedged into the narrow space between the sink cabinet and the bowl. He looked into the basket. Crumpled, lipstick-stained wads of Kleenex. Cellophane wrapper from a tampon. Wrapper from a stick of Wrigley spearmint chewing gum. Several soggy Q-Tips. He picked up the basket, rested it on the sink. Dug under the debris.

Bingo.

"He's going to decide in their favor, I *know* it," Lainie said.

We were eating a late lunch in a delicatessen near the courthouse. The place called itself the New Yorker, though the knishes and the hot dogs tasted as if they'd been made in Korea. Even the mustard was all wrong, a bright yellow stuff that lacked the bite of the grainy brownish blend my partner Frank insisted was essential to a true kosher frank. And besides, you had to pay an additional fifty cents for sauerkraut, which Frank said was outrageous. I wished Frank were here with us right this minute. Frank had a way of explaining law that made him sound like a justice of the Supreme Court. Frank was a comfort to distraught clients. On the other hand . . .

"I just think he needs more time," I said.

"Why?"

"Because this isn't a decision he can make lightly. He gave us fair warning right up front. Remember what he said?"

"What did he say?"

"He said, 'The Court does not intend to be rushed into any decision.' Those were his exact words. He's aware of how much is hanging in the balance. For *both* sides."

"Nothing's hanging in the balance for Toyland," Lainie said. "This is just another *product* for them. They'll put it out in time for Christmas, if it catches on, great, if it doesn't there'll be *another* toy next Christmas and *another* one after that. But this is my *future* we're talking about here. If Gladly makes it . . ."

"I understand, Lainie. But there's no reason to . . ."

"No, I don't think you . . ."

". . . believe Santos will decide for the Tolands. Really. His caution isn't unusual. There are factors he still has to consider, you know . . ."

"What factors?"

"Well, aside from deciding whether there *was* copying . . ."

"He doesn't think there was. He said . . ."

"I know what he said."

"He said he had to be certain in his own mind that Gladly really *was* copied."

"Yes, but I think he knows . . ."

"How can you know what he . . . ?"

"He dismissed that nonsense about Nettleton copying the eyeglasses, didn't he?"

"That doesn't mean he thinks their fucking *bear* was copied from mine."

"Well, maybe not yet."

"Maybe not ever."

"The point is, Lainie, there's more to this than whether or not there was just copying."

"Yeah."

Picking at her fries disconsolately. As far as she was concerned, Santos had already decided, and the case was lost. One eye on me, the other wandering elsewhere. Dipping a fry in the ketchup on her plate. Fine sheen of perspiration on her tanned face, the New Yorker's air-conditioning unit had probably come from Pyongyang, too. Lifting the fry to her lips.

"What he'll be considering in the next week or so . . ."

"He said the end of the month."

"Well, he's shooting for the twenty-ninth at the very latest. What he'll be considering is whether we'd be likely to prevail on the merits should this thing ever come to trial."

"Is that a possibility?"

"Oh, sure. He may, in fact, *order* a trial."

"There goes Christmas," Lainie said.

"No, no. If he goes that route, he'd probably ask for an immediate trial. He knows the importance of Christmas, he's stated that several . . ."

"*How* immediate? *Any* delay would put me out of the running for Christmas. Matthew, you don't understand how *impor-*

tant this is to me."

"I do."

"No, you *don't*," she insisted, and put down her fork, and looked across the table, her right eye focusing for a moment before it wandered away again. I imagined her as a four-year-old girl enduring her first strabotomy. And then another one a year after that. The failure of both operations. At their first meeting, she'd told me she had cried night after night after night, wanting to be like all the other little girls, and knowing she never would. She seemed ready to begin crying again now. "I *know* Gladly is a winner," she said. "And I know her time is *now*." Talking about the bear as if it were a real person. "Not next year or the year after that, but *now*. Why do you think Mattel and Ideal are so interested? Because of my good looks?" She was, in fact, quite beautiful. "They *know* Gladly'll sell in the millions. That bear is my future, Matthew. That bear is my *life*."

And did begin crying.

I told her that I wasn't at all convinced Santos had already made his decision. Told her the judge would be considering other things besides the copying. For example, as I'd started to tell her a moment ago, Santos would be considering whether we were likely to succeed on the merits should the case eventually go to trial. Considering, too, whether deciding for the To-lands would cause irreparable harm to Lainie . . .

"It would only ruin my entire life," she said, sobbing.

". . . or whether money alone could repair your injuries."

"I wouldn't take a million dollars . . ."

"Good, because if you were willing to accept a cash settlement . . ."

"For Gladly? Never."

". . . there'd be no grounds for enjoining them."

"I told you *no*. She's mine."

Again sounding as if she were talking about a living human being and not a stuffed animal.

"Good," I said.

"Yeah, good. What's so good about it?"

She dried her eyes with a paper napkin. She looked across the table at me. Green eyes shining. Trying to focus. Losing the battle. Right eye wandering. Oddly, I felt like taking her in my arms, comforting her as I would a child.

"Everything'll be fine," I said. "Don't worry. Please."

She nodded.

On Wednesday morning, the first thing I heard on Channel 8, the local television station, was that Brett Toland had been shot to death aboard his yacht late last night, and that a former employee named Elaine Commins had been charged with his murder and taken into custody early this morning.

2

I hate the sight of women in jailhouse threads.

Even more so than with men, the clothes seem to rob them of all humanity. Lainie Commins was wearing on this Wednesday morning a shapeless blue smock with the words CALUSA COUNTY JAIL stenciled over the breast pocket. White gym socks. Laceless black shoes. No lipstick, no eye shadow. They had confiscated the heart-shaped Victorian ring for safekeeping. Only the eyeglasses were her own. Everything else she had on, right down to her underwear, belonged to the county. Even her tan seemed to have been confiscated by the authorities; under the harsh, overhead fluorescent lights, she looked pale and somehow faded. She hadn't sent for me, but I was here, and she seemed glad to see me.

"I thought you might need help in finding a good criminal lawyer," I said.

"I want you to represent me," she said.

"I wouldn't advise that."

"Why not?"

"Because I lost the only murder case I ever tried."

"I didn't kill anyone."

"I would hope not. But . . ."

"And I'm happy with the way you've been handling the copyright case."

I looked at her.

"Lainie," I said, "copyright infringement isn't murder. You've been charged with murder in the first degree, and in Florida . . ."

"I didn't murder anyone."

". . . that's a capital felony."

"So they told me."

"Who told you?"

"The detectives who arrested me."

"When was that?"

"After they took me downtown. Before they started questioning me."

"Had they informed you of your rights by then?"

"Yes. I think so."

"Had they informed you of your right to a lawyer?"

"Yes. I didn't think I'd need one. It was all too ridiculous. I thought I'd be out of there in a minute. I don't even own a gun. That wasn't my gun. I was on the boat for no more than . . ."

"You were on the *boat?*"

"Yes."

"Last *night?*"

"Yes. But only for a little while."

"How short a while?"

"Half an hour? No more than that. I didn't kill Brett, I didn't even know he was *dead* until they came to my house and arrested me. Matthew, I want someone I know and trust to defend me, I want *you,* Matthew. Please help me. I didn't murder Brett Toland."

I looked at her again. Behind the glasses, her right eye had begun wandering yet another time. I wondered how often that wayward eye had served to enlist sympathy and compassion.

"If I represent you . . ." I said.

"Yes. Please. Help me, Matthew."

". . . I'd want someone else in my office to do the actual trial work."

"However you want to do it."

I nodded.

"Tell me again," I said. "Did you kill him?"

"I didn't kill him."

I nodded again.

"Your first appearance hearing is at eleven this morning," I said, and looked at my watch. "We've got an hour to talk. Tell me what you were doing on that boat."

I have to tell you that I frankly believed she was making a mistake. I am very good at gathering facts, I will admit that, I am a total bulldog when it comes to sniffing things out and clamping my jaws on them and shaking them till they yelp. But I really don't think I have the requisite shark mentality to try a murder case. I'm not being modest. I just don't think I'm cut out for it. Benny Weiss, admittedly the best criminal lawyer in all Calusa — in fact, maybe in all Florida — once told me that he never asks a person charged with murder whether he committed the crime.

"I don't *care* if a client did it or not," he told me. "I'm only interested in combating the charge against him. So I tell him what the other side has, or what they think they have, and then between us we work out a plan of attack. You'll notice I did not use the word *defense,* Matthew. As far as I'm concerned, this is an *attack,* a relentless *attack* against forces determined to deprive my client of his constitutional right to liberty, whether he committed the crime or not."

Well, the way I see it, the Canons of Professional Ethics notwithstanding, which canons grant to a lawyer the right — but not the obligation — to undertake a defense *regardless* of his personal opinion as to the guilt or innocence of the accused, otherwise an *innocent* person might God forbid be denied a proper defense and our entire judicial system would go down the drain, provided the jury system doesn't flush it out to sea first . . .

But the way *I* see it, if someone has

committed murder — or arson, or armed robbery, or rape, or aggravated assault, or any one of the hundreds of crimes we have designated as affronts to civilization — then he should be punished for that crime. It's a bromide of the criminal justice system that you'll never find anyone in prison who's actually committed the crime that put him there. You won't find any guilty people in a courtroom, either. That's because a lawyer got there first. The day I stand in a courtroom and hear a judge ask, "How do you plead?" and hear the accused answer, "Guilty, Your Honor" is the day I will fall down dead in another coma.

Meanwhile, I bequeath to every criminal lawyer in the world anyone who has stabbed his wife or shot his mother or set fire to his girlfriend's house or poisoned his goldfish or peed in his neighbor's mailbox.

Me, I won't defend anyone I think is guilty.

Warren's friend went by the name of Amberjack James.

He had got the name not because the color of his skin sort of matched the fish's color — what the rednecks down here used to call "high yeller" back when such shit was still tolerated — but because he'd caught the biggest jack ever fished in the waters off Calusa, a hundred-and-ten-pound beauty that now hung mounted on a plaque in the living room of the small house he shared with a girl much darker than he was but only half his age and a lot prettier. Amberjack was thirty-seven. The girl had just turned eighteen. *Less* than half his age, actually. She was in the kitchen fixing lunch while Warren and Amberjack sat on the back porch of the house, looking out at the river and the boat Warren hoped to borrow.

Amberjack's real name . . .

Or rather the name he'd been born with, or rather the name that had been *foisted* upon him at birth since nobody — the way he looked at it — was ever *born* with a name tattooed on his forehead or his belly button, he was just born naked and squawking and helpless till some higher authority *put* a name on him.

In this case the higher authority happened to be his daddy, and the name he'd put on poor powerless little Amberjack was Harry James. This was in honor of a white trumpet player Amberjack's daddy admired, he playing the cornet himself, which was a fine tribute, to be sure, if it didn't so happen that James was also the *family* name, which made the baby come out Harry James James. Never did amount to much of a horn player, Amberjack's daddy, but he left Amberjack's mama a goodly sum of money when he died of cancer at the age of sixty-two, and he'd left Amberjack him-self — in addition to the stupid fuckin name — the thirty-foot powerboat from which he'd caught his record fish two years later, thereby leaving behind forever the name of the honky bugler he'd never heard of, any-way.

It was the boat Warren was here to bor-row.

"What you gonna do with it?" Amberjack asked.

Both men were drinking Coors beer and munching on fried pork rinds they were plucking out of a red and yellow cellophane bag even though Mercedes had yelled twice from the kitchen to stop snackin less they spoil they appetites. The beer was cold and tasty and the rinds were salty and crisp. It was another scorching-hot day here in Calusa. Warren kept thinking it'd be cooler out on the water, on Amberjack's boat. The boat was tied up at a ramshackle wooden dock that thrust out into a narrow canal. The shallow water here near the shore was choked with green. The air was still.

"I just need to borrow it for a few days," Warren said.

"For what?"

"Something I have to do."

"Something legal?"

"Come on, Am, I'm a licensed P.I."

"Cause, nigger, I got to tell you. You use

my boat to run any kind of controlled substance up onto the beach . . ."

"This is nothing like that, Am."

"Then answer my question. Is what you plan to do with my boat *legal?*"

"Yes, it's legal," Warren said, lying in that what he had in mind wasn't *strictly* legal. Not that anyone would condemn him for doing it. Still, it *was* Am's boat, and he had every right to ask Warren what he planned to do with it, just as Warren had every right to *lie* about his plans.

"You even know *how* to run a boat?" Amberjack asked.

"Oh, sure," Warren said.

"Where you gonna take this boat?"

"Out on the Gulf."

"How far out?"

"Twenty, thirty miles."

"Better not go any further'n that," Amberjack said. "She holds a hundred gallons of gas, burns about ten gallons an hour, so plan accordingly. I usually figure I can go a hun' forty miles on a tank of gas."

"I'll be careful."

"What's out on the Gulf?"

"Thought I'd do some fishing."

"Maybe I'll go with you."

"I feel the need for solitude, Am."

"You takin some woman out there with you?"

Warren smiled.

"What I figured all along," Amberjack said, and returned the smile. "Don't get too busy you miss any hurricane coming. There's a good radio on the boat, you keep it tuned to either channel one or channel three. You hear anything sounds like weather, you head right back in, hear?"

"I told you, I'll be careful."

"Never mind careful. You turn around and haul ass the minute you hear any kind of Coast Guard warnin."

"I will."

"I like that little boat," Amberjack explained.

In Florida, a so-called first appearance hearing is normally held before a County Court judge on the morning following an arrest. Quite some time ago, the state's Supreme Court had ruled that even a person accused of a capital crime was entitled to bail. Moreover, the ruling held that unless proof of the crime were "evident" or presumption of the crime "great," bail could not be denied. It was my job to ask for bail and to argue that it should be granted. It was the state attorney's job to argue that the evidence he possessed was so legally overwhelming that a verdict of guilty was inevitable and thus bail should be denied. The judge's job was to decide one way or the other. The decision was exclusively his to make. Or, in this instance, hers.

The presiding judge this morning was a woman named Heather Grant, some forty years old and alarmingly attractive in black, probably because black was a good color for a redhead. Male attorneys tend to prefer homely female judges to pretty ones. I don't know why that should be; no one in the legal profession debates whether a *male* judge has good legs or not. Heather had good legs and good breasts and flaming-red hair and beautiful brown eyes and she was a good dancer besides, as I'd discovered at many of Calusa's charity balls. But she was one of the toughest judges on the County bench, especially where it concerned female defendants, go figure.

Lainie Commins appeared before the Court in her unfashionable jailhouse threads, wearing lipstick, eyeliner, and blush, which her keepers had allowed for this hearing that would merely determine her immediate freedom. Tomorrow morning at nine, a grand jury would decide whether to indict or to dismiss. It was my personal opinion that the state attorney — in this case, an assistant named Peter Folger — would get the indictment he was seeking. But that was no reason to keep Lainie in jail for the next six or seven months or however long it took for her case to come to trial on an exceptionally crowded calendar.

I told Heather that based on my investigation to date — which was bullshit,
since all I'd done so far was talk to my
client — I did not know of any eyewitnesses to the actual shooting, did not
know of any conclusive forensic evidence,
and believed that the prosecution's case
was wholly circumstantial and that there
was no evidence so great or proof so evident as to prevent the automatic granting
of bail as provided by the statutes. Moreover, Ms. Commins had no previous record
of violence, and no possible motive for the
crime — she had, in fact, been seeking
to resolve her differences with Mr. Toland
in a court of law. In short, Lainie Commins
posed no threat to society and was a responsible citizen with roots in the community, who would meet all scheduled
court appearances. I then recited the "Let
Freedom Ring" speech and asked that she
be released on her own recognizance.

I was pretty good, if I say so myself.

Folger went the "Monstrous Beast" route,
telling Heather that the victim had been
shot twice in the face, that this angelic-
looking woman sitting here was in fact a
cold-blooded killer nursing a deep-seated
anger against the victim, that exposure as
an impostor and a thief was sufficient motive for the crime, that the danger of her
fleeing the jurisdiction was very real in light

of the airtight case the people had, and that releasing her on bail would also pose a danger to the state's witnesses, whereby he sang the "Particularly Heinous Nature of the Crime" song and respectfully requested that bail be denied.

Heather set bail at half a million dollars, which I promptly assured her could be secured by the defendant's home, offering to turn over to the Court the deed to her house, her current tax bill and her passport for good measure.

Whatever the grand jury decided tomorrow morning, Lainie was for the time being a free woman.

The first thing I say when I open my eyes is "Where am I?"

Hardly original, it nonetheless startles the ICU nurse into unaccustomed alacrity. Running from the room shouting "Doctor! Doctor!" she provides the first clue that I might be in some sort of medical facility. The second clue comes with the realization that I am lying flat on my back with a great many tubes running into or out of my arm or arms.

Someone leans over the bed.

"Mr. Hope?"

He has a little black mustache and little brown eyes opened wide in expectation and surprise.

"Who are you?" I ask. "Where am I?"

"I'm Dr. Spinaldo. You're at Good Samaritan Hospital. In Calusa, Florida. Do you know where Calusa, Florida, is?"

"My head hurts," I say.

"I'm sure it does," he says. "Do you know your name?"

"What is this?" I ask.

"This is Good Samaritan Hospital in . . ."

"Yes, Calusa, Florida. What is *this?*" I ask, more forcefully this time. "Why are you asking me if I know my own name?"

"You've been very sick," Spinaldo says.

There is now something close to unbridled joy on his face. I expect him to begin crying in ecstasy at any moment. I suddenly like him. And just as suddenly I remember. But not everything.

"Did I get shot?"

"Yes," he says.

"My chest hurts."

"Good."

"My shoulder, too."

"Very good."

I cannot imagine why he thinks hurting so much is good and very good. I do not realize that he's telling me I'm *feeling* things again. He's telling me I'm *awake* again. The problem is I don't remember having been asleep. Euphemism of the week. Asleep. It will later be explained to me that sometime while I was in surgery and they were frantically trying to repair the ruptured blood vessels in my chest, I suffered cardiac arrest and . . .

Well, what happened was my heart stopped for five minutes and forty seconds, and there was subsequent loss of blood to the brain . . .

No blood was being pumped to the brain, you see.

No blood was being circulated *anywhere* in my body.

In short, I was in a coma for seven days, eleven hours, and fifteen minutes, after which time — and with a mighty leap, don't forget — I sprang out of the pit.

A different face suddenly appears above me.

This one I know.

This one I love.

"Daddy," she whispers.

Joanna.

My daughter. Blue eyes brimming with tears. Blond hair falling loose as she leans over the bed.

"Oh Daddy."

Nothing more. And hugs me close.

And the nurse who'd earlier run to fetch the doctor cautions her not to knock over the stand holding the plastic bag of *whatever* the hell is dripping into my arm, I am beginning to feel crotchety already, you see, I want to put on my pants and get the hell out of here.

But now there is yet another face, and I love this one, too, and Patricia leans over the bed, and kisses my cheek, eyes as blue as my daughter's, shining and wet, hair as blond as my daughter's, it occurs to me that I may have a thing for blue-eyed blondes.

But, no, my former wife was a brunette, isn't that so? And lo and behold, here she is *now*, right on cue, the once and future Susan Hope, leaning over me with a smile on her face and a whispered "Welcome back, Matthew," which causes me to wonder where I've *been* because no one has yet explained to me that I've been in a coma, you see, although I am beginning to recall, vaguely, a bar someplace, I am waiting for someone in a bar, I leave the bar — and can remember nothing further.

I feel suddenly exhausted.

All at once, the room seems too noisy and too crowded and too active.

I want everyone to go away.

I want my pants back.

I want to go home.

I feel like crying.

I want to go to sleep again.

I have to pee.

Something is starting in this room on this bright day in April.

It is called recovery.

It is called recuperation.

Section 905.17 of the statutes plainly states that "no person shall be present at the sessions of the grand jury except the witness under examination, the state attorney, designated assistants as provided for in Section 27.18, the court reporter or stenographer, and the interpreter."

This means that a grand jury hearing is a nonconfrontational thing. No defense lawyers there. No cross-examination of the various witnesses. Just the state attorney munching on his own sweet ham sandwich. This further means that should an accused elect to testify, his or her lawyer cannot be present in the room. Which may explain why, in most cases, any good attorney will advise his client not to accept an invitation to go in there and face the music. I explained this to Lainie now, and she nodded gravely and said it seemed unfair. I told her that perhaps the word she was seeking was "Draconian."

I had picked her up at the County Jail after she'd changed back into civilian clothing, the jeans, T-shirt and sandals she'd thrown on last night when the police came to arrest her. I was driving her home to North Apple because we needed to talk further and also because she'd promised to show me the new stuffed animal she'd been sketching when the call from Brett Toland came last night. I was eager to see her drawings because her frame of mind was important to the events that had subsequently transpired. The important thing was that she'd been working on something *new,* you see. She was planning to move on, planning for the *future.* Contrary to her gloomy outlook at lunch, by the time she'd got back to her house, she'd come around to believing that Judge Santos would find in our favor and order the preliminary injunction we were seeking. There was no reason for her to have wanted Brett Toland dead. She hadn't even been *thinking* of Brett when his call came later that night.

Her house on North Apple looked exactly as she'd described it to the Court yesterday morning. I parked my car under a huge shade tree which I could not identify, and looked up to make sure there weren't any birds in it. The car I drive is a slate-blue Acura Legend which Patricia ran into just before our first meeting. She claims I will never forgive her for that. Maybe I won't. Rudyard Kipling once wrote, "And a woman is only a woman, but a good cigar is a smoke." I don't smoke, but I *love* that car. Not as much as I love Patricia, he was quick to amend. But I still didn't want birds shitting all over its hood and its roof.

I followed Lainie up the path to the low cinder-block structure, and then into the house itself. She showed me around briefly, asked if I wanted a cold drink — it was only three-thirty, so I guessed she meant a soft drink — and we each went into the studio carrying a beaded glass of lemonade afloat with ice cubes. I felt as if I'd been in this house before, this work space before. She threw a light switch. The fluorescents came on over the long drawing table she'd described at the hearing, illuminating her sketches for Kinky Turtle. She pointed out the date she'd penciled into the lower right-hand corner of each drawing, just below her signature. Unless she'd altered the notations, the drawings had, in fact, been made yesterday.

"Tell me everything that happened last night," I said.

"From when to when?"

"From when Brett called to the last time you saw him alive."

It occurs to me as she speaks that she would make a compelling witness if ever we decide to put her on the stand. Her eyeglasses do nothing to correct that wandering right eye. But the visual defect gives her a somewhat startled look that attracts unwavering attention. As beautiful as she is, it is the imperfect eye that lends to her otherwise flawless features a skewed look that is totally compelling.

Sitting on a stool in jeans, T-shirt and

sandals, hands in her lap, she tells me she was in the studio working on the sketches when the telephone rang . . .

"What time was this?"

"Around nine o'clock."

"How do you know?"

"Because when we were later talking about my going over there . . ."

Brett is calling to invite her to his boat.

"What for?" she asks him.

"I want to discuss a settlement," he says.

"Then call my lawyer," she says.

"I don't want to drag the lawyers in just yet, Lainie."

"Brett," she says, "the lawyers are *already* in."

"The lawyers are why we *have* this problem, Lainie. All lawyers should be *shot*, Lainie. I want to discuss this face-to-face, just you and me. You're familiar with the toy business, you'll understand the significance of what I want to suggest."

"Okay, try me," she says.

"Not on the phone."

"Why not?"

"Lainie, trust me, my proposal . . ."

"Trust you, Brett?"

"I know we've had our differences . . ."

"Differences? You stole my fucking *bear!*"

"I'm willing to grant there are similarities between your design and ours. But what I'm about to propose . . ."

"Propose it to Matthew Hope."

"Lainie, I promise you this won't compromise your case at all. This isn't a trick. I know you've been made aware of the fact that if money alone could repair your injuries . . ."

"Forget money, Brett. If you're about to . . ."

"No, I'm not offering a cash settlement."

"What are you offering?"

"Come to the boat."

"No. Call Hope. Make your offer to him."

"Lainie, please. For old times' sake. Please. I promise you this is a solution. You won't be disappointed. Come here and let me talk to you."

She hesitates.

"Where's here?" she asks.

"The yacht club."

"Which one?"

"Silver Creek. You've been here."

"You're there now?"

"On the boat."

"Is Etta with you?"

"No, but she's aware of what I'm about to propose. We're absolutely in agreement on it. How long will it take you to get here?"

She looks at her watch.

"An hour? Depending on traffic?"

"I'll be waiting."

"Brett . . . ?"

"Yes, Lainie?"

"This better be good."

She looks at me over her lemonade glass. I think she can sense my disapproval because she says nothing for a moment, and when she does speak it is only to explain what she'd started to tell me earlier, about knowing the time of Brett's call because she'd looked at her watch in order to estimate how long it would take for her to dress and . . .

"Yes, I realize. How long *did* it take you to get there?"

"You're thinking I shouldn't have gone, right?"

"Why did you go?"

"Old times' sake," she says, and shrugs. Brett's exact words on the phone. "We *did* work together for a long time, there *was* a history there. And I thought he might actually be ready to offer something that would simplify matters. No one likes lawsuits, Matthew."

Graciously, she did not add "No one likes lawyers, either."

"What time did you get to the club?"

"Around ten o'clock."

"Silver Creek? On the river and Polk?"

"Yes."

"How'd you get there?"

"I drove."

"What kind of car?"

"A white Geo."

"Anyone know the exact time you arrived?"

"Well, Brett."

"Unreliable witness. Dead, you know."

"*I* didn't kill him."

"Dead nonetheless."

"Stop acting so pissed off."

"You should have stuck to your guns, Lainie. You were right telling him to come to me with his offer. Why'd you change your mind?"

"I told you."

"You weren't so concerned about 'old times' when you brought the copyright suit."

"All right, damn it, I was afraid we'd *lose* it, all right?"

"That's not what you told me ten minutes ago. You told me you were feeling confident . . ."

"I was lying. I was scared shitless. I was sure Santos would eventually tell the Tolands to go right ahead with their bear."

"Then what was all that business about Kinky?"

"I *was* working on Kinky when the phone rang. As insurance. For when Santos decided *against* me."

"In other words, your frame of mind was anything *but* confident, isn't that right?"

"Whose side are you on, Matthew?"

"I can't help you if you lie to me, Lainie."

"I'm sorry."

Head bent. Little cockeyed girl in tight jeans and braless T-shirt, staring down at the hands in her lap now. Lemonade on the drawing table, alongside her "insurance" sketches for a new stuffed animal.

"All right, what happened next?"

She does not answer for a moment. She keeps staring at her hands. Then she sighs heavily, and looks up at me. Bee-stung lips slightly parted. I suddenly think it's a long time since Patricia and I made love. I put the thought out of my mind. It occurs to me that Lainie fully understands her cock-eyed appeal to men. It further occurs to me that I had better be careful here.

"Have you ever been aboard *Toy Boat?*" she asks.

"No."

"Well, she's a marvelous *rig,* as Brett calls her, making her sound like a little *runabout,* when she's actually a ninety-four-foot gaff-rigged yawl with three beautifully outfitted double staterooms and a crew cabin forward . . ."

Walkway lights illuminate the dockside area, and there is a single lamppost at the far end of the parking lot, where Lainie parks the Geo. She has dressed casually but elegantly for this meeting, perhaps because she knows the boat, and doesn't want to be intimidated by its teaked and varnished grandeur, or possibly because she truly believes Brett may be about to offer a real solution to their problem, in which case she wants to look and feel festive when they break out the celebratory champagne. So she's wearing white-laced, blue Top-Siders — she knows the rules of boating — with flaring, bell-bottomed, blue silk slacks and a white silk boat-necked shirt over which she's thrown a blue scarf in a tiny red-anchor print. The red frames of her eyeglasses are the color of her lipstick. The gold of the heart-shaped pinky ring echoes her blond hair, worn loose tonight. The hair catches glints of light from the lamppost as she steps out of the car and strides toward the Toland boat. She feels hopeful. She sometimes thinks her entire life, from the moment she learned her eyes weren't like those of other little girls, has been one long battle — but now there may be a happy ending in sight.

There are lights burning in the saloon.

From the bottom of the gangway, she calls, "Hello?"

Silence.

"Brett?" she calls.

"Lainie?" a voice says, and she sees Brett coming topside from the short ladder leading below. He is wearing white cotton slacks and a loose-fitting white buttonless cotton top slashed in a V over his chest. He hits a switch someplace on his right and light spills onto the cushioned cockpit area where she now sees that a bucket of ice, a pair of tumblers, and several bottles of liquor — she cannot read the labels yet — have been set out on the teak table. "Come aboard," he calls. "I'm so glad you decided to come."

She has been aboard this boat many times before, for cocktail parties, small dinner parties, casual lunches, an occasional sail out on the Gulf. The saloon below is furnished with comfortable couches, and glass-fronted lockers that enclose a television set, a VCR, and a CD player. The dining table seats ten comfortably, and whenever she's been here for dinner or lunch, it has been set with Wedgwood china, Waterford crystal, and damask napkins. The boat is truly luxurious, with Oriental rugs covering the teak decks, and framed Currier & Ives sailing prints hanging on the paneled bulkheads.

In the past, she has felt more comfortable in the informal cockpit area, and she's happy he has chosen this space for their meeting now. Brett is barefoot. She remembers that he once asked a state senator's wife to take off her smart linen pumps for fear she might damage his precious teak decks. "Sit," he says, "please," and indicates with an open-hand gesture one of the cushioned banquettes. She eases in behind the teak table, seeing now that the bottles on it are Johnnie Walker Black, Canadian Club, and Stolichnaya. She also notices a small white porcelain bowl with wedges of lime in it. Brett sits on the cushioned banquette on the other side of the table.

"So," he asks, "what to drink?"

"Do you have any Perrier?"

"Oh, come on, Lainie," he says, smiling. "I promise you'll want to celebrate."

"We'll see," she says, and returns the smile.

He is being his most charming self, which can be charming indeed. Again, she finds herself wishing this will truly be the end of all the turmoil and strife.

"Perrier? Really?" he says.

"Really," she says. "Perrier."

One more time, she thinks, and they'll send me a case every week for the rest of my life.

"Perrier it is," he says, and slides out from behind the table, and surefootedly slips down the ladder. She hears him rummaging below — the galley is modern and spacious, with Corian work surfaces and a four-burner stove, an oven, a microwave, a trash compactor, a freezer and she forgets how many cubic feet of refrigeration, had he once said sixty? Eighty? A lot, that was for sure. He was searching now in one of the fridges for the Perrier she'd requested, and she hears him cursing when something clatters to the deck, and then there's some muttering below, and finally he comes up the ladder again with a green bottle clutched in one hand and a blue-black automatic pistol in the other.

She looks at the gun.

"Some people tried to come aboard last week," he says in explanation, and places the gun on the table alongside the bowl of sliced limes.

"What people?" she asks.

"Two wetbacks," he says.

Meaning Cubans, she surmises.

"What'd they want?"

"They said they were looking for work. Wanted to know if I was taking on hands. *Por favor,* are you takin on some hanns, *señor,*" he says in bad imitation. "Have to be careful these days. Too many boats are being hijacked."

"From a marina dock?"

"Why not?"

"Is that thing loaded?"

"Oh yes," he says. "Sure you don't want a little vodka in this?" he asks, pouring into one of the tumblers.

"Just ice and a lime," she says.

Her artist's eyes are studying the color scheme on the table. The green of the Perrier bottle and the limes, the bone white of the bowl, the amber whiskey in two of the bottles, the black label on the Scotch echoing the black cap on the other bottle, the red and black label on the Stoli, the blue-black dullness of the Colt automatic.

Brett pours himself a hefty blast of Johnnie on the rocks.

"To our future," he says, and clinks his glass against hers. She remembers that it's bad luck to toast with a nonalcoholic beverage. But the moment has passed, the glasses have been touched, the toast has been uttered. Still, she does not drink just yet, hoping to put some distance between the bad-luck toast and the act itself, waiting first for him to take a long swallow of Scotch, and then waiting another decent interval to take the curse off before she herself sips some of the sparkling water.

"So what's the offer?" she asks.

"To the point," he says.

"Directly to the point," she says.

"Good old Lainie."

"Let me hear it."

At first, the offer sounds terrific.

What he's proposing is that instead of Toyland coming out in competition with whoever decides to manufacture *her* bear — Ideal or Mattel, either one, he has ears all over the trade, and he knows there's keen interest at each company . . .

"Which I think is wonderful for you, Lainie, you're so talented, and it's time you were rewarded for the hard years of apprenticeship you've put in . . ."

Which appraisal she doesn't quite accept since she's had half a dozen toys already produced and *marketed,* for Christ's sake, and that ain't no *apprenticeship,* thank you. But she says nothing, just listens for now, sipping at her Perrier, watching him across the table as he pours more Scotch over the ice in his glass.

He tells her that he recognizes a bidding situation might very well develop between Ideal and Mattel, which is why he's willing now to make a preemptive offer that he hopes she'll consider satisfactory. What he's suggesting . . .

She leans forward expectantly. In periods of stress, the eye seems to wander mercilessly. She can feel the tug of the muscle shortened twice by surgery. The eye is losing the battle yet another time.

"Here's what we want to do, Lainie. Toyland is willing to manufacture your bear, using your copyrighted design and your trademarked name . . ."

She recognizes this as a victory.

". . . and compensating you by way of a substantial advance against generous royalties . . ."

"How substantial? How generous?"

"To be mutually agreed upon, Lainie. I promise you, no one's trying to take advantage of you here."

"You'll call the bear Gladly?"

"Just as you have it."

"My design? For the bear *and* the eyeglasses?"

"Exactly to your specifications."

"What's the catch?"

"No catch. I just don't want to have to go through this whole damn mess, Lainie."

Which means he believes Santos will decide against him.

"So if you think what I'm suggesting is something doable," he says, "maybe you can have Matthew call my attorney . . ."

She notices that he does not refer to him familiarly as "Sidney," he is now merely "my attorney," perhaps because he's concluded the infringement case is already lost . . .

". . . so they can work out the advance and the royalties, and prepare transfers of copyright and trademark. How does that sound?"

"Transfers?"

"Yes. Toyland would want an outright assignment of all rights to the bear and its name."

"Outright?"

"Which, I'm sure, any other company would insist on."

"An outright assignment of all rights?"

"Forever," Brett says.

"Forever," she repeats.

"Yes. Well, Lainie, I'm sure this doesn't come as a surprise to you. If we're to try making a success of the bear, we'd have to be certain beforehand that we have the irrevocable right to manufacture it for the life of the copyright."

"I was thinking more in terms of a licensing agreement."

"A transfer, an assignment, a license, all the same thing."

"I don't think so."

"I'm sure neither Ideal nor Mattel would sign a limited licensing agreement."

"It sounds to me as if they might."

She is lying. The feelers from both companies have been tentative pending resolution of the copyright problem.

"Well, perhaps so, who knows, stranger things have happened. But we're willing to go a long way on royalties, Lainie, and on subsidiary rights to . . ."

"What do you mean, a long way?"

"Escalation clauses should the bear really take off. Bonuses premised on performance. A huge share of subsidiary rights . . ."

"Like what?"

"Who knows? A television show? A movie? Whatever. The percentages would be heavily loaded in your favor."

"What sort of control would I have, Brett?"

"We would guarantee the quality of the product."

"But what *control* would I have?"

"I think you know what the Toyland logo stands for. Besides, your compensation would ensure optimum performance on our part."

Which sounds like double-talk to her.

"How does it sound to you in general outline?" Brett asks.

"I'm not sure. I'll have to discuss it with Matthew," she says, and puts down her glass, and is sliding her way out of the banquette when Brett puts his hand on her arm.

"Lainie," he says, "I wish we could shake hands on this tonight."

"No, I can't. Not until I talk to him."

"Santos has promised a decision by the twenty-second."

"Well, he's shooting for that."

"End of the month, for sure. You can lose, you know."

"Then why are you offering a deal?"

"I want things to be the way they were between you and the company."

"Maybe they will. Let me talk to Matthew."

"When will you do that?"

"I'll try him when I get home."

"Will you let me know?"

"As soon as we've discussed it."

He extends his hand. She takes it. They

shake hands. The forty-five is lying on the table, alongside the bowl of limes.

"That's the last time I saw him alive," she tells me.

Warren sat in the dark, waiting for her to get home. This was not going to be a kidnapping, per se. In Florida law, the term "kidnapping" was defined as "forcibly, secretly, or by threat confining, abducting, or imprisoning another person against his will and without lawful authority . . ."

All of which Warren planned to do.

"With intent to . . ."

And these were the key words.

"With intent to hold for ransom or reward or as a shield or hostage, or to commit or facilitate commission of any felony, or to inflict bodily harm or to terrorize the victim or another person, or to interfere with the performance of any government or political function."

None of which Warren planned to do.

So what this would be was false imprisonment, which was defined in the statutes as "forcibly, by threat, or secretly confining, abducting, imprisoning or restraining another person without lawful authority and against his will . . ."

And here's where the difference came in.

"With any purpose *other* than those referred to in Section 787.01," which was the kidnapping section of the statutes.

Add to that the B&E, because he had once again unlawfully forced the door to her apartment the moment he saw her driving off in her faded green Chevy at ten o'clock tonight. He sat just inside that door now, where he could hear her key the moment she inserted it in the keyway. He had dragged a chair in from the kitchen and had placed it just to the side of the door, the bottle sitting on the floor beside him, the cap on it.

Somewhere outside, church bells began bonging the hour.

In the stillness of the apartment, he listened.

Eleven P.M.

He checked his watch.

He was two minutes fast.

Or the church was two minutes slow.

Or maybe it took two minutes for the bells to ring eleven times. This made him wonder if any clock in the world was precise. Because in the second it took for the sweep hand to move to the next number, wasn't the second already gone? Or if a digital watch read 11:02:31, as his watch now read, wasn't it already *past* 11:02:31 by the time the . . . well, there it was already 11:02:32, forget it, 11:02:33, 11:02:34, damn metaphysics could drive a person nuts.

He heard footsteps outside on the covered walkway that led past the apartments. High heels clicking. Lady must've got all dolled up to go do her marketing, he wondered where she was shopping these days.

Footfalls stopped just outside the door.

She was home.

He picked up the bottle, gently lifted the chair out of the way.

Set it down well clear of the door.

Key sliding into the keyway now.

Uncapped the bottle.

Reached into his pocket.

Lock turning, tumblers falling.

He backed against the wall to the side of the door.

Braced himself.

The door opened. She closed it behind her. Locked it. Was reaching for the light switch . . .

"Hello, Toots," he said.

"Warren?" she said, turning toward him, and he clamped the chloroform-soaked pad over her face.

3

She opened her eyes.

The room was pitching and rolling, took her a minute to realize she was on a boat, and that her right wrist was handcuffed to something bolted to the wall or the bulkhead or whatever they called it. It was dark in the V-shaped space where she was lying on her back, she figured she was up front in the boat, the space coming to a kind of a point this way. Some sort of foam mattress under her, this had to be a sleeping compartment.

She remembered Warren all at once, standing there in the dark inside the door to her apartment and she called his name sharply — "Warren?" — like an angry mother or older sister screaming for a rotten kid to get here right this fucking minute if he knew what was good for him, handcuffing her to the wall this way. But nobody came, and all at once she wondered if it *was*, in fact, Warren driving the boat and not some fisherman he'd hired to take her to Mexico and sell her into prostitution.

The boat was moving, that was for sure, so there had to be *someone* up there, or out there, or wherever the steering wheel was, if that's what you called it, she hadn't been on too many boats in her lifetime. She brought her left wrist close to her face in the dark and looked at the luminous dial of her watch, ten minutes past two, where the hell were they?

"*Warren?*" she called again, same imperious Get-Your-Ass-in-Here tone, and this time she heard a sound from what she guessed was the back of the boat, the rear, the *aft*, what*ever*, and she heard footfalls coming down what she supposed were steps, a ladder, and then through the boat toward where she was sitting up now, short skirt hiked kind of high on her legs, still wearing all her clothes, she noticed, including her high-heeled shoes.

A light snapped on.

She squinted her eyes against it.

She could now see that a low wall divided the sleeping area from what appeared to be a dining area with leatherette banquettes around a Formica-topped table, and then another low wall separated this area from the food preparation area — well, a small *kitchen* actually, well, a *galley*, she guessed you called it. So what this appeared to be was a single somewhat smallish section of the boat, what you might call a cabin, she supposed, divided by these very low walls, these bulkheads, and through the cabin came Warren, waltzing on over and ducking his head because of the low ceiling, or overhead, she *hated* boats.

"Okay, what is this?" she asked.

"What is what?"

"Why am I chained to the wall? Where'd you get the hardware?" she asked, rattling the handcuff on her wrist.

"St. Louis P.D."

"You still got the key?"

"Yes, I've . . ."

"Then unlock it," she said, and shook her wrist again.

"Sorry, Toots."

"Well, first we've got the B&E," she said, "I figure that for a good fifteen years. And then we've got the kidnapping . . ."

"False imprisonment," he said.

"Thank you. Which should add another five to your tab. So how about unlocking these cuffs right this fucking minute and turning this barge around and taking me back home, and we'll forget the whole thing, okay?"

"No," he said. "Sorry."

"I ask again, Warren. What is this?"

"It's cold turkey," Warren said.

At nine o'clock that Friday morning, the fifteenth day of September, the grand jury listened to the witnesses Pete Folger had invited to testify on behalf of the people of the state of Florida. At six minutes before noon, the jurors returned a true bill signed by the jury foreman and requesting the state attorney to file an indictment for first-degree murder.

Folger called me in my office ten minutes later. He told me he'd got the true bill he was seeking, and said he was now going to ask that bail be denied my client, and that she be taken into custody. He also mentioned that as a matter of courtesy he would have someone in his office type up a list of the witnesses who'd testified today, in the hope that I would talk to them myself, as soon as possible, and then be willing to discuss a deal that would save his office a lot of time and the state a huge electricity bill.

I called Lainie to tell her the bad news and to advise that I'd be requesting bail be continued as set . . .

"Do you think it will be?"

"Yes, I feel certain it will."

"Good, because I've been invited to a party," she said. "All at once, I'm a celebrity."

"Don't say a word about the case."

"Of course not."

"They'll want to know. Just tell them your lawyer says you can't discuss anything about it. If they persist, walk away."

"I will. Thank you, Matthew."

"The state attorney's already mentioned a

deal. I think that's a good sign."

"Why do we need a deal?" she asked.

"We don't."

"I didn't kill him," she said.

"I know you didn't."

"*Do* you know?"

"Yes, I do. Where's your party?"

"On the Rosenberg yacht," she said.

"Small world," I said.

She had heard him banging around in the galley as she lay on the foam mattress that had no sheet on it, trying to keep her skirt tucked around her legs, everything feeling sticky with salt, she hated boats, her right arm extended uncomfortably behind her head, the wrist handcuffed to what she now realized was some sort of stainless-steel grab rail bolted to the bulkhead. When she sat up, she could see him standing at the small stove on the port side of the boat, to the left of the ladder leading below. Cooking smells filled the vessel.

He finally brought in some scrambled eggs and browned sausage and whole-wheat toast and coffee, carrying everything in on a tray which he put down on the berth in front of her.

The first thing she said was, "Who's driving this thing?"

"We're drifting."

"Won't we run into something?"

"We're thirty miles out. There's nothing anywhere near us."

"Take off the cuff."

"No," he said.

"How can I eat with my hand chained to the wall?"

"Use your left hand. Or I can feed you if you like."

"I don't need your help," she said, and picked up the fork with her left hand and began eating, sitting with her legs crossed Indian fashion on the berth. He watched her.

"You're making a mistake, you know," she said.

"Am I?"

"Yes, Warren. I'm still clean."

"No, you're not," he said.

"Well, I really don't know where you're getting your information, but I can promise you . . ."

"I found some empty crack vials in your bathroom trash basket," he said.

"Why'd you go to my apartment in the first place?"

"I guess I know the signs of cocaine addiction, Toots."

"You had no right."

"I'm your friend."

"Sure, chained to the wall."

"Would you stay on this boat otherwise?"

"Warren, you have to let me go. Really."

"No."

"Warren, I don't need anyone to look after me, really. I'm a big girl now."

"Yes, that's what I thought, too, Toots."

"I'm *not* doing drugs again," she said. "Do you think I'm crazy? Those were *perfume* samples. The vials look . . ."

"Sure."

". . . just like crack vials."

"How about the ones I found in your handbag?"

"I don't know what you found in my handbag. You had no right going through my handbag. You have no right doing *any* of this. What'd you find in my handbag that gives you the right to . . . ?"

"Crack vials, Toots."

"I told you. Perfume samples . . ."

"With rocks in them."

"You're mistaken."

"No, Toots, I'm not mistaken. I know what crack rocks look like."

"Someone must've . . ."

"How about the pipe?"

"Was there a pipe, too? Someone must've dropped all that stuff in my bag. People do all sorts of . . ."

"Sure."

". . . crazy things. To make a person look bad. Or just cheap. Anyway, you had no right. When did you do that?"

"Do what?"

"Go through my bag."

"Last night. Right after I got you on the boat."

"You have no right doing *any* of this. Whose boat is it, anyway?"

"Friend of mine's."

"Keeping me prisoner this way. No right at all. He'll be in trouble, too, you know."

"Nobody's in trouble but you, Toots. That's why I'm here."

"I don't need you here, Warren. All I need you to . . ."

"No."

"I'm not doing dope. I don't need a guardian. I don't need a warden. I don't need you to look *after* me, Warren. All I need you to do is take off these fucking *cuffs!*"

"No."

"Warren, I have to be left alone to do what I want to do."

"I won't let you do crack, Toots."

"I will do *exactly* what I . . ."

"No."

"Then I'm going to scream."

"Go ahead, scream."

"The Coast Guard will come."

"Ain't nobody here but us chickens, boss," he said.

She began screaming.

The boat was a seventy-five-foot Burger worth about four million dollars, large enough to accommodate, without crowding, the two dozen guests who stood talking and sipping cocktails on the aft deck as the sun began its slow descent into the Gulf of Mexico.

The boat was named *Sea Sybil*, after one of its owners, Sybil Rosenberg, whose husband was the attorney David Rosenberg, who was senior partner in the firm of Rosenberg, Katlowitz and Frank, all of whom made a lot more money than I did. In Calusa, Florida, everybody knew how much money everybody else made. There were a lot of moneyed people down here in this Paradise by the Sea, this Athens of Southwest Florida. Most of the money came from Canada or the Middle West; that was because if you drew a zigzagging line south from Toronto, it would pass through Cleveland and Pittsburgh and then hit Calusa before heading for Havana.

Coincidence, or perhaps fate, had thrown Lainie and me together on the same boat for the same sunset bash. Being out on bail could turn into a pleasant pastime in a small town, even if you'd been charged with slaying your mama, your papa, and your pet parakeet. As Calusa's latest Accused Murderess celebrity, I supposed she would be much in demand in the weeks and months to come, and I knew I couldn't confine her to her home or be with her at every function she attended, monitoring every word she muttered. Clearly the center of attention in a circle of sunset watchers on the starboard side of the boat, all of whom seemed eager to know what it felt like to be accused of *murdering* someone, for God's sake, she successfully fended off any attempt to learn what had happened or not happened on Brett Toland's yawl.

As for me, everyone kept asking how I was feeling.

Everyone kept asking what it had felt like.

This evening, I was lying.

It was a way of creating my own fun. I used to do that even *before* I'd got shot one dark and stormless night. I hated cocktail parties, especially sunset cocktail parties, especially sunset cocktail parties on boats. I sometimes felt that the moneyed people who moved down here from unspeakable climes like those in Minneapolis or Milwaukee or South Bend did so only because they liked to look at sunsets.

"I found myself staring into the face of God," I said.

"What did she look like?" Aggie Pratt asked.

A long time ago, I had enjoyed — if that was the appropriate word — an extramarital love affair with Aggie. In fact, Aggie was the reason Susan and I had ended our marriage. I don't think I liked myself very much back then, but that was all in the past, merely yet another sun dropping into yet another vast body of water.

Aggie had eventually divorced her then husband Gerald, and was now married to a man named Louis Pratt who published the *Calusa Herald-Tribune*; I still had difficulty remembering that she was now Mrs. Pratt. She looked very good to me tonight, causing me to wonder what was happening to me. Gray eyes glowing in the fading light of the sinking sun, faint smile on her generous mouth as she made her little God-Is-a-Woman joke, long black hair (Aggie's, not God's) combed straight and sleek as Cleopatra's, short black, scoop-necked cocktail dress exposing treasures I recalled fondly but only vaguely.

Patricia Demming stood beside me in the ring of people wanting to know what *God* had looked like, for God's sake! I couldn't tell from the expression on her face whether or not she knew I was putting them on. Maybe she thought a vision of the Almighty actually had appeared to me one night while I was adrift in limbo. Her red dress — her favorite color, by the way — was also extravagantly low cut, considering the fact that she was supposed to be a staid and serious assistant state attorney, albeit beautiful and buxom and not in any courtroom at the moment, its daring bodice

115

revealing yet *more* treasures I could scarcely remember, where have you gone, Joe DiMaggio?

"Actually he was a man," I said, "and he looked like Joe DiMaggio," winging it.

My former wife Susan was also here aboard the *Sea Sybil* — large boat, small town. As the sun plunked into the Gulf, she and all the assembled guests ooohed and ahhhed the obligatory squeals of delight. She was wearing tonight an extremely short, moss-green cocktail dress that showcased spectacular legs I remembered quite well, thank you, though I wouldn't have wished her to notice me noticing them. The sky suddenly turned a sexy velvety violet — what the hell *was* happening to me?

"What did you and God talk about?" Aggie asked.

"Sex," I said, and my eyes met Patricia's, who was the only one who didn't laugh at the remark.

"Do people even *think* about sex when they're in coma?" a woman named Andrea Lang asked, and Susan responded — with all the authority of someone who'd been married to the apparent subject in question for, lo, those many years — "Matthew *always* thinks about sex," which comment did not sit at all well with Patricia, who turned away and joined the cluster of satellites around Lainie. Thinking better of it an instant later — she was, after all, an S.A. even though one of her colleagues would be trying the case — she sauntered over to the bar and extended her glass to the man behind it. A few moments later, Lainie walked over to where I was now standing alone, I sure know how to clear a room.

She was wearing a short, peach-colored, rayon dress cut fore and aft in plunging Vs, with flaring pleats created by a knotted tie at the back. Drop earrings with red tourmaline stones. Victorian seal ring once again on her right pinky. High-heeled open-toed sandals with red straps. Long blond hair pulled back into a ponytail fastened with a barrette fashioned from tiny seashells. Rimless eyeglasses that lent a touch of the schoolmarm to an otherwise sophisticated look. Right eye askew behind them.

"When do you expect that witness list?" she asked.

"Tomorrow morning."

"What then?"

"We'll see."

"Will you call me?"

"I'll call you," I promised.

We sounded like spies.

She couldn't believe she was hooked again.

Toots Kiley.

That's m'name, folks, she thought. Daughter of James Kiley, who'd heroically named her after Toots Thielemans, best harmonica player in the world, take it or leave it. Nor is Toots a nickname, folks, remember that, it is a proud and proper given name. Toots. To rhyme with "puts" and not "boots," as if you didn't know. But enough already, she thought. You're a fucking crackhead, Toots.

A cop had got her started the first time, that had been the irony of it.

Same cop got her started all over again *this* time, that was the same irony all over again.

Good old Rob Higgins, pride of the Calusa P.D.

First time around, it was cocaine. Sitting in a car with him in Newtown, working a case where she was tailing a woman whose husband suspected her of cheating on him, but who was instead — or so Rob claimed — working in a whorehouse he'd been investigating. "Your lady ain't fuckin *around*," he'd told Toots, "she's just plain *fuckin*." So there they were, sitting in a car outside the place at a little after midnight on a September morning more years ago than she chose to remember, with an hour or so to kill before the next wave of johns arrived before closing time, and all at once Higgins asked, "You feel like doin' a few lines?"

Well now, Toots *knew* what this *meant,* of course, she didn't think he was speaking Martian or anything, she knew the significance of the words "doin' a few lines." The only surprise was that a *cop* was the one asking her if she'd care to snort a little coke. "What do you say?" he asked. This was a time when a well-meaning but ill-informed First Lady was advising ghetto kids to Just Say No. Toots wasn't a ghetto kid. "Why the hell not?" she said.

An hour later, higher than a fucking kite, she'd floated up the whorehouse stairs with Rob and got some very nice pictures of the married lady she was tailing, who was wearing at close to two in the morning nothing but black open-crotch panties from Frederick's of Hollywood and black boots with four-inch-high spike heels, and who was incidentally blowing a black man who was at least six feet four inches tall all over.

It took Toots two years to sober up.

It took her two minutes to fall off the wagon.

She ran into Rob Higgins again the day Matthew Hope was released from the hospital. She was there at Good Samaritan on that bright sunny day at the end of May when a nurse wheeled him out to the curb in a wheelchair, Patricia waiting in her car to pick him up and drive him home. Warren, and Detective Bloom, and Matthew's partner Frank, and even Matthew's former wife Susan were all there to wish him well and to let him know they'd be there for him if ever he needed them, though Patricia looked as if she wished Susan would wade into the Gulf of Mexico and never be heard from since.

Warren had a lunch date with a friend of his from St. Louis, who was in town for a few days — he never said whether the person was male or female, white or black — and Bloom had to get back to the Public Safety Building, and Frank and his wife Leona had no interest in having lunch with a private eye who was now wearing her formerly frizzed blond hair long and straight and hanging over one eye like Veronica Lake, whoever the hell *she* might have been. So Toots stood on the sidewalk outside the hospital with her finger up her ass, watching everybody driving off, and then she walked to where she'd parked her tired green Chevy and climbed in behind the wheel and drove over to the Calusa Square Mall, figuring she'd grab a bite to eat in one of the food courts there.

It so happened . . .

Things happen, you know.

It so happened that Detective Rob Higgins — on his day off, she learned later — was walking into a bar called Frisky's, situated at one corner of the big mall building, just as Toots got out of her car. He spotted her, sauntered over with that detective strut a lot of the plainclothes cops down here affected, asked how she was doing, and asked would she like to have lunch and a beer with him. She told him she'd join him for lunch, but she'd have to skip the beer. She was clean now, you start with a beer, next thing you know . . .

He said, "I've been straight since last January, when I burned two keys of the shit in my fireplace. But a glass of beer can't hurt anybody."

"It can hurt me," she said.

"Then drink milk," he said, and smiled. "Come on in, we'll catch up."

She still didn't know why she agreed to have lunch with him. In retrospect, she guessed it was because Warren hadn't asked her to join him and his friend from St. Louis, who — also in retrospect — she supposed had been a woman, and maybe a white woman at that. Not that there was anything but a professional relationship between her and Warren.

Or maybe it was because she was feeling sort of left out as Matthew drove off from the hospital in Patricia's car, looking small and pale and somehow lost sitting there in the passenger seat beside her, all his friends drifting off in opposite directions, leaving Toots standing alone on the sidewalk, worst thing an addict can feel is alone and lonely.

Why*ever*, she said, "Sure, why not?" and if this triggered any echoes of previous famous last lines, they were entirely lost on her. She had been taught to understand that an addict was *always* an addict, so *watch* it, sister. But somehow she temporarily forgot the admonition when she accepted Rob's invitation to lunch in a place called Frisky's, which looked like a barroom and smelled like a barroom and was populated at twelve-thirty that afternoon with a lot of people doing what looked to Toots like some very serious drinking.

They took a booth at the back, and they both ordered burgers and fries, Rob's with a beer, Toots's with a Coke. Rob started talking about Matthew Hope, what a bum break it was he'd got shot and had to lay there in coma for a week, ten days, whatever it was. Toots told him it had only been eight days or so, and that he was fine now, although it had taken a while for the gunshot wounds to heal and for him to get back his strength — well, a coma, you know. Oh, sure, Rob said. Matter of fact, Toots said, they'd picked him up at Good Sam today, and he'd looked terrific, which was a lie because he hadn't looked like his old self at all, she could still see him sitting there beside Patricia looking somehow withered and . . . well . . . old.

Rob said he'd been watching all the good work she'd been doing since she sobered up, he was really very proud of her, working with Warren Chambers, good man, they were the ones cracked the case got Hope shot, weren't they?

"Well, Morrie Bloom was on it, too," Toots said, not wanting to take all the credit. "And, anyway, it was Matthew's legwork led us in the right direction. It was almost as if he was supervising the case from his hospital bed."

For some reason, Rob looked very attractive to her. Maybe it was because he'd lost ten, fifteen pounds and was down to what he called "fighting trim" or maybe it was because he'd been putting in a lot of time on his boat most weekends and had a great tan . . .

"You like boats?" he asked. "We could maybe go out on my boat one weekend, you like boats."

"Yeah, I do," she said, lying.

The way she felt about boats was that they looked terrific from the shore, but they weren't particularly great to be on. Even so, the notion of going out on a boat with Rob one weekend was somewhat appealing, although she couldn't have said quite why at that moment. Also, he was wearing his hair differently. Back when they were sitting that whorehouse together, he wore his brown hair in a very short crew cut that really made him look like a redneck cop, but now it was longer in back and hanging on his forehead in front, which gave him a sort of boyish look with those clear blue eyes of his, she had never noticed how startlingly blue his eyes were.

It didn't occur to her that the reason Rob might have seemed so attractive to her on this day last May when she was feeling particularly vulnerable and alone was that in the early days of her getting to know cocaine Rob was the man who'd supplied her with the stuff. He was her source. He was the one who introduced her with a courtly bow to the white lady, and later — when the only thing that mattered in her life was scoring cocaine and snorting co- caine — he was the one who taught her how to go out and get it on her own, introduced her to men who would help her earn the money to pay for the stuff she so desperately needed, became her mentor and her guide, her savior and her salvation. It never occurred to her that in her mind Rob Higgins would forever be equated with snow or C or blow or toot or Peruvian lady or white girl or leaf or flake or happy dust or nose candy or freeze or any of the other darling little euphemistic pet names he'd taught her for a drug that could fry your brain whether you sniffed it up your nose or smoked it in a pipe. It never occurred to her that proximity to Rob meant proximity to the white powder that had dominated her life for more than two years. It never occurred to her that Rob would forever be equated with the soaring ecstasy she'd known when she was a user.

"So do you think you'd like to see the boat sometime?" he asked.

"Yeah, maybe," she said.

She had worn to the hospital a short khaki-colored cotton dress with panels that tied in front to create a sarong look, and she could tell from the way he was looking at her that he liked the way it showed off her legs and her breasts. It never occurred to her that she might be in danger. It never occurred to her that Rob Higgins *was* cocaine.

Looking up at her as if the idea has just occurred to him, he said, "How about now?"

On the way over to the marina, he started talking about how many crack users they'd been busting lately right here in little old Calusa — "The fuckin thing's an epidemic," he said, "well, not only here, all over America." That was because you didn't have to *snort* crack the way you did cocaine *powder,* what you did was *smoke* it, which made it appealing to people, especially teenagers, who thought smoking was sophisticated and glamorous, anyway. But smoking it meant you got your high in ten seconds or less instead of the two minutes or so it took with the dust, because the drug went straight from the lungs to the brain.

"Although there are people who say it isn't addictive because of the sodium bicarbonate they use when they're processing the drug."

"What's the sodium bicarbonate got to do with it?"

"You're asking me? It's what makes the crackling sound when you smoke it. The sodium bicarbonate. That's why it's called crack."

"Yeah, but what's sodium bicarbonate got to do with whether or not it's addictive."

"They say it makes it *non*addictive," Rob said.

"Who says?"

"Addicts," Rob said, and laughed.

"That's bullshit," Toots said. "Crack is freebase cocaine, and cocaine's addictive, period."

"Well, not *physically* addictive."

"No, not physically. But . . ."

"As well we both know," he said.

"As well we both know," she repeated, nodding in acknowledgment, smiling in appreciation of the fact that they'd both been there and back.

"You hear all *kinds* of crazy stories from these jerks doing crack," Rob said. "We picked up this guy last Tuesday in a bust we made, he told us Sigmund Freud was a famous coke user, the shrink, you know?"

"Yeah?"

"Yeah. And that he'd written some kind of medical paper, Freud, about how coke cured indigestion and morphine addiction, and how it also helped cure asthma, and how it could be used to arouse sexual desire. Anyway, here we are," he said.

He was all over her the minute they got on the boat.

His hands went up under the short cotton dress, and she felt him hard against her as he pulled her close, and she thought Hey, I thought you were going to show me your boat, but she did nothing to stop him, pressed tighter into him instead, tilting her groin into him, arms going up around his neck, lips responding when his mouth claimed hers. They half fell, half slid onto one of the berths up forward, in a narrow little space as tight as a cave, and he slid her panties down over her thighs and her ankles, and spread her wide to him, and she wondered how long it had been since anyone had touched her down there, sober and celibate went hand in hand. His hands on her buttocks now, lifting her to him, inside her now, clutching her tight against him, enclosing him, rising to meet him, Jesus.

He showed her the crack pipe while she was still lying naked on the bed. Stood before her naked himself, tanned every-where but on his ass and his still faintly tumescent cock, poor baby. It took a moment for her eyes to move reluctantly to the glass pipe in his hands. Naked, he sat on the bed beside her.

"Want to see how it works?" he asked.

"I know how it works," she said, meaning she didn't want a *demonstration,* for Christ's sake, they were both clean. But maybe he meant the *principle* of the thing, a demonstration of how it would work if somebody actually *put* crack in it, because she didn't think he actually had any crack here on this nice boat where he'd just fucked her brains out. What she figured was the pipe was something he'd picked up busting a crack house someplace in New-town, little war souvenir, so to speak. She never expected him to open one of the lockers and lift out a little plastic Baggie full of plastic vials that really did look like the vials perfume samples came in. But there were rock crystals in these vials. There was crack in these vials.

"Where'd you get that?" she asked.

"You pick up things here and there. Let me show you."

"Rob . . ." she started to say, but he said, "Biggest high you ever had, Toots," and suddenly her heart was pounding fiercely, and suddenly she was wet again below, as if anticipating sex, when all she anticipated was cocaine.

Now, four months later, miles and miles from shore again, she sat handcuffed to the bulkhead of another boat and felt the first pangs of a gnawing desire she knew would devour her completely in the days and nights to come.

I kept thinking of *Annie Hall*, where there's a split screen and Woody Allen is talking to *his* psychiatrist while Diane Keaton is talking to *hers* and the psychiatrists are both asking the same question, "How often do you have sex?" and he answers "Hardly *ever*," and she answers "All the *time!*" Or words to that effect, it was an old movie.

Patricia wanted to know what I'd meant by my remark about God.

"I was making a joke. We didn't really talk about sex."

"What *did* you talk about?"

"He wanted to know how I'd like my steak done."

Patricia ignored this.

"It seems to me," she said, "that raising the topic of sex in Susan's presence was tantamount to leading a witness."

"I didn't raise the topic. Andrea Lang did."

"You were the one who first mentioned sex."

"Andrea Lang was the one who asked if people in coma thought about sex."

"Chain of custody," Patricia said. "Tinkers to Evers to Chance. An opening that allowed Susan to testify as an expert. And what's with you and the Cross-Eyed Cooze?"

"She's a client," I said. "You know that. Talking about her is out of bounds."

The professional arrangement Patricia and I have made — as opposed to our personal arrangement, such as it's been since my recovery, but who's griping? — is that we simply do not discuss any criminal case I'm working, this to avoid even the slightest appearance of impropriety between the law firm of Summerville and Hope and the State Attorney's Office. Since Patricia is one of the brightest stars on the prosecution team headed by Skye Bannister — the unfortunate name with which our eminent state attorney was anointed — and since my office handles a great many *non-*criminal legal matters, we normally have plenty to talk about when it comes to sharing shoptalk.

But this wasn't shoptalk tonight.

"She really *should* stop wearing her skirts

so short, by the way."

"Lainie?"

"*Susan*. And she should also stop using your goddamn name."

"It's *her* goddamn name, too."

"Doesn't she have a maiden name?"

"Not anymore. She hasn't been a maiden for many moons now."

"Didn't she *once* have a maiden name?"

"Yes, Susan Fitch," I said.

"So why doesn't she go back to it? Why does she have to keep *clinging* to you?"

"I wasn't aware that she was clinging to me."

"She came to the hospital every goddamn day."

"I wasn't aware of that."

"Even *after* you woke up. *Especially* after you woke up. So tonight you give her an opening she could drive a locomotive through."

"*Andrea* gave her the opening."

"You were the one who started it. I'm surprised she didn't just unzip your fly."

"Andrea? She hardly knows me."

"Or maybe you'd have enjoyed that."

"Would've given me something to tell God about, anyway," I said, and was immediately sorry.

"What does *that* mean?" Patricia asked.

"Nothing," I said. "Let's go to bed."

We were in the second-story bedroom of

131

her house on Fatback Key, where first we'd consummated our then-burgeoning romance, moonlight shining through the skylight in the cathedral ceiling as it had been on that autumn night that now seemed so very long ago. Together, we had found each other again and again and again and were surprised and delighted and grateful each and every time. Tonight Patricia was wearing a lacy white teddy, and I was wearing pajama bottoms, which bedtime attire seemed to predict a replay of that passionate night we shared under a waxing September moon too long ago. If tonight had been a movie, this scene would not have been titled "Are You Getting Enough Lately?"

I started to explain to Patricia that ever since the day she drove me home from the hospital —

And, oh dear God, how small and sad and forlorn I'd felt on that sunny day last May, how pitiably insufficient, how weak and dependent and utterly incapable of coping I'd felt on that bright hopeless day, no pun intended, but oh dear God it *did* seem a Hope-less day because the pallid figure sitting beside Patricia was definitely not Matthew Hope but an impostor who had taken his place.

She could not have known that lying beside her in bed that night four months ago, I had wept silently and secretly, despairing that I would ever regain full strength, cursing God for having allowed me to step into the path of two speeding bullets faster than I was, knowing I would forever be an invalid, a man who'd survived a coma perhaps, but a man who would never be quite himself again, a person to be pitied instead, perhaps despised instead, a person not quite whole.

"Ever since that day," I started to say, and she said, "Yes?" and I said, "Ever since that day . . ." and she waited, and I said, "I've been hoping . . ." and she waited, and I said, "I'm very tired, Patricia, do you think we could talk about this some other time?"

We climbed into bed, and we lay there beside each other in the silent dark, well not *quite* dark since moonlight was splashing through the skylight. I was naked from the waist up, and Patricia was naked and long and supple from the waist down, and I thought If I try to make love to her, she'll back away yet another time because she's afraid I'll break into a million pieces.

I wanted to tell her I would not break into a million pieces.

I wanted to tell her I was all right again. Really.

We lay still and silent under the moon.

And at last Patricia sighed and said, "I hate that bitch," and in a little while we both fell asleep.

4

"Aside from Etta Toland's," I said, "do you recognize any of the other names on that list?"

We were sitting in the garden behind Lainie's house. It was ten o'clock on Saturday morning, and I had just handed her the witness list that Pete Folger had hand-delivered to my office at nine. I had not slept well the night before. Neither had Patricia. Folger was all smiles when he suggested that I ask my client to plead to Murder Two and thirty years, rather than risking the electric chair on the Murder One indictment. He wanted to move this along fast, he said. I wondered why.

Lainie wasn't wearing glasses this morning.

Her hair sleep-tousled, no makeup on her face, wearing a red and black, floral-print, knee-length kimono sashed at the waist, she sat sipping black coffee under the shade of a pepper tree, squinting at the document I'd just handed her. She was wearing the heart-shaped ring on her pinky; I wondered if she slept with it on. Her legs were crossed. A short baby-doll nightgown in the same floral print showed where the kimono ended high on her thigh. She kept jiggling her foot.

"I don't know any of these people," she said. "Who are these people?"

"The witnesses who testified to the grand jury."

"What'd they say?"

"Well, we don't know yet. Enough to get an indictment, that's for sure."

"Does he have other witnesses, too?"

"If not now, then he certainly will by the time we go to trial. But he'll supply their names when I make demand for discovery."

"When will that be?"

"Within two to three months."

"When will you talk to the people on this list?"

"I'll start making phone calls today. If I'm lucky, I can begin seeing them on Monday."

"To take depositions?"

"No. Just informally. *If* they're willing to talk to me. Otherwise, yes, I'll have to subpoena them and question them under oath. You see . . ."

Lainie glanced up from the typewritten list. A spot of sunlight escaped the snare of leaves above her head, shifted uncertainly in her golden hair. She looked at me expectantly. The wandering eye gave her the forlorn appearance of an abandoned child.

"You see, Folger's still hoping we'll plead."

"Why would we?"

"He's hoping that after I talk to these people, whoever they are . . ."

"Well, *who* are they, that's what *I'd* like to know, too."

"I have no idea. But he's hoping we'll recognize the strength of his case and accept his offer."

"Second-degree murder."

"Yes. Second degree means without any premeditated design."

"I just shot Brett on the spur of the moment, right?"

"Well, yes. For second-degree murder, that's what it would have to be."

"Heat of passion, right?"

"Well, no. That's a term used in the section on excusable homicide. That wouldn't apply here."

"Especially since I didn't kill him."

"I know that."

"So why would I settle for thirty years in jail?"

"Well, not to *exceed* thirty."

"For something I didn't do."

"I'm not recommending it."

"More coffee?" she asked.

"Please."

She leaned over to pour. I watched her.

"Was your girlfriend angry?"

"What?" I said.

"Last night. She seemed angry."

"Well . . . no. Angry about what?"

"You and I talking together," she said, and shrugged. The kimono slid slightly off her shoulder, revealing the narrow strap of her nightgown. She adjusted it at once, put down the coffeepot, and looked across the table at me. "Was she?" she asked. "Angry?"

"No."

"Someone told me she's a state attorney."

"That's right. A very good one."

"Do you talk to her about me?"

"Absolutely not."

"I hope not. Milk?"

"Please."

She poured. I kept watching her.

"Sugar?"

"One."

She slid the bowl across the table to me. "Why was she angry?"

"It had nothing to do with you."

"Then who?"

"I'd rather not discuss it."

"Then she *was* angry, right?"

"As I said . . ."

"You'd rather not discuss it."

"Right."

She was jiggling her foot again. Smiling. Jiggling the foot.

"I'd hate to go to the electric chair, you see. Just because . . ."

"Well, I'll try to make sure . . ."

"*Just* because my attorney's *sleeping* with someone," she said, overriding my voice. "Giving away my secrets to some woman in bed," she said. Single eyebrow raised over the crooked right eye. Faint smile still on her mouth.

"I don't know any of your secrets," I said.

"If you knew them," she said.

"I don't care to know them."

"But you *are* sleeping with her."

"Lainie . . ."

"Aren't you?"

"Lainie, if my personal relationship with Patricia Demming intrudes in any way upon my performance as your attorney, I'll immediately withdraw from the case."

"Your performance as my attorney," she repeated.

Still smiling.

"Yes. In fact, if you think I'm *not* representing you properly . . ."

"But I think you are," she said.

"Good. I'm happy to hear that."

"Besides," she said, "anything between us is privileged, isn't that right?"

"Yes," I said.

What secrets? I wondered.

"Isn't it?"

"Yes," I said.

The security guard's name was Bartholomew Harrod.

138

If a jury had been present, anything old Bart said would have been instantly and automatically believed. That's because anyone named after one of the Twelve Apostles could not possibly be lying. Well, Judas Iscariot, maybe. Nowadays, there are women on juries, but back when you and I were young, Maggie, a jury consisted of men only. Put on that jury an Andrew, Bartholomew, James (two of them, no less), John, Thaddeus, Matthias, Philip, Peter, Simon, Thomas, or — well yes, he said modestly — even *Matthew,* and what you had, folks, was a jury of "twelve good men and true." Not to mention Paul, who said he'd seen Christ after the resurrection, and was therefore elevated to Apostlehood and later to sainthood.

There was no jury listening to what Bartholomew Harrod was saying at two o'clock on what was still a bright sunny Saturday, the sixteenth day of September. Sitting outdoors around a circular coffee table with a plastic top and wrought-iron legs painted green were Harrod, and me, and Andrew Holmes, the man in my office who would most likely be trying the Commins case if I myself declined that singular ordeal. That made *three* good men and true, but who was counting Apostles' names?

I had called Harrod immediately after leaving Lainie's house. I'd told him I was defending Ms. Commins and had been offered his name by the state attorney, Peter Folger, whom I was sure he knew and who had suggested that I might want to talk to him as soon as possible. I told Harrod that if he agreed to come to my office, or to meet with me wherever he preferred, we could talk informally about what he'd said to the grand jury, and this might save the trouble of my having to cross-examine him later, a blatant lie, but one that sometimes swayed a reluctant witness.

What worked best, however, was the "America the Beautiful" approach, which basically sketched in the premise that everyone in the United States was entitled to a fair trial. In the interests of justice, then — which certainly Mr. Harrod would want for himself if ever, God forbid, he found himself in a similar situation — in the interests of freedom and justice for all, then, I felt certain he would want the defense to know how the grand jury had arrived at its finding, toward which end a knowledge of his testimony would be enormously helpful, in the spirit of justice and fairness.

I told him that he wouldn't be under oath while we talked, it would all be very informal, although I would appreciate being able to record what he said, just for reference later on. This was another lie, though a smaller one, but neither was anyone under oath while we were talking on the phone. I needed the recording for backup in case we asked him, on the stand *and* under oath, to repeat anything he might say in our informal discussion. That was why I'd asked Andrew Holmes, no relation, the new partner in the firm of Summerville and Hope, to join me when I spoke to Harrod.

I would have preferred sending either of my two investigators, Warren Chambers or Toots Kiley, to interview and record Harrod. But calls to Warren's office and home garnered identical messages saying he'd be out of town for the next week or so, and Toots's machine said only that she was "away from the phone just now" and asked that a message be left at the beep. Which meant that I could not send them independently to do the donkey work and then later testify to the authenticity and genesis of the tape. Which further meant I needed a witness to the taping.

You may well ask why.

Because if I myself tried Lainie's case and called the Apostle Bartholomew to the stand and started questioning him about what he'd said on the tape, he might very well answer, "I never said that." In which case, I would play the tape to refresh his memory. But suppose he then said, "That's not my voice on that there tape" — who

141

would be able to testify to the contrary? Under the Disciplinary Rules — what we refer to in the trade as DR 5-101 — an advocate cannot be called as a witness. So Folger would need no prompting to ask, as the Constable of France had once asked a lowly messenger, "Who hath measured the ground?"

Hence the presence of Andrew Holmes.

Whichever one of us ended up actually trying the case, the other could be called as a witness to the whys, whens, hows and wherefores of the taping.

The tape recorder sat in the center of the coffee table.

The three of us sat around the table in uncomfortable director's chairs with faded green canvas backs and seats. We were in the backyard, such as it was, of Harrod's mobile home in a park thronged with similar homes just off Timucuan Point Road.

In the state of Florida, people who own so-called mobile homes pay no state, city, county, or school taxes. All they have to do is buy a license under Article VII — titled "Finance and Taxation" — of the Constitution of the State of Florida, wherein "Motor vehicles, boats, airplanes, trailers, trailer coaches and mobile homes, as defined by law, shall be subject to a license tax for their operation in the amounts and for the purposes prescribed by law, but shall not be subject to ad valorem taxes."

The license, under Chapter 320.08 of the Motor Vehicle Licenses section, costs twenty dollars flat for a mobile home not exceeding thirty-five feet in length, twenty-five dollars flat for a mobile home over thirty-five feet in length but not exceeding forty feet, and escalating on up to fifty dollars flat for a mobile home over sixty-five feet in length. Even if the tires have been removed from the vehicles, even if the vehicles are sitting on concrete pads, even if water and electricity have been connected to the vehicles, they are still considered "mobile" homes so long as they are not "permanently affixed" to the land.

What annoys many residents of Calusa is that people who own mobile homes are permitted to vote, even though they pay no taxes. To many residents of Calusa, these frankly ugly aluminum monsters are a blight on the land, especially when the land happens to be choice riverfront property purchased long before anyone knew it would one day become valuable.

Harrod clearly appreciated his protected status as a mobile home owner. He clearly appreciated his tiny fenced backyard and the distant glimpses it afforded of the Cottonmouth River, which meandered through the metallic maze like the snake after which it had been named, sunlight glinting off its scaly waters. He seemed to appreciate as well all the attention being lavished on him this afternoon, two lawyers in suits and ties, tape recorder ready to preserve his precious words for posterity.

He was a blue-eyed, white-haired, somewhat grizzled man in his late sixties, who — like so many other senior citizens down here on the white sand shores of the Gulf — had retired some ten years ago, only to realize that doing nothing was the equivalent of being dead. I had read somewhere that George Burns's nephew had once told him he was thinking of retiring, and Burns had said, "What will you do with yourself?" His nephew had responded, "I'll play golf all the time." Burns thought about this for a moment, and then said, "Lou, playing golf is good only if you've got something *else* to do."

Harrod had taken a job as a security guard.

Which is how he happened to be there this past Tuesday night when Lainie Commins drove into the parking lot of the Silver Creek Yacht Club at a little before ten P.M.

"How did you know the time?" I asked.

"Just let me see if we're getting this," Andrew said, and pressed the STOP button and then the REW button, and played back Harrod's opening words. Andrew's suit was the color of wheat. His tie was a green

144

that matched the faded backs and seats of the director's chairs upon which we were sitting. He was twenty-nine years old, and he had dark curly hair and brown eyes and an aquiline nose, which meant it was curving like an eagle's beak, and an androgynous mouth, which meant it had both male and female characteristics, with a thin upper lip and a pouting lower one. Black-rimmed eyeglasses gave him a scholarly look, which was entirely appropriate in that he'd been editor of the *Law Review* at U Mich, and had graduated third in his class.

". . . little before ten," Harrod's voice said.

"How did you know the time?" my voice asked.

"Okay," Andrew said, and simultaneously pressed the PLAY and REC buttons.

"I looked at my watch," Harrod said.

"How come?"

"Dining room quits serving at eleven-thirty. I wondered who might be coming in so late."

"Tell me where you were," I said.

"Little booth at the entrance to the club. I sit in there checking the cars as they come in. People on foot, too, some of the time."

"Is there a barrier?"

"No, I just stop them and either wave them on or tell them to back on up and turn around."

"Is there a light in the booth?"

"There is."

"Was the light on this past Tuesday night?"

"It was."

"Tell me what you saw at a little before ten that night, Mr. Harrod."

"White Geo driving up to the booth, woman behind the wheel."

"Can you describe this woman?"

"She was Lainie Commins."

"Did you know Lainie Commins at the time?"

"No, I didn't."

"Then how . . . ?"

"I asked her what her name was and she told me it was Lainie Commins and said she was there to see Mr. Toland. Brett Toland, that is. Who was killed that night."

"She gave you her name and also Mr. Toland's name?"

"Yes. That's what they usually do. If they're here to join somebody for dinner, or to go on one of the boats. The boats sometimes give cocktail parties, fifty, sixty people invited to them, it gets hard keeping track. I'll tell you the truth, there's no way I can really *double*-check with the person who's the member. I just keep my eye on a guest, make sure they're going where they *said* they were going, the dining room, or one of the boats."

"What did this woman who said she was Lainie Commins . . . ?"

"Oh, she was Lainie Commins, all right. I seen her since, identified her picture at the hearing, in fact. She was Lainie Commins, no question."

"What'd she look like?"

"Blond hair, eyeglasses, wearing a white shirt with a blue scarf had some kind of anchor design on it."

"What color?"

"I told you. Blue."

"The anchors, I mean."

"Oh. Red."

"Was she wearing slacks or a skirt?"

"Couldn't see. She was inside the car."

"Where'd she park the car?"

"Near the lamppost at the far end of the lot."

"Did you see her when she got out of the car?"

"Yes, but I don't remember whether she had on slacks or a skirt."

"But you were watching her."

"Yes. Wanted to make sure she was going to the Toland boat, like she said."

"How was she wearing her hair?"

"What do you mean?"

"Loose? Up? Tied back?"

"Oh. Loose."

"But you didn't notice whether she was wearing slacks or a skirt."

"No, I didn't."

"Watched her as she got out of the car . . ."

"Yes."

"What'd she do then?"

"Went to the walkway along the dock, started looking for the Toland boat. *Toy Boat*, she's called."

"You were watching Ms. Commins all this time?"

"Watching her."

"Did she find the boat?"

"She found it. Stopped at the gangway, looked up at the boat, then yelled out 'Hello?' Like a question, you know. Hello? When she didn't see anybody on deck."

"You could see all this from the booth?"

"I could."

"How far away from the boat were you?"

"Fifty, sixty feet?"

"Light on in the booth, dark outside, but you could see . . ."

"There were lights along the dockside walk. And in the saloon. I could see her plain as day."

"But you didn't notice whether she was wearing slacks or a skirt."

"Didn't notice that, no. Not a leg man, myself," he said, and smiled. I smiled, too. So did Andrew.

"What happened then?"

"She yelled out his name. Mr. Toland's.

Like a question again. Brett? And he came up out of the saloon and she went aboard."

"Then what?"

"Don't know. Soon as I saw she was expected, I went back to my own business."

"Which was what?"

"Watching television. I have a little Sony in the booth, I watch television when it's slow."

"What were you watching?"

"*Dateline.*"

"This was now what time?"

"Oh, ten after ten. A quarter past?"

"Did you see Ms. Commins when she left the boat?"

"No, I did not."

"You wouldn't know whether *Dateline* was still on when she left the boat, would you?"

"Goes off at eleven, it's an hour-long show. Dining room closes at eleven-thirty, which is when I go home. Night watchman comes on then."

"Does *he* sit in the booth, too?"

"No, he patrols the docks, the dining room, the whole area. There's no traffic after the dining room closes."

"You didn't happen to see Ms. Commins coming off the boat at about ten-thirty?"

"No, I did not."

"Didn't happen to see her driving out of the parking lot a few minutes after that?"

"No, I did not."

"How come? You were sitting right there in the booth . . ."

"I didn't see nobody come off that boat at ten-thirty," Harrod said. "And I didn't see the white Geo leaving the lot at that time, neither."

You were on the boat?

Yes.

Last night?

Yes. But only for a little while.

How short a while?

Half an hour? No more than that.

"Thank you, Mr. Harrod," I said. "We appreciate your time."

"Hello, you've reached Warren Chambers Investigations. I'll be out of town for the next week or so, but if you leave a message I'll get back to you as soon as I return."

No clue as to when Warren had recorded the message.

Same message on the machine at his home number.

I tried Toots again.

"Hello, I'm away from the phone just now, but if you'll leave a message at the beep I'll get back to you as soon as I can. Thanks. Bye."

Which meant that Andrew and I had to keep our four o'clock appointment with a tape recorder and a man named Charles Werner.

When you're a member of the police force, you see all kinds of things, people doing all kinds of things. You answer a Family Dispute call, you go in, find a man in his undershorts, woman wearing nothing but panties, man yelling she threw hot grits on his head, woman yelling he's full of shit, you see all kinds of things. It's like a police officer isn't a human being anymore the minute he puts on the uniform. He becomes *just* the uniform, nothing inside it. Woman ain't ashamed to be seen wearing only her panties, big fat woman with breasts hanging down to her navel, you aren't human to her, you're just the Man come to see to this little dispute here, you're just an anonymous part of the system, not a human being at all, just the Man.

You see a dead person laying in his own blood in the street, people screaming and crying all around him, you tell them to back off, go home, ain't nothing to see here, let's go, let's break it up now, you're not a human being same as the ones screaming and yelling, you're just the Man. And you're not supposed to be affected by the blood underfoot swarming with flies, or the brain matter spattered all over the fender of the car, or the fact that the kid laying there with his skull open is only fourteen years old, you're the Man come to set it all straight.

On Amberjack's boat here in the middle of the Gulf, Warren Chambers was the Man again. The Man come to see about this little matter of Toots Kiley's addiction, the Man come to set it all straight. So it didn't matter he had to take the handcuffs off and lead her to the head and stand outside the door where he could hear her peeing behind it. There was no more embarrassment here than there'd been with the fat lady in her panties, he was just the Man here to settle this thing, the Man here to get her sober again. Wasn't anybody behind that door pissing, wasn't anybody outside here listening. The lady in there was invisible, and the Man outside here was anonymous.

"I *still* don't know how to flush this fucking thing," Toots said from behind the door.

"You finished in there?"

"I'm finished."

"I'll show you again. Unlock the door."

She unlocked the door. Stood by the sink in the small compartment, washing her hands while he demonstrated the use of the flush yet another time, not that she seemed too interested in learning about it. The thing wasn't working properly, anyway, he'd never been on a goddamn boat that had a toilet worth a damn. He had to run the pump over and over again till he finally got water in the bowl. Toots dried her hands on a paper towel, and was about to toss it in the toilet when he gave her a look would kill a charging rhino. She wadded the towel and dropped it in the sink. He picked it up, opened the door under the sink, tossed the towel into a metal basket fastened to the inside of the door, closed the door again, and took the handcuffs from the pocket of his windbreaker.

"Come on," she said, "we don't need those."

"I don't want you hitting me upside the head," he said.

"What good would that do? I don't know how to run a boat."

"Even so."

"Come on, Warr. I'm not a desperado."

"Not yet."

"I'm not hooked. You're making a mistake. You see me clawing at the walls?"

"Bulkheads."

"You see me?"

"That's not what happens, Toots."

"That crack you found, somebody was trying to make me look bad, that's all."

"Sure."

"Come on, let me go upstairs, get some air. You keep me chained to the wall like an animal I'm liable to go crazy."

"I don't want you jumping overboard."

"Why would I do that?"

"You've kicked it before, Toots. You know *exactly* what you're liable to do."

"I can't swim. Why would I jump over-board?"

"Gets too bad."

"It's not *going* to get bad. How many times do I have to tell you I'm . . ."

"How do you feel now?"

"Terrific. How do I look?"

She put her hands on her hips, lifted her chin like a model, turned to him in profile, took in a deep breath. She was wearing the same short black skirt she'd had on when he'd snatched her from the condo on Thursday night, wrinkled now, that and the thin yellow blouse, also wrinkled, her legs bare, the high-heeled black shoes up forward where she was handcuffed to the wall when she wasn't complaining about the toilet facilities.

"You look fine," he said.

"So let me go upstairs, okay?"

He looked at her closely.

She didn't seem any the worse for wear, considering she hadn't had a hit since sometime Thursday. He didn't know whether she'd beamed up at a crack house someplace before coming home with her new stash, the ten jumbo vials he'd found in her handbag, four big juicy rocks in each vial. But that would've made it late Thursday night, say ten, eleven o'clock, and this was now a little past three on Saturday afternoon, which made it — what? Forty hours or so since she'd been off the pipe? Eight hours to go for two full days, yet she wasn't showing any of the signs he'd expected. Either she was a damn good actress or she was really telling the . . .

No, he thought, don't fall for that shit.

She is Tootsie Pipehead, and I am the Man.

"Please, Warren," she said. "Just for a few minutes. Smell a little fresh air."

"Just for a few minutes," he said.

Two reasons she wanted to go up on deck.

First was to keep on working him, make him believe she was sane and sound, just a dear old friend wanting a breath of fresh air, look at me, do I look like a person craving *cocaine,* for Christ's sake? I am little Miss Goody Two-Shoes, and all I want is to go back to the Land of the Free and the Home of the Brave. One thing she *didn't* want was to show him what she was *really* feeling this very fucking minute. Because if she could convince him she was really straight, that this was all some kind of *bizarre* mistake, why then she could get him to turn this fucking tub around and take her back to Crack City. If she could keep him thinking she was just the Nice Little Girl Next Door, breathing in all this clean fresh healthy air ten thousand miles from shore, here in the middle of fucking nowhere, keep him from knowing how much she was missing the shit right now, keep him from knowing how everything inside her was screaming for a hit right now, couldn't *sleep* for dreaming of crack, couldn't stop *thinking* of crack every minute she was awake, if she could only keep him from knowing what she was thinking and feeling here at the railing of the boat as she looked out at a clear blue afternoon sky over inky-blue water, trying to appear calm and cool and dignified though her skirt and her blouse were wrinkled and her mind was screaming crack.

Ten seconds was all it took.

Two glass stems stuck in the glass bowl of the pipe. You drop the crack pellet in the larger stem and heat the frog with a butane torch till it melts down to a cooked brown ooze. You suck on the shorter stem like you're pulling a lover's tongue into your mouth, kissing that sweet mother crack, fine white cloud swirling up in the bowl of the pipe, swirling, sweet suicide flying to your brain in ten seconds flat, man, you got a piece of the mountain, man, you are beaming up, man, Scottie got the *rock*, man, you are in *explosion* mode!

And oh that first sweet flash, oh that incomparable rush, puffing at the mother lode, sucking on the source, warp speed now, oh how good, oh how fucking *ecstatic*, oh come fuck me, crack, come be my lover, come be my man, come make me laugh out loud, come make me strong and powerful, come make me happy, happy, happy, make me come, make me giggly happy, crazy happy, I am so *alive,* so fucking *married* to this delicious fucking Rock of Gibraltar!

God, how she wanted it.

Now!

Right this fucking minute.

But no, just be Shirley Temple here at the boat's rail, blond hair blowing in the wind, she once blew a Japanese man for the twenty dollars she needed for the rocks. He kept telling her he liked "bronze," she thought he meant the metal, realized he was talking about girls with yellow hair, the things she'd done for crack, the twists she'd worked for crack. She'd blow a thousand fucking Japs right this minute if somebody would only return her pipe and the rocks she'd bought last Thursday night, a hundred and fifty bucks' worth of the shit, he hadn't thrown it *overboard,* had he? Only a crazy person would do that, he wasn't a crazy person.

So first, let him think everything's hunky-dory sweetie, here's Peggy Sue Got Married, sniffing in the good salt air, not a *thought* of any controlled substance on *her* mind, oh dear no, cocaine, what is that? Crack, what is that? I never heard of such things, sir, I am just a little farm girl from the heartland of America, far from the shore, adrift on a sea of little-girl happiness, sniffing in the good clean ocean air. Me a druggie? Oh dear no. Me a crackhead? What does that mean, sir, crackhead?

Let him think I'm clean and sober, let him think he's made a mistake, it was just somebody trying to set me up, frame me, putting evil substances in my trash basket and my purse, trying to make people think I'm *using* again when I wouldn't even know where to go to score.

And *then* find where he stashed the rocks he took from my bag Thursday night.

Stuff had to be *somewhere* aboard this tub, he *couldn't* have thrown it overboard, could he?

You son of a bitch, she thought, tell me you didn't throw it overboard.

She was sure he'd kept it. Because some well-meaning jackasses, you know, they didn't realize how desperate you could get when you were forced to kick it cold turkey. So they kept some of the stuff around thinking they could give you just a little bit of it if you started acting crazy, just a teensy-weensy little bit to take the edge off if you started bugging. Just till you straightened out a bit, you know? And then let you go without anything for a slightly *longer* time this time, before they gave you another hit of the pipe, acting as a sort of tender, loving counselor, you know, helping you through this terrible ordeal of what was known in the trade as Drug Withdrawal, never once realizing that cold turkey is cold turkey, man, and cocaine plays no fucking part in rehabilitation.

But he'd been a cop once, he knew better than to try *weaning* a crack addict from the pipe, he'd worked sections in St. Louis could curl the hair on a dachshund. So why *would* he have kept any of it? Coast Guard out here stops the boat, finds ten jumbos and a pipe, there goes Warren Chambers *and* the cute little blonde he's got handcuffed to the wall. Nice story, Sambo, you're helping the cunt kick it cold turkey, then what are you doing with this shit, can you tell us that? No *way* he would've kept it.

But just in case . . .

Just on the *off chance* he had a soft heart for someone so severely afflicted, addicted, *yearning* for the rock, *aching* for the rock, *dying* for the rock, then maybe there was one chance in a hundred million that he had kept some of the stuff to ease her pain when push came to shove, and *maybe*, if only she could convince him to give her free rein of the boat . . .

Shit, she wasn't going to jump over the side.

Or hit him on the head.

Or do anything else foolish.

So if only she could sort of roam around, you know, loose, you know, instead of chained to the wall, the fucking *bulkhead*, then maybe she could find the stuff and . . .

"Let's go," he said.

"What?"

"Time to go back down."

She wanted to hit him.

Instead, she smiled dazzlingly and said, "Sure, whatever you say," and held out her right hand for the cuff.

5

Charles Nicholas Werner lived in a Spanish-style house that had been built in Calusa during the early thirties, shortly after the area was rediscovered, in effect, by a railroad man named Abner Worthington Hopper. Before then, the city's growth was lethargic at best, the 1910 population of 840 people growing to but a mere 2,149 a full decade later. But then came Hopper, and suddenly the town became a proper city of more than 8,000 people, and all at once Calusa was on the map as a resort destination. Building his own Spanish-style mansion on choice Gulf-front property, Hopper then built a hotel to accommodate the multitude of guests he and his wife Sarah invited down each winter. The mansion was now the Ca D'Oro Museum and the hotel was a fenced derelict perilously close to U.S. 41.

The museum housed an only fair collection of Baroque art, of which Calusa was inordinately proud; when you were the self-proclaimed Athens of Southwest Florida, you had to boast about your cultural treasures, however second-rate they might be. Restoration groups were constantly promising to remodel and refurbish the hotel, which had deteriorated over the past six decades from lavish and lush to comfortable and cozy to faded and worn to shabby and decrepit. Recent talk was of tearing it down and replacing it with a shopping mall. *Sic transit gloria mundi.*

The Werner house was the only hacienda-type structure on either side of the narrow canal running behind it. Pink stucco walls and a roof of glazed orange tiles, arched windows that smacked of Saracen influence, exotic-looking peaks and minarets greeted Andrew and me as we walked from where I'd parked my Acura to the arched mahogany front door. There was a fair amount of boat traffic on the canal. This was the beginning of the weekend — well, four o'clock on what remained of Saturday afternoon — and a popular boaters' activity was cruising the backwaters of the city's myriad canals, ogling the sometimes lavish homes on their banks. A wrought-iron doorbell fashioned to look like an opening black rose was situated on the jamb to the right of the door. Andrew pressed the push button positioned like a single white eye at the center of it. We heard footsteps approaching the door.

Despite the wealth down here in sunny Calusa, there are very few live-in housekeepers anymore, and seeing one of them in a proper maid's uniform is as rare as spotting a wild panther. The maid who answered Andrew's ring was in her early twenties, I supposed, a beautiful black woman wearing a black uniform with a little white cap and apron and collar. We told her who we were and whom we were here to see, and she said, *"Pase, por favor. Le diré que está aquí."* I wondered if she had a green card.

We were standing in a hallway floored with blue tile and lined with Moorish columns. Beyond, at the center of the house, was a secluded cloister riotously blooming with flowers. Late afternoon sunlight pierced the colonnaded stillness. We could hear the maid's footfalls padding through the house. Out on the canal, the sound of a boat's engine spoiled the sullen stillness.

Werner, wearing shorts and sandals and nothing else, came from somewhere at the back of the house, walking briskly toward where Andrew and I were waiting. He was a short, gnomic man who looked a lot like Yoda, somewhat bandy-legged, very brown from the sun, with twinkling blue eyes and a fringe of white hair circling his head. His handshake was firm. He told us he was happy to be of assistance and then led us to the back of the house where a pool sparkled and shimmered under the sun.

I detected for the first time a faint Southern accent when he asked if we'd care for anything to drink, "Some whiskey, gen'lemen? Beer? Iced tea?" But we told him we didn't want to take up too much of his time, and got to work at once, setting up the recorder on a low white plastic cube and sitting around it on expensive Brown Jordan lawn furniture. The boat that had earlier entered the canal was now making its way back to the Intercoastal. A sign on a stanchion across the canal warned NO WAKE ZONE. We waited until the boat was clear, and turned on the recorder.

Werner told us essentially what he had told the grand jury. At ten forty-five this past Tuesday night, he had been guiding his sloop — a twenty-five-foot centerboard, under power, and with a spotlight showing the way — toward his slip at the club's dock. There are sixty slips in the marina. He had passed on the approach to *his* slip the yawl *Toy Boat*, with its cockpit lights on and a blond man and woman sitting at the table drinking. He had recognized the man as Brett Toland, with whom he had a passing acquaintance at the club.

"Did you recognize the woman?" I asked.

"I had never seen her before in my life," Werner said.

I kept trying to pinpoint his accent. I

164

guessed maybe North Carolina.

"Have you seen that same woman since?"

"Yes, suh," Werner said. "I was shown her photograph at the grand jury hearing."

"Just *one* photo?" I asked. "Or were there . . . ?"

"They showed me at least a dozen photographs. I picked hers out of the lot."

"You identified her from a photograph."

"I did."

"Can you now tell me who she was?"

"She was the woman charged with killing Brett Toland. She was Lainie Commins."

"You say you were under power as you came into the club."

"I was."

"How fast were you going?"

"Idle speed."

"And you say your spotlight was on?"

"It was."

"Pointing in the direction of the Toland boat?"

"No, suh, pointing at the water."

"Ahead of the boat?"

"*Dead* ahead as I came past the club marker, and then toward the dock as I came closer in."

"How much light was there in the cockpit of the Toland boat?"

"Enough to see who was sitting there."

"Two blond people, you say. A man and a woman."

"Brett Toland and Miss Commins, yes, suh."

"You saw them clearly?"

"Clear as day. Sitting there drinking."

"Did you say anything to them?"

"No, suh."

"Didn't greet them in any way?"

"No, suh."

"Didn't call to them?"

"No, suh. I was busy bringing my boat in. Watching the water, watching the dock."

"Did *they* call anything to you?"

"No, suh."

"Was your slip alongside the Toland slip?"

"Oh, no. Much further down the line."

"How many boats down the line, would you say?"

"Six or seven boats."

"Could you still see the Toland boat after you passed it?"

"Could've if I'd looked back, but I didn't look back. I was bringing a boat in at night, with just a spotlight showing me the way. I kept my eyes on the water all the time."

"You say this was around ten forty-five, is that right?"

"Just about on the dot."

"How do you know that?"

"There's a clock on my dash."

"Lighted?"

"Yes."

"And it said ten forty-five?"

"Almost."

"Is it a digital clock?"

"No, it's what they call an analog. With hands. Black hands on a white dial."

"Then how can you know so exactly . . . ?"

"The hour hand was almost on the eleven, and the minute hand was almost on the nine. So it was *almost* ten forty-five."

"You looked at the clock as you passed the Toland boat?"

"I did. And it said almost ten forty-five."

"Took your eyes off the water . . . ?"

"Just for a second."

". . . to look at the clock."

"Yes, suh."

"Why'd you do that?"

"Wanted to know what time it was, I guess."

"Why'd you want to know what time it was?"

"Wanted to see what time I was coming in."

"Was the water dark?"

"Not where the light was shining."

"But you took your eyes *off* the water . . ."

"Just for a second."

". . . to see what time it was."

"Yes, I did."

He was beginning to get annoyed, I could see that. On the phone, I had sold him "a friendly little informal interview," but now I was coming at him like Sherman entering Atlanta. He didn't like it one damn bit. He was a Southerner, however, and a gentleman, and I was a guest in his home, and he had agreed to talk to me, and so he went along for the rest of the ride.

"So when you say you kept your eyes on the water all the time, you didn't actually . . ."

"Just for a second, I told you."

"To look at the clock."

"Yes, suh."

"Could it have been *earlier* than ten forty-five when you looked at . . . ?"

"No, suh."

"Could it have been ten *twenty*-five, for example?"

"No, it could not have been earlier than about ten forty-five."

"And at that time you continued under power . . ."

"I did."

". . . past the Toland boat . . . which slip was that, by the way, would you know?"

"No, I would not."

"You looked at the clock as you were passing the Toland boat, and then turned right back to the water?"

"Yep. Bringing the boat in."

"To which slip?"

"Number twelve. That's my assigned slip."

"Some six or seven boats down the line. From the Toland boat, that is."

"Yes."

"Did you look at the clock again as you were coming into your slip?"

"I don't believe I did."

"Did you look at it before you cut the engine of your boat?"

"No."

"Before you left the wheel?"

"No."

"Before you made her fast to the dock?"

"No, suh."

"Didn't want to know what time you were getting in?"

"Already knew that," Werner said curtly, and rose in dismissal. "It was almost ten forty-five."

From my home phone, I called the next two witnesses on the list Folger had given me, a man and wife named Jerry and Brenda Bannerman, who lived in West Palm Beach. They graciously agreed to see Andrew and me tomorrow, provided we didn't mind coming to their boat. We arranged to be at their yacht club by twelve-thirty, which meant an early rising and a three-to-four-hour drive across the state.

Etta Toland wasn't quite so gracious.

Although we'd known each other socially before the infringement matter came up, on the phone she called me "Mr. Hope," and told me at once that she had no interest in doing a taped, informal reprise of her grand jury testimony. On the other hand, she would be *delighted,* Mr. Hope, to come to my office on Monday morning and testify under *oath,* because — as she so delicately put it — "I want to bury your fucking client."

I asked her if ten o'clock would be convenient.

"Ten o'clock would be fine, Mr. Hope."

I thanked her for her courtesy, and she hung up without saying goodbye.

I looked at my watch.

It was almost six o'clock and I was supposed to pick up Patricia at seven.

All during dinner that night, I kept wondering why Patricia didn't want to make love anymore. I figured it had something to do with the fear of losing me. Fuck me and my brains would curdle again. Fuck me and I would lie in coma again for the rest of my life, a fate *some* people might have wished for me, but not Patricia, certainly not Patricia, who loved me. But she had also loved someone named Mark Loeb, and I think he loomed large in the equation. Mark was one of the partners in the firm she worked for at the time — Carter, Rifkin, Lieber and Loeb, he was the Loeb. She was thirty-one years old at the time, this must have been five years ago. He was forty-two. They had celebrated his birthday not a month earlier. October the fifteenth. Birth date of great men.

They'd been living together for almost two years, in a little apartment on Bleecker Street in the Village. It was his apartment, she'd moved in with him. Her own apartment had been uptown on Eighty-ninth near Lex, which was a longer subway ride to the office on Pine Street. His apartment was nicer, and closer to the office. It had seemed the right thing to do at the time. Everything had seemed so right at the time, they were so very much in love.

He was Jewish, and so it had always seemed so ironic that he was the one who'd wanted to go uptown to see the tree in Rockefeller Plaza. He'd never had a tree in his own home while he was growing up, never had a tree during his marriage to a Jewish girl, who'd divorced him after five years of what she called turmoil and anguish — just before Christmas, incidentally, but that was a coincidence. He'd always thought of Christmas as a time to escape, get down to St. Barts or Caneel, get away from the insistent Christian barrage that made him feel excluded in his own city, made him feel somehow . . . un-American.

Because New York was his city, you know,

he'd been born here and raised here, had only once in his life lived outside of it, and then not too distant — in Larchmont, with his ex, whose name was Monica. Patricia had met her at a party once. This was three years after the divorce, Mark hadn't expected to see her there, he seemed flustered when he introduced them, three years after the divorce. She was a tall and gorgeous brunette who made Patricia feel like a frump. He'd apologized afterward. Never would have gone there if he'd known, and so on. In Patricia's apartment later — they hadn't yet started living together — it was as if seeing her again . . . seeing Monica . . . he realized he truly loved Patricia.

At the time, the firm had been litigating an important case, a mere matter of tax evasion that could have sent their client to prison for the next fifty years and cost him millions in fines. December eleventh fell on a Friday that year, which also happened to be the day the trial ended in an acquittal for their client. So they'd gone out to celebrate with the other partners and their wives, and afterward Mark suggested that they all go uptown to look at the tree in Rockefeller Plaza. None of them wanted to go except Lee Carter, who wasn't Jewish, but his wife said she had a headache, which Mark thought was a euphemism for *Let's go home and fuck, Lee*. So they all went home and Patricia and Mark got into a taxi and headed uptown.

This was pretty late. Neither of them knew what time they turned off the lights on the tree. She guessed they both had some vague idea that the tree couldn't stay lit all night long, but they didn't know exactly what time the plug was pulled. Neither of them was paying any attention to the time, anyway. It had been a wonderful victory today, and a great party, and they'd each had too much champagne to drink, this was now maybe eleven-thirty, maybe later, when they climbed into a taxi, and told the driver to take them uptown to Rockefeller Plaza.

There were still people skating on the ice.

The tree was still lighted.

They got out of the cab and stood on the sidewalk on the almost deserted street, holding hands, looking up at the tree. Below them, on a sunken ice-skating rink, young girls in short skirts were cutting fancy figures on the ice, and old men with their hands behind their backs were plodding along like ocean liners. The giant tree with its multicolored lights dazzled the night air above them.

And suddenly, all the lights went out.

On the tree.

The rink below was still illuminated, a glowing rectangle in an otherwise suddenly black landscape. Well, there were lights on the street corners, and some lights on in the windows of 30 Rockefeller Plaza, across the street, but everything suddenly felt dark in comparison to what it had been not a moment before. There was a collective disappointed ohhhhh as the lights on the tree went out, but the skaters below went about their determined circling of the rink, and the few people on the street above began dispersing, some heading into the Plaza itself, where some of the store windows were still lighted, others walking down toward Forty-ninth, Patricia and Mark walking — well, strolling really, still hand in hand — toward Fiftieth.

The two men who attacked them seemed to materialize out of nowhere. They were both black, but they could just as easily have been white; this was the Christmas season in New York, and muggers at that time of year came in every stripe and persuasion. The mink coat was what they were after. That and Patricia's handbag, which happened to be a Judith Leiber with a jeweled clasp that looked like money. One of them hit her on the back of the head while the other one grabbed her handbag. As she started to fall forward, the first one circled around her and yanked open the flaps of the coat, popping the buttons. He was starting to pull it down off her shoulders when Mark punched him.

The punch rolled right off him. The man was an experienced street fighter and Mark was merely a downtown lawyer who'd taken his girl uptown to see a Christmas tree. Jewish, no less. The irony. The man hit him twice in the face, very hard, and as Mark fell to the pavement, he turned toward Patricia again, determined to get that fucking coat. The other man kicked Mark in the head. Patricia screamed and took off one of her high-heeled shoes and went at the man who was kicking Mark, wielding the shoe like a hammer, striking at his face and his shoulders with the stiletto-like heel, but the man kept kicking Mark, kicking him over and over again, his head lurching with each sharp kick. There was blood all over the sidewalk now, he was bleeding from the head, she almost slipped in the blood as she went at the man again. "Stop it!" she yelled. "Stop it, stop it, stop it," but he kept kicking Mark, kicking him, until finally the man trying to get her coat off yelled "Let it be!" and on signal they vanished into the night as suddenly as they'd appeared.

She was still wearing the mink.

One of the sleeves had been torn loose at the shoulder.

They'd got the Judith Leiber bag.

Mark Loeb was dead.

A month later, she joined the D.A.'s Office.

I figured she didn't want this to happen to her again.

Didn't want to lose another man she loved.

But, Patricia . . .

"Something?" she asked, and smiled, and reached across the table to take my hand.

"No, nothing," I said.

The top of Andrew Holmes's Chrysler Le-Baron convertible was down, and the sky above was so blue I wanted to lick it right off the page. Every so often a fat white lazy cloud drifted overhead, shading the car as it floated past. It was a beautiful Sunday morning in the state of Florida, and like college boys on spring break, we drove first toward Okeechobee along Route 70, and then through Indiantown toward West Palm Beach, the jackets to our seersucker suits lying on the backseat, our ties loose, the top buttons of our shirts unbuttoned. We were wearing suits and ties only because we were making a business call. Lawyers wear suits and ties when they're conducting business. When we found Jerry and Brenda Bannerman on their powerboat — a forty-five-footer rigged for deep-sea fishing — they were wearing, respectively, cutoff jeans and a thong bikini.

Jerry was a man in his mid-forties, tanned and fit, his cutoffs belted around his snug waist with a length of white line. His wife Brenda was in her late thirties, I guessed, a toothy, leggy brunette with blue eyes that matched her skimpy swimsuit. They were both swabbing the deck when we came marching up the dock of their club, a mile or so from their oceanfront West Palm condo.

Stowing the buckets and mops at once, they offered us a light lunch, and sat with us around a cockpit table under blue canvas, all of us chatting idly like good old friends, eating the delicious shrimp salad Brenda had prepared, sipping at iced tea in tall glasses afloat with lemon wedges. Jerry told us that he, too, was a lawyer. Brenda said that she'd been a legal secretary before they married, yet another revolting development. Too much expertise here, I was thinking. Andrew later told me he was thinking the same thing.

They told us they'd bought two apartments in their condo at a bargain price three years ago, and had broken through the walls to make one huge apartment overlooking the Atlantic. The *Banner Year*, as they called their boat, had been purchased after Jerry's firm won a huge class-action suit and declared extravagant Christmas bonuses. They had been all over the state of Florida with it, had even jumped off to Bimini one fall — but that was another story.

"We hit a hurricane," Brenda said.

"Wouldn't want to experience *that* again," Jerry said.

Brenda served little cookies with chocolate sprinkles on them.

She poured more iced tea.

It was time to get to work.

"As I told you on the phone," I said, "all we want to know . . ."

"Sure, let's cut to the chase," Jerry said. "Did the S.A. offer you a deal?"

"He suggested we might want to make one after listening to his witnesses."

"Might be a good idea," Jerry said.

"Okay to turn this on?" Andrew asked.

"Sure," Jerry said.

"I hate the way my voice sounds on tape," Brenda said, and rolled her eyes. She had moved out into the sun. The three of us were still under the Bimini top, but she was now sitting aft of us, her face and the sloping tops of her breasts tilted up to the sun.

Andrew hit the REC and PLAY buttons. The tape began unreeling.

"What I figure he was trying to do," Jerry said, "was . . ."

"Who do you mean?" I asked.

"Folger. Your state attorney. Aside from establishing that we heard shots, of course . . ."

This was not heartening news.

". . . was establish a timetable. I could tell by the questions he asked me . . ."

"And me, too," Brenda said.

". . . that he had other witnesses who'd seen the accused on the boat before we came along."

"How could you determine that?"

"Well, he asked if we'd seen a security guard in the booth near the gate, for example, so I figured . . ."

"Me, too," Brenda said.

". . . that the guard had some significance. So what could the significance be if the guard hadn't seen the accused going aboard the boat where later we heard the shots?"

Shots again.

Witnesses to the shooting.

"He also asked . . ." Brenda said.

"Folger," Jerry said.

". . . whether we'd seen a sailboat coming in under power and tying up in slip number twelve, I think it was . . ."

"Twelve," Jerry affirmed with a nod. "Which was another link in the time sequence, I figured."

"Like whoever was on that sailboat must've seen the accused before we came along," Brenda said.

"Folger was trying to establish that the accused was still on the Toland boat when we heard the shots," Jerry said.

I bit the bullet, so to speak.

"What shots?" I asked.

"Well, gunshots," he said.

"What time was this?"

"Around twenty to twelve."

"Tuesday night," Brenda said, nodding.

"This past Tuesday night. The twelfth," Jerry said.

"Eleven-forty P.M.," Brenda said, nodding again.

"You heard these shots coming from the Toland boat?"

"Oh yes."

"Yes."

"What were you doing near the Toland boat?"

"Walking toward where we'd parked the *Banner Year*."

"We were staying a few nights," Brenda said.

"Sleeping on the boat."

"Came over through Lake Okeecho-bee . . ."

"Spent a night in Clewiston . . ."

"Went down the Caloosahatchee to Punta Rosa . . ."

"And then took the Intercoastal north to Calusa."

"We've got courtesy privileges at Silver Creek."

"Got there around seven that night," Brenda said.

"Showered ashore . . ."

"Got all tarted up . . ."

"Went in for dinner around nine."

"They stop serving at ten-thirty."

"Dining room closes an hour later."

"I had a delicious broiled lobster," Brenda said.

"I had the red snapper."

"Finished a bottle of really good Chardonnay."

"Headed back for the boat around eleven-thirty, I guess it was."

"Just ambling back to the boat," Brenda said.

"Just taking our good sweet time."

"Nowhere to go but to bed."

There are cars moving out of the parking lot as they enter it at the dining room end. Late diners like themselves heading home. Headlights blinding them as they move toward the waterfront planking that runs past the boats parked in their slips. The activity is short-lived. The sound of automobile engines dies on the still September night. Now there is only the sound of water lapping at dock pilings and boats. The occasional sound of a lanyard clanking against a mast. Marina sounds. The sounds boat people love.

The walkway is lighted with low all-weather mushroom-shaped lamps that illuminate the path and cast some reflection onto the tethered vessels bobbing dockside. The Bannerman boat is in slip number three. As they recall it again now, *Toy Boat* was tied up at slip number five that night. This would make Werner's recollection of the geography accurate. He had told us he'd tied up his boat at slip number twelve, some six or seven boats down the line from the Tolands.

The cockpit lights are still on as the Bannermans, arm in arm, approach the luxury yawl. There is no one sitting at the cockpit table now, but there are lights burning in the saloon. It has taken them ten minutes or so, looking over all the parked boats, admiring some, dismissing others, to amble their way from the dining room to this point just abreast of the Toland boat. It is twenty minutes to twelve when . . .

"We heard shots."

"Three gunshots."

I looked at them both. Not many people know what gunshots sound like. It is not like in the movies. In the movies, even the smallest caliber gun sounds like a mortar shell exploding an inch from your ear. I am not an expert on *all* guns, but I do know what an Iver Johnson .22-caliber Trailsman Snub revolver sounds like when it is fired three times from a car parked at the curb, the first bullet taking me in the shoulder, the second taking me in the chest, the third going Christ knew where because by then I didn't even *hear* that next shot, possibly because I was suddenly gushing blood and screaming in pain and falling into a deep black hole in the sidewalk. The sound of the gun that catapulted me into an eight-day coma was nothing more than a small *pop,* an insignificant *crack.*

"What'd these gunshots sound like?" I asked casually.

"We know guns," Jerry said.

"We keep guns."

"We go to the range every Saturday."

"We know what a gun sounds like."

"These weren't backfires."

"They were gunshots."

"Coming from the saloon of the Toland yawl," Jerry said.

"Three shots," Brenda said.

"What'd you do?" Andrew asked.

"What do you mean?"

"Well, you say you heard three gun-shots . . ."

"We did."

"So what'd you do?"

"Went back to our boat. Went to bed."

"Didn't report the shots to anyone?" I asked.

"Nope," Jerry said.

"Why not?"

"None of our business."

"When *did* you come forward?"

"When we heard this man had got killed."

"Brett Toland."

"We called the S.A.'s Office right away, volunteered what we knew."

"Which was that you'd heard three shots coming from the Toland boat at eleven-forty last Tuesday night."

"Yes."

"Yes."

"Did the state attorney ask why you didn't report those shots?"

"He did."

"What'd you tell him?"

"That we weren't eager to confront anyone who had a gun in his hand."

"Is there a telephone on your boat?"

"A radio."

"Why didn't you use the radio to report . . . ?"

"We didn't want to get involved."

"But you're involved now. You're a witness in a . . ."

"It doesn't matter now."

"It matters to Lainie Commins. If you'd reported those shots when you heard them, someone might have apprehended who-ever . . ."

"We didn't say anything that linked those shots to Ms. Commins," Jerry said.

"We didn't *see* her on the boat, so how could we have implicated her in any way?" Brenda asked.

"My guess is they've got someone who can place her there around the time we heard the shots," Jerry said. "That's why the careful timetable. Wouldn't you say?"

"Yes. But if you'd reported those shots *immediately* . . ."

"No, we couldn't do that," Jerry said.

"Why not?"

"We just couldn't," Brenda said.

"Why not?" I asked again.

"We didn't want anyone rummaging around."

"Rummaging around?"

"*Our* boat."

I looked at them both again.

"Why didn't you want anyone on your boat?" I asked.

"Turn that thing off," Jerry said, and nodded toward the recorder.

Andrew hit the STOP button.

Jerry looked at his wife.

Brenda nodded okay.

"We had a little pot aboard," Jerry said.

"Marijuana," Brenda said, explaining to the two squares in the seersucker suits.

"Just a few ounces," Jerry said.

"For recreational use," Brenda said.

"We were on vacation."

"Just the two of us on the boat."

"Just a little for our own use."

"Not enough to hurt anybody."

Except Lainie Commins, I thought.

185

6

Etta Toland arrived at 333 Heron Street at the stroke of ten on Monday morning. She was dressed casually — disdainfully, my partner Frank later said — in jeans, a loose-fitting, tunic-style, melon-colored blouse, low-heeled very strappy sandals, and a brown leather belt with a hand-crafted brass buckle in the shape of a lion's head. Her shoulder-length black hair was pulled to the back of her head and fastened there with a brass barrette. She wore no lipstick. The lids over her dark almond-shaped eyes were subtly tinted with a tan liner. It was obvious that she expected to get the hell out of here as fast as she could and get on with the more important business in her life.

This was for real.

This was under oath.

Her personal attorney, Sidney Brackett, was there in my office and so was a woman from the State Attorney's Office, presumably to protect Etta's rights, though depositions are customarily open-ended and nonleading, and no one does any cross-examination. I expected that if

186

I asked Etta to reveal anything that constituted privileged communication — as, for example, a conversation between her and her psychiatrist, if she had one — I would at once hear from either Brackett or Mrs. Hampton, which was the ASA's name, Helen Hampton. But I didn't intend to tread any dangerous ground, and my partner Frank was there to nudge me in case I did.

I should tell you that people say Frank and I look alike, though I have never been able to see the slightest resemblance. I am thirty-eight years old and Frank is forty. I am an even six feet tall and I weigh a hundred and eighty-five pounds. Frank is five-nine and a half and he weighs a hundred and sixty. My face is long and narrow, what Frank calls a "fox face." By contrast, he calls himself a "pig face." There are also "rhino faces" and "turtle faces" in the system of categorization he invented. I am originally from Chicago, he is from New York. We both have black hair and brown eyes, true, and we both have corner offices at Summerville and Hope, but that's *all* we have in common.

Frank has been nicer to me since I survived becoming a vegetable.

Everybody has been nicer to me, in fact.

In fact, that's precisely the goddamn trouble.

Neither Frank nor I knew anything Etta Toland had told the grand jury. Like most depositions, this was a fact-finding exploration, or, if you prefer, a fishing expedition. But we could assume, as had the pot-smoking lawyer-boater Jerry Bannerman, that Assistant State Attorney Peter Folger had used Etta to establish yet another time sequence in the inexorable order that linked Lainie Commins to the murder of Brett Toland. Since the Bannermans had testified to hearing shots at eleven-forty on the night of September twelfth, I figured that was a good enough place to start, so I asked Etta where she'd been at about that time.

"Home," she said. "Waiting for Brett's call."

"You were expecting your husband to call you?"

"Yes."

"Did you know where he was?"

"Yes, he was aboard *Toy Boat*. With Lainie Commins."

"Why were you expecting him to call?"

"To tell me how it had gone."

"How what had gone?"

"His meeting with Lainie. He asked her to come to the boat so he could offer a solution to our problem."

"By problem . . ."

"Her suit for a permanent injunction."

"What was the nature of this solution, can you tell me, Mrs. Toland?"

"He offered to buy her off."

"Buy her off?"

"He offered a cash settlement if she would drop her claim."

"A cash settlement?" I said, surprised.

"Yes. Five thousand dollars."

"Are you saying your husband offered Ms. Commins . . . ?"

"I don't know if he actually ever *made* the offer. She may have shot him first, for all I know. I never saw him again after he left the house, you see. Or spoke to him, for that matter. But that's what he was planning, yes. That's what he and I had discussed."

"You'd discussed offering Ms. Commins five thousand dollars if she'd drop her infringement claim."

"Yes."

"Did you and your husband discuss any *other* possible offer?"

"No. Well, the *price*, yes. We were trying to determine how *much* she was going for. But there was never any doubt in our mind that she'd agree to a cash settlement."

"You didn't, for example, discuss manufacturing Ms. Commins's bear yourself and . . ."

"No."

189

". . . and compensating her by way of a substantial advance against generous royalties?"

"Why would we do that? She designed the bear while she was working for us. In fact, the bear was *Brett's* idea. And we have a witness to prove it."

"What witness?" I said at once. "You offered no witnesses at the . . ."

"Brett remembered only later."

"Remembered what?"

"That Bobby Diaz was there."

"Who's Bobby Diaz?"

"Our design chief. He was there."

"Where?"

"In Brett's office. When he first told Lainie about his idea for a cross-eyed bear."

"When was this?"

"Last September."

"And your husband remembered it only *after* the hearing?"

"Yes. In fact, that's what prompted him to invite Lainie to the boat last Tuesday night."

"To make an offer of a cash settlement."

"Yes. Because now we had a witness."

"Did you tell this is your attorney?"

"We planned to. If Lainie didn't accept the offer."

"So, as I understand this, at eleven-forty you were waiting at home for your husband's phone call . . ."

"Yes. To learn whether she'd accepted the offer or turned it down."

"Did you think she might actually *accept* such an offer?"

"Brett and I were confident she would."

"An offer of five thousand dollars to drop . . ."

"The bear was ours," Etta said simply. "We have a witness."

"Did your husband, in fact, call you at any time that night?" I asked.

"No," Etta said. "My husband was being murdered by Lainie Commins that night."

I let that go by.

"Did *you* try to reach *him* at any time that night?"

"Yes."

"How?"

"By telephone."

"You called the boat?"

"Yes. Well, the cellular phone number. There's a cellular phone on the boat."

"At what time did you call the boat?"

"Eleven forty-five? Around then. I was ready for bed, in fact. When I didn't hear from Brett, I thought something might be wrong. So I called the boat."

"And?"

"I got no answer."

"What did you do then?"

"I got dressed and drove to the club."

"Why?"

"It wasn't like Brett not to call when he said he would."

"Did you think the meeting might still be going on?"

"I didn't know what to think."

"How long did it take you to get to the club?"

"Ten, fifteen minutes?"

"Just for clarification," I said, "by 'the club,' I'm assuming you mean the Silver Creek Yacht Club."

"Yes."

"Where you keep your boat."

"Yes."

"What time did you get there, Mrs. Toland?"

"A quarter past twelve."

"How do you know what time it was?"

"I looked at the dashboard clock just as I was nearing the club."

"How'd you happen to do that?"

"I knew it was late, I guess I was wondering if they could still be on the boat discussing the offer. I guess I wanted to know just how late it actually was."

"Is the clock in your car a digital clock?"

"No. It has hands."

"Then you can't say *exactly* what time it was, can you?"

"It might have been a minute or so later."

"Twelve-sixteen, would you say? Twelve-seventeen?"

"More like twelve-sixteen."

"You said earlier that you hadn't heard from your husband since he'd left the house . . ."

"That's right."

"What time was that?"

"Around eight."

"Are you aware that he called Ms. Commins at nine? From the boat?"

"Yes, he said he was going to."

"Didn't call her from the house, is that right?"

"No. Said he wanted to call from the boat."

"Why?"

"Lend urgency to it. Tell her he was already on the boat, ask her to meet him there, discuss a solution calmly and sensibly."

"Didn't ask you to come along?"

"No. He didn't want it to seem we were ganging up on her."

"So he left the house at eight . . ."

"Yes."

"And this was now sixteen minutes past twelve as you were approaching the club . . ."

"Yes, the big stone pillars at the club's entrance."

"What did you do then?"

"I made a right turn in front of the restaurant, where the driveway swings around the oval there, and I headed for the marina parking lot."

"Toward the booth there at the entrance to the lot?"

"Yes."

"Was there anyone in the booth at that hour?"

"No."

"Were there any lights on in the booth?"

"No. Listen, let's just *get* to it, okay?"

Frank raised his eyebrows.

I looked surprised.

"Get to what?" I asked.

"Your *client*," she said.

"I'm sorry, what . . ."

"Elaine Commins," she said. "In her little white Geo. Racing past that booth and out of the parking lot."

My heart sank.

I was silent for a moment. Helen Hampton kept watching the tape recorder. Sidney Brackett sat with his arms folded across his chest.

"You just said there weren't any lights on in . . ."

"There were lights *outside*."

"Where?"

"Hanging on either side of the booth."

"Overhead lights?"

"I saw her."

"Even though . . ."

"I saw her! It was Lainie. I looked her dead in the eye as she went flying out of that lot.

194

Lainie Commins. Fresh from killing my husband!"

"Did you know he was dead at the time?"

This from my partner Frank, who'd been silent until this moment.

"No, I did not know he was dead."

"No one had yet informed you . . ."

"Of *course* not!"

". . . that your husband was dead?"

"No."

"Then you had no reason to assume, even if you did actually *see* Ms. Commins driving out of that lot . . ."

"Oh, I *saw* her, all . . ."

". . . that she'd killed your husband, isn't that right?"

"Until I *found* him, do you mean?"

She said this quite sweetly, nailing Frank right between the eyes. No, she was saying, I had no reason to connect a woman racing from the scene of a crime until I'd actually *found* the scene of the crime. But we are coming to that, counselors. Just keep asking your dumb questions, and we will slowly but inexorably get to my husband Brett Toland with two bullets in his head.

Wish to or not, we had to hear it.

"Can you tell us what happened next?" I asked.

What happened next . . .

And next . . .

And next . . .

And next . . .

. . . was that she'd driven her car to a parking spot facing slip number five, where *Toy Boat* was tied up, and she got out of the car and walked up the gangway to the boat, calling her husband's name because there were lights on in the saloon and she figured he might be down there, though she had no idea at the time that he might be down there *dead.*

Far out on the water, she can hear a buoy's foghorn moaning to the night. The wooden ladder creaks under her weight as she takes the four steps down into the saloon with its Oriental rugs and its pais-ley-covered couches and glass-fronted lockers and Currier & Ives prints, walks through the saloon and past the closed door to the head on her right, and down the passageway into the master state-room.

She does not see her husband at first.

What she sees at once is a gun on the bed.

Blue-black against the white bedspread.

She knows this gun, it is her husband's. But it is odd that he would leave it here in plain sight on the bed, and besides . . .

Where is he?

"Brett?" she calls.

And sees him in that instant.

Lying on his back, on the carpet, on the

deck, on the far side of the bed.

He is naked.

A white towel is draped open around his waist.

His face is covered with blood.

He is red with blood.

Quite calmly . . .

She is amazed that she does not scream.

Quite calmly, she lifts the cellular phone from where it is resting on one of the cabinets, and quite calmly dials 911 to report that she has just discovered her husband murdered aboard their yacht.

Her watch reads twenty minutes past midnight.

The police arrive five minutes later.

If anyone in Calusa needs confirmation that the crime business here is in very good health, thanks, all he has to do is take a quick glimpse at what was once called the Public Safety Building. The old tan brick facade of the building is still there, but in place of the discreet lettering that had announced the police facility in the dear dead demure days, there are now bigger, bolder, bronze letters informing the public in no uncertain terms that this is the home of:

CALUSA
POLICE
HEADQUARTERS

The day was hot and still. There seemed to be even less wind than was normal for September. It has always struck me as odd that the school year down here starts in August, when a person can wilt just stepping out of bed. September is no picnic, either. Sultry is perhaps the best word to describe September in Calusa, although at night cool breezes often blew in off the Gulf. It rained a lot in September. You expected the rain to cool things off, but no, all it did was cause steam to rise momentarily from the sidewalks. Tourists knew what Florida was like in the wintertime, but year-round residents knew the *real* Florida. Sometimes in September, when the days got steamy and sullen, an alligator waddling up Main Street wouldn't have surprised anyone. September in Florida was what Florida was all about.

There were no alligators coming up Main Street on that hot and sunny morning of September eighteenth. I walked past the pittosporum bushes lining the sidewalk in front of the police facility, and glanced up, as I usually did, at the very narrow windows resembling rifle slits in a fortress wall. But there were no snipers behind them because they were designed for protection against heat rather than siege. Where once a person walked through a pair of dark bronze doors into an open space containing only a reception desk with a young woman behind it, there was now a metal detector unit with an armed Calusa P.D. blue standing to the right of it and another one sitting at a desk behind it. The one behind the desk conducted a hands-on search of my briefcase. He also asked who I wanted to see, and called upstairs to make sure I was expected.

Upstairs is where the real changes have taken place. On the third floor, the old orange-colored letter elevator is gone, a victim of high-tech delivery systems. The old somewhat cozy reception area has been enlarged to some four times its original size, and transformed into a bustling space that resembles a warship's battle room, with computer terminals beeping and blinking, phones ringing, civil service employees mingling with P.D. blues and plainclothes cops in a frantic boil resembling a famous borrowed television show. A bank of four elevators is on the entrance wall. The other three walls have more doors in them than a bedroom farce, constantly opening and closing, people coming and going in handcuffs or without.

Where earlier there had been no need for what in bigger cities is called a detention cage, there is now a rather large so-called Conditioning Unit, which makes the cell sound like a brainwashing center, but staid, sedate Calusa has never quite admitted to itself that crime is as rampant here as it is anyplace else in the United States. Calusa would rather believe that the miscreants dragged into this facility day and night are not "criminals" in the strictest sense but merely misguided souls who've somehow fallen afoul of the law and must be temporarily "conditioned" until the matter can be straightened out.

This morning, there were half a dozen recently arrested individuals in the C.U., as the huge cage was euphemistically called. One of them was a black woman wearing pink satin shorts, a red bikini bra, and red high-heeled shoes. I imagined she'd been picked up for soliciting sex on U.S. 41, near the airport. The other five people in the cage were men, three of them black, two of them white. The biggest of the black men was obviously drunk and kept shouting to anyone who'd listen that he wasn't no *African* American, damn it! He was a plain ole *American* same as anyone else born in this country.

"Do I look like I drink goat's milk and blood? You see flies eatin *my* eyes, man? Fuck Africa!" he shouted to me as I went by. "You hear me? *Fuck* Africa!"

One of the white men said, "Fuck *you,* man!" and then threw a finger at *me* when he realized I wasn't the detective, lawyer, or state attorney he was waiting for. Nobody else paid any attention to me.

I found Morris Bloom in his office at the far end of the corridor.

"Got yourself another winner, I see," he said, and grinned and extended his hand.

I told him I thought Lainie Commins was innocent.

He said, "Sure."

I told him Pete Folger had already offered me a deal.

"What has he got, Morrie?"

"Is this on the record?"

"He suggested I talk to his grand jury witnesses."

"Well, I was one of them," Bloom said, nodding.

"Can we talk?"

"No tape."

"However."

"Sure."

In every man's life, there are two cowboys who once beat him up and taught him the meaning of fear. I keep expecting my particular cowboys to show up again one day, to pay me back for what Bloom taught me to do to them. That is the kind of thing cowboys never forget. So one day I'm sure they'll be waiting around the next corner. In fact, when those bullets came banging out of that parked car last April, I thought it might have been my cowboys coming to get me at last. I can tell you this. I will never be able to repay Detective Morris Bloom for what he taught me to do. What he taught me to do was almost kill them.

The walls of his office pretty much told the story of his life. Resting on a shelf was a boxing trophy he'd won while serving in the United States Navy. Hanging on one of the walls were a pair of laminated front-page stories from the New York *Daily News* and Long Island's *Newsday*, headlining the daring capture of two bank robbers in Mineola, Long Island, by a young police officer named Morris Bloom. Hanging on another wall were several framed photographs of the detective squad he'd subsequently commanded up north, together with a citation plaque from the Nassau County chief of detectives. On yet another shelf was a Snoopy doll his then-nineteen-year-old son had given him on a Father's Day some years back, the hand-lettered sign around its neck reading: *To the best bloodhound in the world. Love, Marc.* A framed picture of Bloom's wife Arlene, a smiling dark-haired, dark-eyed beauty, rested on his desk alongside a humidor of Cuban cigars he offered to rank but never smoked himself.

A heavyset man in his mid-forties, an inch over six feet tall and weighing either side of two hundred pounds, depending on how many pizzas he'd had this week, he stood waiting for my first question. There was a look of ineffable sadness on his face, as though he were certain my case was already a lost cause. But the look, exaggerated by shaggy black brows and soulful brown eyes, was *always* there, a bad failing for a cop. Arms folded across his chest, he waited. He was a blunt, plainspoken man. I knew there'd be no bullshit in this office today.

"Etta Toland says that you and Cooper Rawles were the first detectives to respond when the blues called in a homicide."

"That's right," Bloom said.

"What time did you get to the boat, Morrie?"

"Twenty to one."

"Can you tell me what you found?"

"Sector patrol car angle-parked into the walk running past the boats, I think it was Charlie Car, it's in the report. Patrol sergeant's car was alongside it, also angle-parked. Coop and I were driving one of the squad's sedans, we parked alongside the sergeant's car, his driver still behind the wheel. His name's Brannigan, he's supervisor in Sector Three. He took me to where the victim's wife . . ."

"Etta Toland."

"Yeah, was sitting in this little sort of outdoor . . . I don't know boats, Matthew, I don't know *what* the hell you call it. A little outside area with a table and ban-

quettes around it, what looked like banquettes."

"The cockpit," I said.

"I thought that was airplanes."

"Boats, too. But different."

"Anyway, she was sitting there alone, her
hands in her lap, staring down at her
hands . . ."

"Lights on, Morrie?"

"What?"

"In the cockpit."

"Oh. Yeah. Why?"

"Just wondered. Go ahead."

"Coop and I went to her, and he handled
the questioning while I took notes. You get
a feel whether the white guy or the black
guy should do the talking. I didn't get a
sense it would make any difference at all
here. So he talked, and I wrote."

"What'd she tell you?"

"How she'd gone on the boat around a
quarter past midnight and found her husband dead downstairs. Coop asked her did
she touch anything and she said No, just
the phone, and Coop asked did she call
anyone but the police, and she said No, just
the police. So we all went downstairs to take
a look."

"Mrs. Toland, too?"

"No, no, she stayed upstairs in the cockpit, whatever. I went down with Coop and
the M.E., who'd arrived by then."

"What'd you find?"

"A dead man lying on his back on the far side of the bed, blood all over him. Looked like he took two in the face, which the M.E. said either one could've been the cause of death. We later found another spent bullet. Because we were *looking* for it, Matthew. There were three ejected cartridge cases, you see. We figure the third bullet missed him entirely, maybe it was the first one she fired, maybe her hand was shaking, who knows, you ought to ask her. Anyway, we later dug out the bullet from the wall behind the bed, near the door to the bathroom. Your client must've pumped the slugs into him from two, three feet away, very nice, Matthew."

"And left the gun behind," I said.

"Yeah, on the bed."

"You think she shot him and then placed the gun neatly on the bed?"

"I just report the facts, Matthew. The S.A. decides what'll play to the jury."

"Does Folger think that'll play, Morrie?"

"Gee, I guess not, since you say he's already offered you a deal."

"Was the gun on the bed the murder weapon?"

"That's what Ballistics says."

"You have a report?"

"We had it before we brought your client in."

"Was the gun test-fired?"

"Of course."

"What were the results?"

"The ejected cartridge cases and the bullet we recovered on the boat were fired from the .45 Colt automatic pistol we found on the bed. The bullets the coroner removed from the victim's head were *also* fired from that gun. It's the murder weapon, Matthew, no question about it."

"Have you traced the gun?"

"Purchased by one Brett Toland."

"Uh-huh."

"There's more, Matthew."

"Okay," I said, and sighed.

"We took your client into custody around seven that morning. As permitted by Miranda, we . . ."

"Brought her here?"

"Yes."

"Questioned her here?"

"Yes."

"I'm assuming, since she was in custody . . ."

"Come on, Matthew."

"Then she *was* made aware of her rights, correct?"

Bloom merely cocked a baleful eye at me.

"Okay, okay. I was just wondering why she didn't call *me* right then. Put an end to it right then."

"Said she didn't need a lawyer, this was all ridiculous."

"Uh-huh."

"Even agreed to let us print her. Though I guess you know, under the Miranda guidelines we don't *need* permission to take fingerprints. We asked solely as a courtesy."

"And she said okay?"

"Said she was innocent."

"She is."

"They *all* are, Matthew. I have never met a guilty felon in my entire lifetime."

"This one *is* innocent, Morrie."

"Then why are her prints all over the murder weapon?"

I looked at him.

"Palm prints?" I said. "Fingerprints?"

"Both."

"You still don't have her at the scene. She left that boat at ten-thirty. She was home in bed by . . ."

"Not according to four eyewitnesses."

"All eminently reliable. One of them is Toland's loving wife, another one was on a moving boat in the dark, and the last two were drunk and going back to their boat to smoke pot."

"You don't know that, Matthew."

"It's what they told me yesterday."

"I guess you can prove . . ."

"The point is," I said, plunging ahead

207

regardless, "Lainie Commins wasn't even *on* that boat when the murder took place. She got there at ten, drank a nonalcoholic drink, listened to what Toland had to say, advised him that she'd talk it over with her lawyer, and left the boat at ten-thirty, without once budging from that cockpit."

"Then what was her scarf doing downstairs?"

"What scarf?"

"A Gucci scarf. Tiny red anchors on a blue field."

"Where'd you find . . . ?"

"The master bedroom. Downstairs."

"You don't know it's hers."

"She identified it as hers."

"I can't believe . . ."

"That's when we called in the state attorney, Matthew."

I was shaking my head.

"That's when we charged her with first-degree murder."

Still shaking my head.

"I'm sorry, Matthew," he said. "But she did it."

No, I was thinking.

"No," I said.

But it looked a hell of a lot like yes.

"I didn't kill him," Lainie said.

"Lainie," I said, "your fingerprints are on the gun."

She was sitting in my chair behind my desk. I was pacing the floor of my office. My partner Frank was half-sitting, half-leaning on the corner of my desk, his hands in his pockets, his shirtsleeves rolled to his forearms. He was wearing suspenders today. He looked like Larry King interviewing a celebrity — except that Larry King had a fox face. Anyway, this was not a celebrity. Not yet, anyway. This was merely a woman who'd been indicted for murder in the first degree. With the thumb and forefinger of her left hand, she kept twisting the Victorian seal ring on her right pinky. The digital clock on my desk read 4:03 P.M.

"How do you know they have fingerprints?" she asked.

"Folger has a forensics report."

"That's impossible. They're lying to you."

"They know I'll be seeing the report."

"Even so."

"How'd your fingerprints get on that gun?"

"Oh. Yeah," she said. "Right."

Frank and I both looked at her.

"Now I remember touching it," she said. "The gun. When I asked Brett if it was loaded. I sort of put my hand on it. Ran my hand over it."

"Why?"

"I don't know. I'd never touched a gun in my life. I guess I wanted to see what it felt like."

Frank raised his eyebrows.

"Lainie," I said, "you told me you got to the boat at a little before ten, and left half an hour later."

"That's right. That's exactly what I did."

"Folger has the security guard seeing you go aboard at a few minutes past ten . . ."

"That's exactly right . . ."

". . . and he's got another witness coming in on a sailboat at ten forty-five, and spotting you and Brett Toland drinking at the cockpit table."

"No, he's wrong about the time. I left the boat at ten-thirty."

"Did you see that sailboat coming in?"

"Yes, but it was before I left the boat."

"Were you still there at eleven?"

"No. I was home by eleven."

"Folger has two witnesses who heard shots at eleven-forty."

"I was already home by then."

"Shots coming from the saloon. Three shots."

"I didn't go down to the saloon at all. Brett and I sat in the cockpit all the while I was there."

"Then you couldn't have been below, firing the shots they heard."

"I couldn't have been *anywhere* on the boat. Not at eleven-forty. I was home by eleven."

"Your fingerprints were on the gun,"

Frank reminded her.

"I told you how they got on the gun."

"How'd your scarf get down there in the master cabin?" he asked.

Good old Frank. Straight New Yorker style. No bullshit.

"I told the police all about that," Lainie said.

"How come you never mentioned it to me?" I asked.

"I told you that Brett asked *everybody* to take their shoes off."

I saw the faint flicker of disapproval that flashed in Frank's eyes. He knew, as I knew, but apparently Lainie did not know, that the word "everybody" was singular and that she should have said "his shoes" or "her shoes," but certainly not "their shoes." Or perhaps she knew the correct construction and was merely trying to avoid saying "*his* shoes" lest she fall into a sexist-pig trap. Besides, what did her *shoes* have to do with her scarf?

"You didn't tell me he asked you to take off your shoes," I said.

"I told you he asked *everybody* to take off their shoes."

Again.

"Because of his precious teak decks," Lainie said.

"You told me he asked a state senator's *wife* to take off her shoes. You didn't mention anything about *your* shoes."

"Well, I must have forgotten. He asked me to take them off."

"How could you have forgotten something the police had already questioned you about?"

"Because I told them exactly what happened and I thought that was that. Brett asked me to take them off, and he carried them below when he went looking for the Perrier."

"The scarf, too?" Frank asked.

Lainie looked at him.

"He took my shoes *and* my scarf, yes," she said.

"Why'd he take the scarf?" Frank asked.

"Because I didn't need it. It was a warm night."

"So he carried it below, together with your shoes."

"Yes."

"When did he ask you to take off your shoes?" I asked.

"When I reached the top of the gangway."

"Asked you to take them off . . ."

"Yes."

". . . and then took them from you and carried them below."

"Not right that minute. He carried them below when he went looking for the Perrier."

"Did he ask you for the scarf, too?"

"No, I handed him the scarf. Because I didn't need it."

"What time did you leave the boat, Lainie?"

"Around ten-thirty."

"At any time before that, did Brett Toland offer you a cash settlement to drop your suit?"

"No. Never. Who told you that?"

"Do you know a man named Bobby Diaz?"

"Of course I do. How would *he* know what Brett told me?"

"Was he present at a meeting last September, during which Brett Toland mentioned his idea for a cross-eyed bear?"

"Never. There was never such a meeting. The idea for the bear was *mine.*"

"And you're sure Brett didn't offer you a cash settlement last Tuesday night?"

"I'm positive."

"And you're equally certain you left the boat at ten-thirty?"

"Yes."

"Drove out of the parking lot at ten-thirty?"

"Yes."

"Then Etta Toland couldn't possibly have seen you driving out at a little after midnight."

"I was home asleep by midnight."

"Then you weren't racing out of that parking lot at a little past midnight, is that right?"

"I told you. I was home asleep."

"Did you drive home barefooted?" Frank asked.

"No, I put on my shoes before I left the boat."

"Went below to put them on?"

"No, Brett went down to get them for me. I was never anywhere on that boat except the cockpit."

"But he forgot your scarf, is that it?"

"I guess we both did."

"When did you discover you'd left it on the boat?" I asked.

"When the police wanted to know about it."

"What time was that?"

"When they came to the house."

"Were you asleep when they came to the house?"

"Yes."

"What time was that?"

"Six in the morning."

"So you'd been asleep . . . what time did you say you went to bed?"

"I didn't. It was around eleven-thirty."

"So you'd had six and a half hours sleep by the time the police came to see you."

"Yes. Six, six and a half."

"Didn't miss the scarf when you got home, huh?" Frank asked.

"I guess not."

"Didn't notice you'd left it behind."

"No."

"How come?"

"I guess I'd had a little to drink."

"You told me you were drinking Perrier," I said.

"I also had a vodka-tonic."

"When was that?"

"After Brett made his proposal."

"Thought it was a good proposal, did you?" Frank asked.

"I thought it sounded good, yes. I wanted to check it with Matthew, but it sounded good to me, yes."

"But you didn't call Matthew when you got home."

"It was late."

"Eleven o'clock."

"Yes."

"And you were in bed by eleven-thirty."

"Yes."

"How many drinks did you have?" I asked. "On the boat."

"Just one. Well, maybe a bit more than one. I think Brett freshened it for me. Poured a little more vodka into the glass."

"You didn't tell me any of this."

"I didn't think it was important."

"Is there anything else you didn't tell me?"

"Nothing else. I didn't kill him. And besides, I thought you guys were my lawyers."

"We are," I said.

"Then stop *yelling* at me!"

"Lainie, did you go below at any time last Tuesday night?"

"No."

"Not the saloon . . ."

"No."

"Not the master stateroom . . ."

"No. I told you. We sat on deck, in the cockpit, till I left the boat."

"Without your scarf," Frank said.

"Yes, without my goddamn *scarf!*" she said.

"Did anyone see you leaving the boat?"

"How would I know?"

"Did *you* see anyone?"

"Yes, I saw the man in the booth as I drove out."

"He says he didn't see you."

"Then he must be blind. I drove right by him."

"See anyone else?"

"People coming out of the restaurant."

"Did you know any of them?"

"No. I mean, how could I tell? I was just driving around the oval, they were just people."

"So you drove past the guard booth . . ."

"Yes."

"Say anything to the guard?"

"No."

"He say anything to you?"

"No."

"Wave at you? Anything like that?"

"No."

"And then you came around the oval in front of the restaurant . . ."

"Yes."

"And saw these people coming out . . ."

"Yes."

"Then what?"

"I drove to the pillars at the club entrance and made a left turn onto Silver . . . oh, wait a minute."

We waited.

"That's right," she said.

"What's right?"

"I almost hit this car parked on the side of the road."

"What road?"

"Silver Creek. To the right of the entrance. I was making a left turn out of the club, and this car was parked just beyond the stone pillar on the right there. I guess I was cutting the corner too tight. I almost hit it."

"What kind of car?"

"I don't know. It was dark."

"What color?"

"I don't know. I almost didn't see it. The headlights were off, it was just parked there."

"Anybody in it?"

"No one."

"Did you notice the license plate?"

"No. It was all very dark. I started to make

the turn and saw the car and realized how close it was. I just yanked the wheel over and drove on by. I may have yelled something, too, I don't remember."

"Like what?"

"Like you *jackass,* you *jerk,* something like that."

"But if no one was in the car . . ."

"I know, it was just a reaction."

"This was at ten-thirty, correct?" Frank asked.

"Yes. Ten-thirty. Yes."

"Did you see anyone wandering on foot in the parking lot at that time? While you were driving out?"

He was thinking the same thing I was. First, why would anyone park a car just outside the club entrance when there was a parking lot inside those stone pillars? And next, where was the person who'd left the car there? The Bannermans had heard shots at eleven-forty that night. If someone had been prowling the lot an hour or so earlier . . .

"*Did* you see anyone?" I asked.

"Nobody," Lainie said.

7

He kept remembering what Amberjack had told him about keeping an eye on the weather. Warren didn't want to get caught out here on a small craft some thirty miles from shore in case any storm was on the way. Not much traffic out here, just your occasional fishing boat and now and then a big motor cruiser passing by in the distance. But the way he figured it, all of these boat people knew more about weather than he did, so as long as there was *anybody* out here, he didn't feel foolhardy. Minute he saw any boats heading in, he'd be right behind them. Meanwhile, if there was any danger he expected he'd begin hearing Coast Guard advisories on the weather channels.

A big storm was already raging below-decks, however, and her name was Toots, who'd come past being irritable and jumpy and quivery, all of which he'd expected in the twenty-four to thirty-six hours following her last hit on the pipe, whenever that had been. The symptoms always outlasted the initial big crash every crackhead experienced sooner or later, one time or another.

So she'd come past the inconceivable craving during the first three days, and she'd also come past the insomnia and fatigue and now he could hear her below, crying hysterically again, today was going to be one fine clambake, Clyde. This was now Tuesday morning, so assuming she'd scored Thursday night sometime, it was now Crash-Plus-Four-Days and . . . what? Ten, twelve hours? He'd tried giving her some breakfast ten minutes ago, she'd knocked the tray out of his hands, spattered eggs and coffee all over Amberjack's spanking-clean bulkheads and deck. She'd been like this since late last night, these crazy mood swings, fine one minute, screaming and yelling the next.

Made a man want to start smoking again.

What worried her most was that she'd remain this way forever. Like when she was a little girl and she made a funny face and her mother warned her she'd freeze that way. She didn't think she could bear this forever. Last time she'd kicked the habit, it hadn't been this bad. Then again, cocaine wasn't crack, well yes it was, well no it *wasn't!* Whatever the fuck it was, she could not endure the thought that her present condition might turn out to be something permanent, she might be trapped eternally on this roller coaster that kept plunging her into hell through flames and then leveled off onto a grassy plain in a shaded valley before it started its climb again which was when she wanted to scream and scream and scream.

The last time around, when she was on cocaine but not freebase, she'd done whatever had to be done to get the white powder. Whatever. Anything. You named it, she would do it. Yessir, whatever you say. You, too, ma'am, this is Tootsie La Cokie, didn't you know? I will eat your pussy, suck your cock, take you in my ear, my nose, my armpit, my ass, wherever you want to put it, whenever you'd like it, I'll do it if you just give me the candy or the money to buy it.

She was sure he still had the stuff hidden somewhere on the boat.

Thing to do was to get it from him.

Convince him to give it to her.

Any which way he wanted.

The man's name was Guthrie Lamb.

He was telling me he'd been a famous private detective for more years than I'd been on earth, having started his agency back in 1952, when he used to operate out of New York City. He had moved down here twenty years ago, which accounted for his longevity and good health at the age of sixty-something.

He did, in fact, look entirely fit.

I had no way of knowing what he might have looked like when he first put in an appearance as a Famous Detective, to hear him tell it. But he was still a tall, youthful-looking, wide-shouldered man who, I guessed, was capable of handling himself in any situation calling for physical exertion. In fact, if ever I ran into my cowboys again, I would not have minded Guthrie Lamb at my side — particularly since he seemed to be carrying a very large gun in a highly visible shoulder holster. His eyes were a pale blue, but they appeared deeper against the pristine white of his hair and his eyebrows. He had a wide glittering smile. I wondered if his teeth were capped.

I had called him early this morning because there was no way on earth I could raise either Warren or Toots on the telephone, and the last time I'd done my own legwork, I'd got myself shot, thanks. There were three other private detective agencies in town, none of them any good, and Benny Weiss had recommended Mr. Lamb highly. There were rumors in town that he had changed his name from Giovanni Lambino or Limbono or Lumbini or something like that, but why this should have been anyone's business but his own was quite beyond me. It certainly wasn't *my* business.

My business was finding out if anyone at the Silver Creek Yacht Club had on last Tuesday night noticed a car parked just beyond the pillar on the right-hand side of the entrance gate.

"What kind of car?" Lamb asked me.

"I don't know."

"What color?"

"She couldn't tell."

"No light at the gate?"

"She said it was dark."

"Have you ever been there at night?"

"Yes, but I never noticed."

"Well, I'll check it. Usually, if there are pillars, there are lights on top of them."

"Yes."

"Maybe one of them was burned out."

"Maybe."

"So we'll see. What time was this supposed to be? When she saw the car."

"Ten-thirty."

"Drove through the gate, you say, and was making a left turn . . ."

"Yes."

"When she noticed the parked car and swerved away from it."

"That's what she told me."

"Well, let me see who saw what out there. Did we discuss my rates?"

"I'm assuming they're standard."

"What's standard by you?"

"Forty-five an hour plus expenses."

"I usually get fifty."

"That's high."

"Expertise," Lamb said.

"I pay Warren Chambers forty-five an hour and he's the best in the business."

"I'm better," Lamb said, and grinned like a shark.

When she called to him from below, her voice was so soft he almost didn't hear her. The boat was drifting, drifting, he hadn't put a hook down, there was nothing to hit out here, nothing to run into, just a huge circle of water wherever you looked. Faint breeze blowing, a few whitecaps out there, fishing boat far out on the horizon to the west, where Corpus Christi, Texas, was the next stop.

"Warren?"

Almost a whisper.

"Yes?"

"Can you come down here, please?"

He went to the ladder, took a step down, bent, and peered into the boat. She was sitting on the bunk up forward, wrist in the handcuff fastened to the grab rail on her right, legs over the side of the bunk, ankles crossed. The high-heeled pumps that matched the short black skirt were on the deck. He went down the ladder.

"I'm sorry," she said.

"That's okay," he said.

"I shouldn't have knocked that tray out of your hands."

"Well, listen."

"Really, I hate being this way," she said, and smiled. "Besides, now I'm hungry."

"I'll fix you something," he said, and went to the stove.

"If you have some cereal, that'll be good enough."

"No eggs?"

"I'm not sure I can keep them down."

"That's not supposed to be one of the symptoms."

"It's the boat rocking."

"Oh."

"I'm sorry I lied to you, Warren."

"Did you?"

"Well, sure, you know I did. You're right, I'm hooked. Or *was*. I know I'll be thanking you for this when it's all over."

"No need for that."

He was standing at the countertop alongside the stove now, shaking cornflakes from their box into a plastic bowl. He poured milk over them, found a tablespoon in the utensil drawer, put bowl and spoon on a tray and carried it to the bunk.

"Some coffee?" he said. "I can heat it up again."

"I'd like that," she said.

He went back to the stove, turned on the gas under the coffeepot. Blue flame licked at its bottom. The boat rocked gently.

"Boy, it's funny the way this comes in waves," she said.

"Bit of a chop today," he agreed, nodding.

"No, I mean the craving for it. You think it's gone, and then all at once it's back again." She shoveled a spoonful of flakes into her mouth. Chewed. Swallowed. Shifted her weight on the bunk. "What'd you do with my stash?" she asked.

"The jumbos I found in your apartment?"

"Yes."

"Deep-sixed them."

"You didn't."

"I did, Toots."

"Terrible waste."

"Not the way I look at it."

"I'd love one of those rocks right this minute," she said, and looked at him.

"I can't help you," he said. "They're on the bottom of the ocean."

"I don't believe you, Warren."

"I'm telling you."

She shifted her weight again. He realized all at once that her legs were bare. She'd taken off her panty hose. He saw them crumpled against the bulkhead now, a wad of sand-colored nylon.

"I keep wondering where I'd be if I was a vial of crack," she said. "Did you used to play that when you were a kid, War-ren?"

"No, I never wondered where I'd be if I was a vial of crack."

"I mean if you couldn't find one of your toys or games. Didn't you used to say Where would I be if I was a fire engine? Or a doll? Or a . . . ?"

"I didn't play with dolls."

"Where on this boat would I be?" she asked in a cute, feigned little-girl's voice.

"No place," he said. "There's no place on this boat you'd be. Cause they ain't no crack on dis here boat," he said in a thick, feigned watermelon accent.

"Wanna bet?" she asked, and smiled, and shifted her weight again, her legs parting slightly, the black skirt edging higher on her thighs. "I'll bet if I asked you really nice, you'd tell me where you've hidden that crack, Warren."

"You'd be wasting your time, Toots."

"Would I?" she said, and suddenly opened her legs wide to him. "Tell me," she said.

"Toots . . ."

"Cause, honey, right now I'd do anything for some of that shit, believe me."

"Toots . . ."

"Anything," she said.

Their eyes met.

She nodded.

"Not this way, Toots," he said softly, and turned away from her, and walked swiftly to the ladder and climbed the steps and was gone.

She stared at the empty space he'd left behind him.

What? she thought.

What?

What you expected from a firm that called itself Toyland, Toyland was a yellow-brick road leading to a gingerbread house with white-sugar icicles hanging from the roofline and jelly-drop doorknobs and mint-clear windows. You did not expect a low yellow-brick factory in a Cyclone-fenced industrial park off Weaver Road, the Toyland, Toyland boy-girl logo sitting on the rooftop in three-dimensional bliss. What you expected when you stepped into that fanta-sized gingerbread house was a band of bearded elves on high stools at low tables, wearing red stocking hats and whistling while they worked. What you got was a reception area with a glass-tiled wall beaming late morning sunshine, two teal-colored doors flanking a circular desk centered on the opposite wall, and huge framed glossy photographs of the company's several hit toys and games hanging on the other two walls. Among these toys were a green frog wearing scuba-diving gear; a menacing treaded black tank whose helmeted commander was a little blond girl; and a red fire truck with a yellow water tower which, from the photographic evidence, shot a real stream of water.

I was here to see the man Etta Toland claimed was a witness to Lainie Commins's thievery, the man who'd been present at a meeting last September when Brett Toland first proposed his idea for a cross-eyed bear. Robert Ernesto Diaz's office was at the end of a long corridor lined with doors painted in various pastel shades, as befitted Toyland's image. Etta had defined him as the company's design chief. His office at once fortified that concept.

A rangy man with black hair, a black mustache, and dark brown eyes, Diaz stood behind a huge desk cluttered with what I assumed were models of future toys. A bank of windows behind the desk streamed sunlight onto a wall bearing a huge poster for Francis Ford Coppola's *Dracula*, or Bram Stoker's, or whoever's, flanked by a pair of Picasso prints. A Toys "Я" Us catalog was open on the desktop, resting beside a digital clock that read 11:27, and a pair of clay models for a very slender somewhat buxom doll . . .

"Our annual bid to dethrone Barbie," Diaz said with a rueful grin.

. . . and models in five different colors for a helicopter which I assumed would fly if you put batteries in it, and four painted ceramic models of men and women in space suits, which looked very much like Mighty Morphin Power Rangers to me, but I currently had *one* infringement suit going against the company.

"Toyland's already begun cutting steel on the helicopter," he said, "but we haven't yet decided on the color. Which one do you favor?"

Diaz saw my puzzlement and immediately defined "cutting steel."

"Tooling up," he explained. "Making the molds we'll be using for years and years to come, I hope, I hope, I hope. The helicopter's my design. It's called Whurly Burly, and the pilot's a blond girl like the one in Tinka Tank, which you may have seen on the wall in reception, and which was a big winner for us three Christmases ago. I designed *her,* too. Kids love blond dolls. Even black kids love blond dolls. Six hundred thousand dollars' worth of tooling on that bird, plus another four for R&D . . . research and development . . . in hope it'll fly *next* Christmas. That's a million dollars going in. But we're betting a lot more on Gladys — which I guess is why you're here."

"That's why I'm here," I said.

"A terrible thing, terrible," Diaz said, shaking his head. "To kill a man over a *toy?* Terrible."

I said nothing.

"Look, she must have felt enormously threatened, I realize that. If that bear's going to be under the tree by next Christmas, it's got to be in the stores no later than May. By next month, all your major chains — Kmart, Wal-Mart, Toys "Я" Us, F.A.O.'s — will be planning exactly which toy is going to be in which aisle on which shelf come spring."

"That early," I said.

"That early. October. Everything planned by then. With Tinka Tank, we had the choicest location in every goddamn store in America. There wasn't a girl alive who didn't want that toy. We're hoping the same thing will happen with Gladys. Test her *this* Christmas, have a runaway toy *next* Christmas."

I did not mention that if Judge Santos decided in Lainie's favor, either Mattel or Ideal would be testing *Gladly* and not *Gladys* this Christmas.

"Say we put out twenty, twenty-five thousand bears for the test launch," Diaz said, "which we've now got priced at a hundred and a quarter. If we see we've got a sure winner, we can drop the price to ninety-nine, keep her under that forbidding hundred-dollar price point. Mass-producing her will cost about a third of that, something like thirty-five dollars a bear, including the glasses, which are expensive to make. My guess is we'll have sunk close to two million dollars in Gladys before we *really* begin marketing her. If we sell only a million bears next Christmas, you're going to see some very long faces around here. But if she's a *big* seller next year, she'll be even bigger the year after that and the year after that and then we're in clover. So I think you can see the urgency here."

"Yes."

"Of a decision on who owns what."

"Yes."

"So we can start moving. If we're going to get those test bears out there plugging for us, the judge not only has to decide *correctly*, he has to decide *soon*. So Brett wouldn't have died for no reason at all."

I missed the logic of this.

"Why weren't you called as a witness?" I asked.

"At the hearing, do you mean?"

"Yes, the hearing."

"From what I understand, Brett didn't remember until it was too late."

"Remember what?"

"That I'd been there at the meeting."

"What meeting?"

"When he told Lainie about his idea for the bear."

"When you say 'From what I understand . . .' "

"That's what Etta told me."

"When was that?"

"Last week sometime. After what happened."

"After Brett's murder, do you mean?"

"Yes."

"Etta told you that he'd suddenly remembered . . ."

"Yes."

". . . the fact that you'd been there at this important meeting."

"Yes. Well, I *was* there, you see."

"Before the hearing, did you happen to mention this to either of the Tolands?"

"Well, Brett already *knew* I was there, you see. So I figured if he wanted me as a witness, he'd let me know."

"But he didn't, as it turned out."

"No, he didn't."

"Because apparently he'd forgotten all about it till the day he was murdered."

"Apparently."

"But you remembered being at the meeting."

"Oh yes."

"Do you still remember being there?"

"Well, of course."

"Tell me about it."

It is one of those steamy sulky September days in Florida, when everything and everyone seems wilted by the heat and the humidity and the promise of more heat and humidity. Bobby Diaz — he is familiarly

233

called Bobby by everyone at Toyland — is working here in his office when Brett buzzes him and asks him to come down the hall a minute.

"Do you remember the actual date of this meeting?"

"No, I don't. I'm sorry."

"Or the time."

"I don't remember, I'm sorry."

But he does remember that it was in the afternoon sometime and that he had just taken a call from an insider at Toys "Я" Us who'd phoned to whisper in his ear that the company thought Toyland's new video game, *Rush to Judgment*, was "entirely fresh." In fact, he would've hurried down the hall to report this to Brett, anyway, even if Brett hadn't buzzed him first.

"Down the hall" is where Brett's huge corner-window office is. A secretary sits behind a desk in an anteroom adjoining it, but she scarcely glances up at Bobby as he raps his knuckles on her desk in passing greeting. Walking into Brett's office is like walking into a rich kid's playroom. There are toys and dolls and games strewn on every flat surface, including the floor. Brett himself sits behind a very large desk similarly covered with toys in various stages of development. As Bobby recalls it now, last September they were still searching for a good face for a doll they'd since abandoned, and a dozen or more models of the tiny doll's head are scattered on Brett's desk like the remnants of a mass decapitation. During the conversation that follows, Brett keeps rolling one of these miniature heads between his fingers. Bobby tells Brett the good . . .

"Was Lainie in the office when you got there?"

"No, she wasn't."

"Go ahead."

He tells Brett the good news he's just received from his informer at Toys "Я" Us, and Brett immediately gets on the phone to call, first, his wife in her own large (but not *as* large) office down the hall, and then Toyland's sales manager, asking him to stand by for a possible confirming call and big order from Toys, and then his production manager in the Bradenton factory (which explains why there are no elves here in the Calusa building) to tell him they may have to up their initial run order on *Rush*, as the game is familiarly called in-house. Idly picking up two of the tiny doll heads, he asks Bobby to sit down, and offers him a wrapped mint from the jar he keeps on his desk (he's just quit smoking for the fifth time). As Bobby unwraps the hard candy, Brett tells him all about this idea he's had for a teddy bear.

Rolling the heads between his fingers the

way Queeg rolled the stainless-steel marbles in *The Caine Mutiny* (but reforming smokers can be forgiven their little physical tics), Brett says that he suddenly remembered a hymn they used to sing in church when he was a Baptist growing up in Overall Patches, Tennessee . . .

"Did he actually say that?"

"No, no. I don't know *where* he was from in Tennessee. I just made that up."

"But you're not making up the rest of this, are you?"

"Of course not. I'm telling it just the way I remember it."

The way *Brett* remembers it in that meeting last year is that one of the lines in the hymn was either "Gladly the cross I'd bear" or "Gladly the cross I'll bear," either one of which referred to joyously carrying the cross for Jesus. It doesn't matter what the line actually was, he says, it's an old hymn in public domain. The only thing that matters so far as Toyland is concerned was that all the kids thought there was actually a cross-eyed bear named Gladly.

"What I'd like to do," Brett says, "is come up with a cross-eyed teddy bear."

Sucking on the mint, Bobby looks at him.

"A teddy bear with crossed eyes, okay?" Brett says.

"O-kay," Bobby says slowly and skeptically.

"Which, when you put eyeglasses on him, the eyes get uncrossed."

Bobby is beginning to get it.

"We tell the kids to kiss the bear on the nose and put the glasses on him, and all at once the bear's eyes are straight," Brett says.

"How do we do that?" Bobby asks.

"I don't know how we do it. Am I a designer? We have this cuddly little bear who happens to have a handicap . . ."

"Visually challenged," Bobby says.

"Strabismally challenged," Brett says, nodding. "It's called strabismus. When you're cockeyed."

"Must be millions of kids in America who have to wear glasses," Bobby says, sucking pensively on the mint now, beginning to recognize the possibilities inherent in Brett's brainstorm.

"And who *hate* wearing glasses," Brett says. "This way we give them an *incentive* to wear glasses. Because they can see what the glasses do for the bear. The glasses *fix* the bear's eyes."

"I think it's terrific," Bobby says. "We'll get endorsements from every optometry association in the world."

"Who do we get to design her?"

"Lainie," they both say at once.

Brett reaches for his phone.

Lainie has worn to work, on this insufferably hot day in September, a very short green mini, a darker green T-shirt with no bra, strappy green sandals to match. The heart-shaped ring is on her right pinky. She is bare-legged, and her blond hair is massed on top of her head, held up and away from her neck with a green plastic comb. She looks sticky and sweaty and somehow desirable . . .

"Well, she's a very sexy girl, you know," Bobby says now.

. . . and vulnerable, her wandering eye giving her a slightly dazed appearance. Bobby is fearful at first that her own affliction might cause her to bridle at the notion of a bear similarly handicapped, but, no, she takes to the idea at once, expanding upon it, even making a few on-the-spot sketches of what the bear might look like with and without glasses.

"Does Toyland's finished bear look anything like those first sketches she made?"

"I don't remember what those sketches looked like."

"Do you recall exactly how Brett proposed the idea to her?"

"He told her essentially what he'd told me."

"Do you know exactly what her response was?"

"I told you. She was very enthusiastic."

"Yes, but her exact words."

"I don't remember."

There seemed to be a lot of things Bobby Diaz didn't remember. I wondered if he was related to Rosa Lopez, who claimed she'd seen O.J.'s Bronco parked on the street earlier than it could have been if he was out doing murder. Murders.

"How did the meeting end?"

"He told Lainie to get to work on it. Said he wanted drawings by the end of the month."

"The end of last September?"

"Yes."

"Working drawings?"

"I don't remember if he said working drawings or not."

"Did you see the drawings Lainie supposedly delivered by the end of the month?"

"No, I did not."

"Did you see *any* drawings Lainie delivered?"

"Well, I saw drawings. I don't know if they were Lainie's or not."

"When did you first see these drawings?"

"Before we made up the prototype."

"When was that exactly?"

"When I saw the drawings? Or when we made the bear?"

"The drawings."

"I don't remember."

"When did you have a finished bear?"

"The prototype?"

"Yes."

"In May sometime."

"This past May."

"Yes. We had a working model by the fifteenth."

I remembered that Lainie claimed to have designed *her* bear in April.

"Lainie Commins left Toyland in January, isn't that so?"

"Yes, I believe that's when it was."

"Did she discuss this with you?"

"What? Leaving Toyland?"

"Yes."

"I don't remember."

"Well, you're Toyland's design chief, aren't you?"

"I am."

"And she was working in the design department . . ."

"Yes."

"So didn't she tell you she was leaving?"

"Well, yes, I'm sure she did. I thought you meant did we discuss *why* she was leaving, or what she planned to do *next,* or . . ."

"Well, did you?"

"I told you. I don't remember."

"Did you ever see her again? After she left Toyland?"

Diaz hesitated.

"Did you?" I asked.

"I don't remember," he said.

Which in Spanish was *No me acuerdo.*

Which, according to O.J.'s Dream Team, meant "No" in many Spanish dialects like Rosa Lopez's.

Oh?

Sí.

The way Guthrie looked at it, women's lib was the biggest con mankind had ever foisted on the female gender. First we — meaning Guthrie and every other conniving male in America — convinced women that they deserved the same sexual freedom men had enjoyed for centuries. This sounded good to the feminists. Why *should* men be the only ones to decide when sex was appropriate or indicated? Why shouldn't women be the aggressors whenever they felt like it? Why shouldn't *women* demand sex when they wanted it, initiate it when they wanted it, be the equals of men in every respect as concerned sex.

Men like Guthrie were very sympathetic to these attitudes and ideals.

Men like Guthrie agreed it was definitely unfair that for all these eons women had been used and/or abused sexually but had never been granted the opportunity of calling the shots themselves. Men like Guthrie agreed that this was a despicable situation. In repentance, they were willing to do everything within their power to see to it that women enjoyed equal sexual rights. This meant that women could introduce the sex act, and encourage the sex act, and follow through on the sex act, all without stigma, humiliation or disapprobation. Women thought this was terrific. Freedom at last. Men thought it was terrific, too, because it meant they were getting laid a lot more often with a lot less hassle.

And since there was now nothing wrong with going to bed with a man whenever the spirit moved one, so to speak, then why not take the liberation a step further and move *in* with a man who pleased a person spiritually and sexually besides? Why not indeed? Men encouraged this new notion. Whereas back in the Dark Ages, a man couldn't get into a woman's pants, so to speak, without pledging his troth to her and perhaps not even then, now it became possible for a man and a woman to live together on a sort of trial basis, which — if it worked out — might lead to marriage. But now that women had liberated themselves, there was no need for them even to be *thinking* about old-fashioned, restraining concepts like marriage. It was perfectly okay to share an apartment and incidentally to share the rent and the bills and everything else that went along with living together, *vive la liberté! Et l'égalité, aussi.*

Guthrie was all for women's lib.

He also thought it was wonderful that women now felt so confident and secure that they could walk in the street practically naked or else wearing only clothes they used to wear *under* their clothes. Pick up a fashion magazine like *Vogue* or *Elle* or *Harper's Bazaar* and you saw pictures of women wearing practically nothing at all, which only a few years ago would have got the publisher of *Penthouse* arrested, but which nowadays was an expression of female freedom, more power to them, and God bless them all.

The manager of the Silver Creek Yacht Club was a redhead named Holly Hunnicutt, which name Guthrie found provocative, and she was wearing a suit that looked like the sort frails used to wear when Guthrie was plying his trade back in the Big Bad Apple, a pale pastel-blue number with huge lapels and big breast pockets, you should pardon the expression. She was wearing the jacket over a short tight skirt, no stockings, just suntanned legs. Whenever she uncrossed those legs you could see Miami on a clear day. Under the jacket, she was wearing nothing but herself so that whenever she leaned over her desk, you could see Mount St. Helens in Washington even on a rainy day. Guthrie Lamb felt as if he were back in the pulp magazines again, the *days* of the pulp magazines, that is.

Holly Hunnicutt was too young to know what pulp magazines were. Guthrie guessed she was twenty-two, twenty-three years old, managing this swank yacht club here in one of Calusa's more desirable areas, close to Manakawa County and Fatback Key. Guthrie himself lived in a rooming house not too far from Newtown, one of the city's worst areas. He was wondering if Holly Hunnicutt — God, that name! — might be interested in one day visiting his cozy little room at the Palm Court, as it was aptly called since there were four spindly palm trees out front. Show her his newspaper clippings or something. His private-eye license. Which some people found quite impressive. Meanwhile, he was asking her whether anyone on Tuesday of last week had reported an outage of the light on top of the right-hand pillar at the entrance to the club.

"No, I don't believe so."

"Then the light was on that night?"

"I believe so, yes."

"Is there any way you could check?"

"Well, I guess I could call the electrician . . ."

"Yes, please do," Guthrie said, and flashed his dazzling smile which had cost him twelve thousand dollars for implants, not to mention the time and the pain. Holly found the dental work impressive, he guessed. At least she smiled back at him and bent over her desk to punch a few buttons on the phone, causing her jacket to fall somewhat open again, which Guthrie, gentleman that he was, pretended not to notice.

Holly spent a few moments on the phone with someone named Gus, which was a good name for an electrician, as opposed to a private investigator, who should have a classy name like Guthrie, Guthrie felt. During that time, she ascertained that Gus had not in recent weeks changed any lightbulbs on either of the two pillars at the club's entrance, and unless they had burned out last night after he'd gone home, they were still working. If she liked, he could circumvent the timer on the lights — which was set to go off at seven twenty-nine P.M., sunset in Calusa these days — and see if the lights came on now, which according to Guthrie's watch was three-twenty P.M. Guthrie heard all of this because Gus the electrician was on the speakerphone. He heard Holly, in person, tell him "No, that won't be necessary," and then she hit a button on her phone, and Gus disappeared, and she crossed her long sleek legs and settled back in the big leather chair behind her desk, and smiled, and asked, "How else can I help you, Mr. Lamb?" which Guthrie felt was provocative, but did not say.

"I'd like to talk to any of your employees who were working here last Tuesday night, the twelfth," Guthrie said.

"Why?" she asked.

"Very good," Guthrie said, and smiled. "I hate mysteries as much as you do. What I'm trying to learn is whether any of them might have noticed a car parked just outside the entrance pillars last Tuesday night. On the right-hand side. Facing the club, that is. As you go in. Did you, for example, happen to notice such a car?"

"No, I didn't."

"Which narrows the field," Guthrie said, and smiled again.

But not considerably.

It turned out that the yacht club employed forty people, among whom, and in addition to Holly Hunnicutt herself, were an assistant club manager, a dockmaster and two dockhands, three security guards and a night watchman, an electrician — Gus, of course — four maintenance men, a restaurant manager and assistant manager, a bartender, a hostess, ten waiters and/or waitresses, a chef, three assistant chefs, two dishwashers and four busboys. Not all of these people had been working last Tuesday night. Two had called in sick, and one had gone back to Cuba.

Of the remaining thirty-seven, only ten

had seen a car parked on the shoulder outside the club, but not at the hour Lainie Commins had specified. The time estimates varied, but they were consistent in being somewhere between eleven-thirty and midnight, rather than the ten-thirty Lainie had reported as the time she'd driven out of the club.

A waiter and a waitress who'd seen the car were reluctant to say so because they'd been outside necking, when they should have been in the restaurant helping to set up for Wednesday's lunch. In any case, neither of them was of much help in identifying the car because they were otherwise busily occupied. The waiter seemed to remember pressing the waitress against the car as he fumbled under her skirt. She seemed to remember something hard, cold and metallic against her buttocks, but she may have been understandably confused.

The remaining eight waitresses were absolutely positive they had seen: a dark green Acura, a blue Infiniti, a black Jaguar, a bluish-black Lexus, a brown Mercedes, a blue Lincoln Continental, a black Cadillac, and/or a grayish BMW. All of them agreed there was no one in the car. All of them further agreed that the car's lights were off. One of the assistant chefs said he'd seen the car — he was the one who claimed it was very definitely a blue GS 300 Lexus —

at twenty after eleven when he'd stepped onto the road for a peaceful smoke, but that it was gone when he left for home at a little before midnight.

Most of which added up to zilch.

Guthrie walked to where he'd parked his own car — neither an Acura, Infiniti, Jaguar, Lexus, Mercedes, Lincoln Continental, Cadillac, *nor* Beamer, but instead a little red Toyota — unlocked the trunk, and took from it his Polaroid camera and his casting kit.

Then he went out to the shoulder of the road outside the club, where eight different witnesses had seen eight different cars at eight different times on the night Brett Toland was killed.

There are people who maintain that if you haven't seen Calusa by boat, you haven't seen Calusa at all. The house I was renting was on one of the city's many beautiful canals, and the boat tied up at the dock was a sailboat I'd bought a few months before I got shot. When I was married to Susan, we owned a sailboat she'd named *Windbag*, but no one ever said she wasn't clever. I might have named the new boat *Windbag II*, but Patricia was very touchy about my former wife, and so the boat still wasn't named some seven months after I'd bought her.

Patricia, who doesn't much care for boats, suggested the name *Wet Blanket*. Which is no worse than two lawyers I know who have boats respectively named *Legal Ease* and *Legal Tender*. Another of my friends owns both a discount furniture store and a boat with a big red mainsail. He calls her *Fire Sail*. A dentist I know has a high-powered speedboat he has named *Open Wide*. A gynecologist who has since been sent to prison for molesting one of his patients used to have a boat called *Wading Room*. Another doctor who is still around *should* have been sent to prison for naming his boat simply *Dock*.

In Calusa, Florida, there are as many cute names for boats as there are boats on the water. In the entire United States of America, in fact, there are almost as many cute names for boats as there are cute names for beauty salons. The naming of beauty salons and boats seems to bring out the worst instincts in everyone on the planet. Show me a city that does not have a beauty salon called *Shear Elegance* and I will show you a city that does not have a boat named *Sir N. Dippity*.

My partner Frank says I should name my new boat *Wet Dream*.

The boat, still unnamed, was bobbing on the water at the end of my dock that Tuesday night while Patricia and I sipped after-dinner cognacs on my screened-in patio. All the lights were out. A week ago at about this time, Brett Toland was getting himself shot, allegedly by my client. I put down my glass. I put my arm around Patricia. I kissed her.

Once upon a time . . .

But that was then.

We met at a motel on the South Tamiami Trail. We sneaked into the room like burglars and fell into each other's arms as though we'd been apart for centuries rather than days, not even days, a day and a half, not even that, twenty-eight hours since we'd kissed goodbye yesterday morning. She was dressed for work, wearing a dark blue pinstripe tropical suit with wide lapels, "My gangster suit," she called it, an instant before she hurled the jacket onto the bed. My hands had been on her from the moment the door clicked shut behind her, "Lock it," she whispered under my lips, but I was unbuttoning the front of the long-sleeved white blouse instead, "Oh, Jesus, lock it," she whispered, but I was sliding the tailored skirt up over her thighs, my hands reaching everywhere, my hands remembering her, my mouth remembering her, "Jesus," she kept murmuring under my lips, we were both crazy, kicking off the high-heeled shoes, a garter belt under the skirt, dark blue stockings, "For you," she whispered, "for you," lowering her panties, silken and electric, the skirt bunched up above her waist, her legs wide, entering her, "Oh, Jesus," she said, "Oh, Jesus," I said, clutching her to me, pulling her onto me, enclosing, enclosed, "Oh, Jesus," she said, "I'm coming," she said, "this is crazy," she said, "this is crazy," I said, we were crazy, we were crazy, we were crazy.

But, as I said, that was then.

And this was now.

And now, Patricia returned my kiss gently, afraid I would break, and then put her head on my shoulder and said, "This is nice, Matthew, sitting here."

"Yes," I said.

In a little while, she told me she had a busy day ahead tomorrow . . .

"Yes, me too," I said.

. . . and really ought to be running on home.

Before I got shot, *mi casa* was *su casa* and vice versa.

But that was then.

And this was now.

8

He was trying to explain my condition to Patricia and me. What had *been* my condition. What my condition *would* be in the weeks ahead. What my condition could possibly *become* in the months ahead. The word "possibly" frightened me. I had just taken a mighty leap out of a very dark pit, what the hell did he mean by *possibly?* Patricia sat by the bed, gripping my hand.

Spinaldo explained that I had flat-lined briefly while they were attempting to remove the bullets from my chest . . .

"That's not what you told us," Patricia said.

Not for nothing was she the best prosecuting attorney in the entire state of Florida.

"When we were here at the hospital," she explained, turning to me. "Frank and I." She turned back to Spinaldo. "You told us there'd been a loss of blood to the brain for five minutes and forty seconds. That isn't briefly."

"No, it isn't," Spinaldo agreed. "But Mr. Hope has since reported that he recalls comments made during surgery . . ."

I did indeed.

Oh shit, he's flat-lined . . . he's in cardiac arrest . . . let's pace him . . . Epinephrine . . . keep an eye on that clock . . . one cc, one to a thousand . . . still unobtainable . . .

". . . and this would seem to indicate that he'd remained *aware* at some time during the arrest. I can only believe that the open cardiac massage we performed . . ."

Hands inside my chest. Massaging my naked heart.

". . . did much to prevent total nonperfusion."

"What's nonperfusion?" Patricia asked.

I was letting her do all the talking.

I could think good, but it wasn't coming out good.

"Total ischemia," Spinaldo said.

Doctor talk. Worse than lawyer talk.

"And what's that?"

Good old English. Good old Patricia. I squeezed her hand. Hard.

"Total loss of blood to the brain."

"But you're saying that didn't happen."

"It would appear so. I have to assume the brain was still getting *something*. You have to understand that the brain is the ultimate organ. It gets what it wants, and it gets it *first*, above all the other organs. It's selfish. It has strategies for self-preservation in any crisis. The lidocaine helped, I'm sure. Turned what was most likely a ventricular tachycardia into a *sinus* tachycardia. But

253

the brain was in there grabbing whatever oxygen it needed, struggling to autoregulate its blood supply. I'm guessing, of course. The point is . . . you were aware."

There'd been darkness, there'd been intense light. There'd been unfathomable blackness, there'd been searing glare. There'd been no present, all was then. There'd been no past, all was now. Voices gone, concerned voices gone, lingering voices in the dark, voices swallowed in the then and the light. Whispering voices, pattering footfalls, flurries of movement, a circling of moths. Cold everywhere, hurting in the dark, shaking in the dark, sweating and hot . . .

Yes.

I'd been aware.

"Moreover," Spinaldo said, "you began *talking* seven days after the cardiac arrest."

"One word," Patricia said.

She was thinking Seven days is a full *week*.

"Nonetheless. Any speech at all would indicate to me that his brainstem reflexes were intact, and that he was emerging out of a semicomatose state several days *before* he recovered full alertness."

"Master of suspense," Patricia said, and squeezed my hand again.

I did not feel like the master of anything at the moment.

I could not remember what had happened to me.

Everyone kept telling me I'd been shot.

Spinaldo said I would probably *never* remember all the details of the actual event. Spinaldo said this had to do with the way memory is moved from so-called short-term areas to long-term areas, where hardwired recollection is summoned up either consciously or unconsciously.

Here's a loss-of-memory joke from the good doctor:

"The nice thing about recovering from a coma is that you get to meet new people every day."

Some joke.

This was a week after I blinked up into his face.

I was already beginning to lose hope.

Guthrie Lamb could have chosen to become a cop instead of a private investigator, but the money wasn't as good. Also, he hated all the paramilitary bullshit that was part and parcel of being a police officer. Guthrie hated any organization that evaluated a person by the uniform he was wearing. This was why he much preferred the company of naked broads.

Even so, he was forced to work with cops because there was no way he could otherwise get access to police and FBI files. This was a serious failing of the private-eye business. You had to depend on the people who were *really* empowered to investigate murders and such.

In fact, the last time Guthrie had ever heard of a private eye solving a murder case was never. It was one thing to gather information for an attorney who was defending a poor soul charged with murder, but it was quite another thing to be hired by some old tycoon who wanted you to find out who had murdered his beautiful blond daughter. Guthrie had never been hired by an old tycoon. Tell the truth, he had rarely come across too many beautiful blond daughters, either, dead or alive. What Guthrie did mostly was skip-tracing, or tailing wayward husbands for some woman wanted a divorce, or looking for some guy went out for a cup of coffee, didn't come back in five years, his wife was beginning to get a little worried. Never once in his lifetime as a Famous Detective had he ever been hired to find out who'd killed somebody.

Even working for Matthew Hope this way — who seemed like a nice guy, by the way, except he'd got chintzy about Guthrie's hourly rate, which, okay, it *wasn't* the fifty an hour Guthrie had mentioned, but Hope could at least have gone to forty-seven fifty, couldn't he? No, he'd stuck to what he was paying Warren Chambers, whoever the hell he was, and if he was so good why wasn't Hope using him *this* time? Guthrie hated hassling over money. It made a person seem mercenary.

But even on a case like this one, which was in *fact* a murder case, Guthrie wasn't actually looking for a murderer, he was simply looking for an automobile that may or may not have been parked outside the yacht club while a murder was being committed. Unless, of course, the person who'd left the car there was also the person who'd done the murder, in which case it could be said that Guthrie *was,* after all, looking for a murderer, though to tell the truth that would be stretching it.

A private eye was a private eye, period.

In the old days, when Guthrie was first starting in this business, the police were definite enemies. There wasn't a time back then that the police wouldn't at one point or another accuse the private eye himself of being the murderer, can you imagine? Big bulls from Homicide would drop in on him, maybe rough him up a little, haul him downtown to the cop shop, throw a scare into him, warn him to stay out of their way and keep his nose clean. If it wasn't for the cops back then, any self-respecting private eye could have solved the most complicated murder case in ten seconds flat. But no, the cops were always interfering, making it difficult for a hard-working, hard-drinking shamus to get his job done.

Nowadays, the cops seemed actually glad to see him.

Broke the routine, you know?

Guy coming in from left field with a plaster cast of a tire track, this was impressive. At least, that's what Detective Nick Alston said to him at nine forty-four that Wednesday morning, when Guthrie unveiled his handiwork, first snipping the white cord he'd tied around his package, and then peeling off the layers of brown wrapping paper to reveal — ta-*ra!*

"That's very impressive," Alston said. "Where'd you get that?"

"I made it myself," Guthrie said proudly.

"No kidding? That's very impressive."

Alston had never been what anyone would call handsome, but the last time Guthrie had seen him, his brown eyes were shot with red, and his craggy face looked puffy and bloated, and his straw-colored hair looked stringy, and there was a beard stubble on his face, and it was plain to see he'd already begun drinking at ten o'clock in the morning. Today, at nine forty-five now, he was clean-shaven, and he was wearing a neatly pressed suit and tie over a pristine white button-down shirt, and his hair was combed, and he looked . . . well . . . presentable.

Guthrie was impressed, too.

He basked in the glow of Alston's approval of the cast he'd made at the scene, feeling very much like a sixth-grade pupil showing a clay ashtray to his teacher. The cast really was a very good one, if Guthrie said so himself. Sometimes they turned out lousy. But Guthrie had first sprayed shellac over the tire track in the sandy soil on the shoulder of the road, and then had used only the very finest grade of art plaster of Paris for his mixture. He had spread it over the water in the bowl, not stirring it, permitting it instead to sink eventually to the bottom of the bowl, and only then adding more plaster until the water couldn't soak up anything further. After he'd poured the mixture onto the track, eyeballing it to a thickness of three-eighths of an inch or so, he reinforced it with snippets of twigs and twine and a few toothpicks for good luck, carefully laying on the material so that none of it touched the track itself. Pour on another layer of plaster, allow it to harden — you knew this was happening when it got warm to the touch — and *voilà!* The perfect specimen lying on Alston's desk.

"So what would you like me to do with this fine work of art here?" Alston asked.

Guthrie knew he was joking.

Or hoped he was.

"Nick," he said, "I would like you to seek

a match in either your own files or the Feeb files. I have Polaroids, too," he said, and dropped a thick manila envelope onto Alston's desk. "I would like you to do me that favor, Nick."

"How's Gracie these days?" Alston asked casually.

Gracie was a hooker Guthrie had once sent around to Alston's place as a favor when he was still a falling-down drunk.

"She's fine. Asked about you just the other day, in fact."

Alston said nothing for several moments. Then, still looking down at the plaster cast, he said, "I'd like her to see me sober."

"Done," Guthrie said. "I'll send her over tonight."

"No, just tell her I'll call," Alston said.

"Happy to," Guthrie said, and waited.

"What's this in reference to?" Alston asked, opening the envelope and looking at the very good Polaroids Guthrie had taken, if he said so himself.

"A homicide," Guthrie said. "I'm working for the defense attorney."

"Who?"

"Matthew Hope."

"What happened to Warren Chambers?" Alston asked.

What they do is they treat you like an invalid. Which is what you are. This means

260

that the moment I began speaking, they started a daily assessment of my *functional* status in addition to my *neurological* status. Test after test after test, tests enough to bend the mind and twist the tongue. Let us consider, for example, the Post Traumatic Amnesia Scale, and the Wechsler Adult Intelligence Scale, and the Bender-Gestalt Test and the Minnesota Multiphasic Personality Index, all designed to determine the extent of injury or lack thereof.

They shave your scalp with an abrasive, and with elasticized tape they attach needle electrodes to it. Ten to twenty small electrodes on the scalp in a defined spacing. You feel like Frankenstein's monster waiting for the bolt of lightning that will make you come alive. In metabolic insults such as mine . . .

Spinaldo kept using the term "metabolic insult." I felt I should challenge him to a duel.

. . . in metabolic insults such as mine, then, the electroencephalogram usually shows slow diffuse waves. Recovery occurs in tandem with the resolution of slow waves toward normal brain wave patterns.

Every day, Spinaldo told me I was on the way to recovery.

I kept wondering when that would be.

The yellow CRIME SCENE tapes were still

up around the slip where *Toy Boat* was nudging the dock, but I had called the State Attorney's Office beforehand, and had been told by Pete Folger that the prosecution had already gathered all the evidence it needed, and that I could visit the boat anytime I wished. I was surprised, therefore, to see a uniformed police officer standing at the head of the gangway as Andrew and I approached that Wednesday morning.

I told him who we were, and handed him a card.

He told us who he was, and explained that Assistant State Attorney Peter Folger had asked the police department to send an officer down to "extend every courtesy to Attorney Hope." This was code. What it meant was "Stay with him every minute and make sure he doesn't do anything that will damage our case against Lainie Commins."

I told the officer — whose name was Vincent Gergin, according to the black plastic nameplate over the breast pocket of his blouse — that my associate and I merely wanted to take some Polaroids of the crime scene with a view toward better orientation. I also told him we might look around the boat a bit to see if there was anything the S.A.'s Office might have overlooked. He said, "No problem."

I hate that expression.

I said, "Fine. In that case, we'll go aboard."

He said, "Fine. In that case, I'll just go with you."

We all went down the gangway and onto the boat.

Andrew was there for the very same reason he'd accompanied me when we talked to Folger's witnesses. Whichever one of us later tried the case, the other would be called as a witness to whatever we happened to discover on the boat this morning. Quite frankly, I wasn't expecting to find a damn thing. Say what you will about the office Skye Bannister runs, his investigators and criminologists are enormously efficient in picking a crime scene clean.

Here was the cockpit where Lainie and Brett had sat — according to her — from ten to ten-thirty. Here was where he had made a generous offer, according to her, or a merely insulting offer, according to his widow. Here was where, according to Lainie's first story, she'd sipped Perrier that (oh-yes-I-remember-now) turned into a couple of vodka-tonics in her next version. Here was where she'd given Brett her Top-Siders and her scarf, something she'd neglected to tell me at first, which scarf was later found by the police in the boat's master bedroom. She had not remembered the scarf until the police questioned her about it the following morning. She had not remembered either the scarf *or* the shoes until I later questioned her about them.

I was wondering now what else she had forgotten to tell me.

Perhaps prompted by the Tolands' obsession with keeping their decks pristine, I now took off my own shoes and asked Andrew to remove his as well. Officer Gergin looked at us both as if we were slightly deranged and made not the slightest move to unlace his highly polished black brogans.

We all went below.

There is something about a room where a murder has been committed. This was not in actuality a "room"; there are no *rooms* as such aboard seagoing vessels, although "staterooms" are called rooms and "shower rooms" are called rooms, but these are truly compartments, as was this "dining *saloon*" we passed through which was, in fact, a dining *room.* Enough already. Shoeless, we padded in our socks to the master stateroom, Gergin clumping along behind us in his thick-soled regulation shoes.

If there is one area aboard a boat that truly *looks* like a room, it is the stateroom. Perhaps this is because it's dominated by a bed, in this case a queen-size bed with cabinets flanking it and reading lights above it. The master bath, or the "en suite head" as it was nautically called, was on the port side of the bed, and there was a bank of dressers and several closets on the starboard side. Just opposite the foot of the bed, and flanking the entrance door to the cabin, there were glass-doored, floor-to-ceiling bookcases.

"We'll be taking pictures in here," Andrew said.

"No problem," Gergin said.

I normally feel like strangling people who say "No problem" or, especially, "*Hey,* no problem." What the phrase *really* means is, "Yes, there is *ordinarily* a problem in honoring such a request, but in this single instance, and however irritating it may be, an exception will be made, although it is truly a severe pain in the ass."

That is what "No problem" means.

And don't let anyone tell you otherwise.

"We'll be looking around, too," I said.

"For what?"

"Don't know."

"No problem," Gergin said, and shrugged, and then planted himself squarely in the door to the stateroom, where he could watch Andrew taking his pictures and me rummaging around.

Two shots to the head, the coroner's report had said.

A third that had missed.

No stench of cordite here.

But the place reeked of murder.

The chalked outline of Brett Toland's body was traced on the carpet alongside the bed. Bloodstains had turned black on the carpet. Raw wood showed where the third bullet had been pried from the wall alongside the bathroom door.

Gergin yawned while Andrew took his Polaroid pictures.

This was where the police had found Lainie's scarf.

I didn't know where to begin.

I didn't even know what I was looking for.

I started in the bathroom, looking in the cabinet under the sink and finding nothing but extra rolls of toilet paper and boxes of Kleenex and a six-pack of Irish Spring soap bars. I then looked in the mirrored cabinet over the sink and found several toothbrushes and a tube of toothpaste and a wide assortment of nonprescription medicines, and several prescription drugs as well, but nothing that would help me to prove my client was innocent of the crime with which she'd been charged.

If that was what I was looking for.

Andrew was still taking pictures.

I went to the cabinet on the starboard side of the bed, and opened the latched door. There was a pair of pom-pommed slippers with low heels on the floor of the cabinet. Nothing else. I closed the door and slid open the drawer above it. A pair of reading glasses, a packet of tissues, a tube of lipstick. I figured this was Etta Toland's side of the bed.

I went around to Brett's side.

Ran the same search of the cabinet base and drawer, and found nothing of importance. But I wondered if this was where he'd stored the forty-five that had later been used to kill him.

Walked back to the combination bookcase and entertainment center fitted with a television set, a VCR, and a CD player.

Started looking through the books.

Pulled out a copy of *Great Expectations*. Leafed through it. Placed it back on the shelf. Found *The Rubaiyat*. Blew dust off it. Opened it. Flipped through it. People sometimes tucked letters or scraps of paper into books. But there was nothing. The dust wrappers had been removed from all of the books. Not uncommon on a boat, where moisture caused paper to twist and curl. Took down a copy of Stephen King's *It*. Big book, some two and a half inches thick. Black cover with the initials SK in red in the lower right-hand corner. Opened the book. Closed it, or *It*, put it back on the shelf. Started looking at some other books. Blew dust off them. Leafed through them. Put them back on the shelves again. There were a lot of books here. Hundred best books in the English language, it looked like. Some of them never read, judging by the dust on them. Began looking through the videocassettes in their black vinyl cases. The cover art on one of them showed a woman's hands spread over the crotch of her lacy white panties. The ring on her pinky . . .

"How long you guys gonna be down here?" Gergin asked.

I put the cassette back on the shelf.

"You can leave us if you're bored," I said.

"Hey, no problem," he said.

"We won't be stealing anything."

"Who said you would? It's just it's a little stuffy down here, the air-conditioning off and all."

"Why don't you go upstairs?" I suggested. "Get yourself some air."

"No, that's okay," he said.

I looked at some other cassettes.

Gergin scratched his ass.

"Did you get any pictures of the cockpit?" I asked Andrew.

"Do we need any?"

"Oh, sure," I said, and looked him dead in the eye.

We'd been working together for a good long time.

"Okay to go up alone?" he asked Gergin.

Gergin smelled a rat.

The wrong one.

"I'll go with you," he said, and they both

left the stateroom.

I waited till I heard Gergin's heavy footfalls on the topside deck. I took the cassette down from the shelf again. It was titled *Idle Hands*. The ring on the woman's right pinky finger was identical to Lainie's Victorian seal ring with its heart-shaped face and its floret-covered band.

Without a second's hesitation, I lifted my jacket and tucked the cassette into my trousers against the small of my back.

This was embarrassing.

Three attorneys who represented a person, watching a compromising videotape of that person. *Idle Hands* indeed. A tape that could easily be defined as pornography by prevailing community standards in that Lainie Commins, all by herself and looking quite cockeyed without her glasses on (or anything else but white panties and a gold Victorian ring, for that matter), was exposing her genitals, pubic area, buttocks and breasts below the top of the nipples, with less than a full opaque covering; was engaging as well in masturbation, which act constituted the commission of an abominable and detestable crime against nature, or suggested that such a crime was being or would be committed; was also exposing her genitals in a presumed state of sexual stimulation or arousal; all of this presum-

269

ably done willfully (as witness the knowing albeit goofy smile on her face), which activities predominately appealed to the prurient, shameful or morbid interests, and were without serious literary, artistic, political or scientific value. Boy oh boy.

"Are you telling me you slipped this tape under your jacket while the cop was topside?" Frank asked.

"I did."

"Boy oh boy," he said.

"Do you intend to show this to the state attorney?" Andrew asked.

I merely looked at him.

"In which case," he suggested, "I guess we'd better ask Miss Commins about it."

Lainie arrived at our offices on Heron Street at a little before two that afternoon. She explained that we'd caught her working and asked us to please excuse the jeans, sandals and T-shirt she was wearing. She was also wearing the omnipresent Victorian ring on the pinky of her right hand. I asked her to please have a seat, and then I put the *Idle Hands* tape in our VCR, told her we were going to step outside for fifteen, twenty minutes, and asked her to hit the PLAY button after we were gone.

A half hour later, we rejoined her.

"So?" I said.

"Where'd you get this?" she asked.

"In the master stateroom of the Toland boat."

"Yeah," she said, and nodded bleakly.

We all looked at her. Andrew seemed not to understand quite what was going on. Then again, he was but a mere callow youth. I was wondering what Lainie meant by "Yeah." She didn't seem ready to amplify just yet. Frank caught my eye. The *prompt,* he was saying. Give the lady the *prompt.*

"Did you know this tape was on the boat?" I asked.

She hesitated, trying to determine which of the three of us would be most sympathetic to her story. I was guessing she was guessing Andrew. Instead, she pitched it to Frank.

"He was trying to blackmail me," she said.

"Toland?" Frank said.

"Yes."

"He showed you this tape, and . . . ?"

"No."

"Then . . . ?"

"Said he *had* it."

"Said he had a video of you in the nude?"

"Said he had *this* video," she said, and nodded at the cassette vehemently, as if willing it to burst into flame — as well it might have, considering its subject matter.

"But he didn't show it to you?"

"No."

"Just said he had it."

All of this from Frank in his clipped, no-nonsense New Yorker style. Sometimes I admired him.

"Yes, just said he had it. Showed me the case, the holder, whatever the hell it's called, with my hands on the cover. But it was empty. Told me he'd have been stupid to bring the actual cassette there to the boat with him. Told me it was safe at home. Warned me that unless I dropped the infringement suit, all of kiddieland would learn about that tape."

"All of . . . ?"

"Kiddieland. He meant everyone in the toy world. He would let it be known that the woman designing toys for children . . . well . . . was . . . well . . . doing what . . . what you saw me doing on the tape."

"And out the window goes your teddy bear," Andrew said, nodding.

"No," she corrected. "Out the window goes my *life.*"

"When was this?" I asked.

"When was what?"

"When did he tell you he had this tape?"

"While we were sitting upstairs."

"In the cockpit?"

"Yes."

"Drinking . . ."

"Yes."

"Engaged in pleasant conver—"

"Until he tried to blackmail me."

"But until then . . ."

"Until then, yes, he was telling me he thought he knew a way out of our problems, thought we could settle my claim without lawyers, and so on."

"Is that when he mentioned the tape?"

"Yes."

"Was this before or after he carried your shoes and your scarf down to the master stateroom?"

"I didn't know where he carried them."

"But before or after?"

"After. He took my stuff with him when he went down for the drinks."

"Did you know which tape he was referring to?" Frank asked.

"Yes."

"You knew this tape existed?"

"Well, of *course* I knew," she said, and turned to Andrew with an exasperated look on her face.

Andrew shrugged sympathetically.

"I mean, this wasn't *Candid Camera,*" she said.

"When was this taped?" Frank asked.

"Earlier this year. Sometime in March."

"Who shot it?"

"Man I met."

"Who?"

"Listen," she said, "I'm not on the witness stand here."

"Thank *God* you're not," Frank said.

"Lainie," I said gently, "would you like to tell us about it?"

The way Lainie tells it — and she tells it exceptionally well, first removing her eyeglasses to heighten the Poor Little Cockeyed but Extravagantly Sexy Waif look — the bills begin mounting and the savings begin dwindling the moment she leaves her weekly-paycheck job with Toyland back in January. Her own business, Just Kidding, is not yet established and there is an unexpected dearth of the free-lance assignments she was hoping for — in fact, counting on . . .

"I didn't think it would be that difficult," she said. "I had a track record and a good reputation, and I figured the jobs would just pour in. Frankly, I even began wondering if the Tolands weren't engaging in a little industrial sabotage. Bad-mouth me in the trade, you know, in hope I'd come back when I was on the ropes. The thing is, Toyland is the only game in town down here, so I was sending résumés to people who'd known me in New York or on the Coast, trolling, you know, networking, and it was taking a long time for people to get back to me. Meanwhile, the bucks were shrinking and . . ."

Getting a bit desperate, she begins searching the want ads, first for *any* kind

of job requiring an artistic background —
a graphic designer for an ad agency, for
example, or an art director for a magazine
— and next for any job with the descriptive
word "creative" in its newspaper listing, as
for instance designing daily menus for a
restaurant. The difficulty is that she's looking for something part-time, so that she can
continue designing on her own while earn-
ing enough money to pay the mounting
bills. She left the job at Toyland with two
thousand dollars in savings. By the end of
February, she is down to six hundred dollars and is scanning the ads advertising for
part-time waitresses or hostesses or cash-
iers or landscape assistants or . . .

And her eye stops.

The ad reads:

LINGERIE MANNEQUINS
TO MODEL FAMOUS
IMPORTED BRANDS
PART TIME — EXCELLENT SALARY
CALL BUTTERCUP ENTERPRISES
365-72 . . .

"I thought it was legitimate," she says
now. "Besides . . ."

. . . ever since she moved to Florida, she's
spent a lot of time on the beach . . . well,
her house on North Apple is merely a five-
minute drive or a twenty-minute walk to

the Whisper Key Beach . . . and surely the thong swimsuit she used to wear before the Calusa P.D. cracked down on such "indecent exposure" as they'd labeled it, was very close to parading around in lingerie, wasn't it? In fact, rather more revealing than any lingerie she ever wore in the privacy of her own bedroom or under her clothes on the street. Besides, she truly does think the ad is legitimate, a wholesaler or retailer seeking someone to model famous imported brands like Chantelle or Lise Charmel or Hanro of Switzerland. She's always felt she had a fairly decent figure, so why not use it to good advantage now in a part-time job paying excellent wages.

She calls the number listed at the bottom of the ad.

A well-spoken woman who sounds somewhat matronly and British explains that the job is modeling very expensive lingerie like Chantal Thomass or Rien or Wacoal in a retail venue — the exact word she uses, "venue" — at flexible hours, and at a starting rate of thirty dollars an hour. She asks how old Lainie is . . .

"Thirty-three," she says.

"Mm," the woman says.

Lainie catches her breath.

"It's just that most of our mannequins are younger," the woman says.

"What age were you looking for?"

"Well, most of our mannequins are in their early twenties."

O-kay, Lainie thinks, and immediately figures she's out of the running. Thirty-three. Ancient in the lingerie-modeling trade.

"But I do have a very youthful figure," she says.

"Would you feel comfortable telling me your dimensions?" the woman asks in her pleasant voice with its mild British accent.

"Thirty-four, twenty-five, thirty-four. B cup."

"You don't have any visible scars or blemishes, do you?"

"No," she says, and wonders if she should mention her wandering right eye, but that's neither a scar nor a blemish, though it's been a pain in the ass all her life.

"Tattoos?" the woman asks.

Tattoos? Lainie thinks.

"No," she says. "No tattoos."

"Although some of our mannequins *do* have tattoos," the woman says. "Discreet ones, of course. A tiny butterfly on the shoulder. A little rose on the hip."

"I don't have any of those."

But I can *get* one, she thinks. If a tattoo is required, just let me know, I'll run out and . . .

"Well," the woman says, and is silent for what seems an inordinately long time, no doubt studying the statistics she's written down, no doubt trying to determine whether a thirty-three-year-old woman with a mere B cup and no tattoos is suitable for modeling higher priced lingerie like Simone Perele or Aubade or Gossard.

"You're not married, are you?"

"No," Lainie says at once.

"Mm," the woman says. "Is there anyone who'd be likely to object to your modeling lingerie?"

"No," she says.

Why would they? she wonders.

"Then do you think you'd like to come in for an interview?"

"Yes, I would," Lainie says. "Yes."

She waits.

"What would be a convenient time for you?" the woman asks.

The offices of Buttercup Enterprises, Inc., are in a strip mall on U.S. 41, situated at street level between a pet shop and a garden supply store. Lainie parks her white Geo nose-in, facing a battery of lawn mowers and spreaders, garden hoses on reels, huge sacks of fertilizer and seed, and variously priced rakes, hoes and spades racked against the front window of the store. In the pet shop on the other side of Buttercup, white puppies frolic and a very fat fluffy kitten dozes in the glancing afternoon sun. She raps on the glass. The kitten doesn't stir.

The flowers painted onto the plate-glass windows flanking the entrance door to Buttercup resemble sunflowers more than any buttercups Lainie has ever seen. She wonders immediately if the company would like her to design a new logo for the window. The lettering is none too elegant, either. It is the simplest form of graphic, what graffiti writers called Bubble, a sort of ballooning, overlapping face that any child could master in moments, a totally inappropriate font for a firm specializing in high-style lingerie. She would have chosen something like DESDEMONA (and here she visualizes it in her head) or HARRINGTON (again visualizing it) as more appropriate to the nature of the business.

She does not yet know what the nature of the business actually is.

The man who interviews her is perhaps thirty years old, a good-looking man dressed in a white linen suit and white patent-leather shoes, wearing under the suit jacket a vibrant blue cotton sports shirt, open at the throat, no tie. He looks like he just stepped out of the pages of *GQ*, his black hair slicked back wetly in a look too fashionable for staid Calusa. Pleasantly, cordially, he offers her a chair in front of his wide desk — ebony top, polished chrome legs and trim — and sits in a black leather chair with the same chrome appointments as the desk, a mate to the chair in which Lainie sits and crosses her legs demurely. She is wearing a straw-colored suit, lighter panty hose, a mossy-green silk blouse, low-heeled sandals of the same color. The office is modestly but nicely decorated, modern prints on the walls, a pair of Chagalls, one Calder. A triangular black plastic nameplate on his desk announces C. WILSON in white letters.

"Call me Chris," he says, and smiles. "So," he says, "I understand you're interested in modeling for Buttercup."

"Yes," she says. "But I do have some questions about the job."

"Certainly," he says. "What would you like to know?"

"Well, it doesn't involve any traveling, does it?"

"What do you mean by traveling? You would have to travel back and forth to the venue, of course."

The word *venue* again.

"Do you have transportation?"

"Yes, I have my own car."

"Good."

"But, I meant traveling out of town," she says. "Would the job entail . . . ?"

"Oh no. No, no, no," he says, reassuring her with his pleasant smile. "All of the venues are right here in Calusa. Most of them on the Trail, in fact."

Meaning U.S. 41, the Tamiami Trail, which is good because what she wants to do is spend *most* of her day in the studio on North Apple, designing toys while she does this modeling thing only part-time. This seems to suit Mr. Wilson quite well . . . Chris . . . since the venues are open from twelve noon to two A.M., and she can more or less choose her own work schedule depending on how much time she wishes to spend at it and how much money she chooses to earn . . .

"It's all entirely flexible, you see, entirely dependent on you yourself, Lainie . . . if I may call you Lainie," he says. "Which is a very pretty name, by the way, if you choose to use it."

"I'm sorry?" she says.

"Some of our mannequins prefer using different names."

"Different?"

"Other than their own names."

"Why?" she asks.

"Personal idiosyncrasies," he says, and shrugs.

She still does not smell a rat.

By this time in her recitation, Matthew and Frank are way ahead of the pleasantly smiling Mr. Wilson. Even young Andrew seems to have caught the drift. But Lainie, to hear her tell it, is still blissfully unaware.

"We do insist on a minimum of four hours a day."

Which would be perfect, she thinks. Four hours a day in a five-day week would come to twenty hours a week at thirty dollars an hour, for a total of six hundred dollars a week. Her fixed expenses are something like twenty-five hundred a month, so, actually, this *would* work, particularly if she could choose her own . . .

"There should be some lingerie in your size in the dressing room," Mr. Wilson says.

Chris says.

She blinks at him.

"We stock only the finest imported brands," he says, "Felina, lejaby, Jezebel, La Perla, I wonder if you'd mind trying something on for me? Just any bra, garter belt and panties, whichever color suits you. There's matching hosiery in there as well," he says, "you'll find it. If you'll tell Clarice your shoe size . . ."

Who's Clarice? she wonders.

". . . she'll bring you a pair of heels as well."

Smiling pleasantly.

"You mean you want me to . . . uh . . . try it on now?"

"If you would."

"Well, I . . . I didn't know I'd be . . ."

"If you'd prefer coming back some other time . . ."

"No, no. It's just . . ."

"Whatever makes you comfortable," he says.

Chris says.

"Well . . . did you want me to come back in *here?*" she asks. "After I'm dressed?"

"Yes."

*Un*dressed, she thinks.

"In the lingerie?" she says.

In my *underwear,* she thinks. *Their* underwear, actually, she thinks. Buttercup's high-priced line of underwear. But thirty dollars an hour, she thinks.

"Yes," Chris says. "Because that's what you'd be doing, you know," he says. "Modeling lingerie, you see. For upward of thirty dollars an hour."

Still smiling.

Upward of thirty, she thinks.

"Well . . ." she says.

"Maybe you'd like to think it over?" Chris says, and starts to rise.

"No, no," she says. "Hey, I guess you have to see what I look like."

"Only if you feel comfortable about it."

"Yes," she says. "I do."

"Shall I ask Clarice to come in then?"

"Sure."

"Show you where the dressing room is?"

"Sure."

Clarice, she learns, is a nineteen-year-old college dropout who is trying to earn enough money so she can go to Jackson, Wyoming, "away from this freakin *heat*," she says, where she can become a ski instructor, though she's never skied in her life. She tells Lainie that she only helps out here once a week because she and Chris have a sort of a thing going, but most of the time she models under the name of Kristal at a venue on the South Trail and Beaver Street, "appropriate, huh?" she says, and smiles a dazzling teenybopper smile, and *still* Lainie doesn't catch on, sweet little cockeyed girl who grew up singing hymns in l'il ole Winfield, Alabama.

What is finally explained to her by Clarice is that Buttercup Enterprises, Inc., runs a string of lingerie-modeling shops along the Trail. These shops have names like Satin and Lace, or Midnight Lingerie, or Silk 'n' Garters, or Lace Fantasies, and their ostensible purpose is to sell lingerie. Toward that end, the chain employs what Clarice calls "a bevy of young girls" to *model* the lingerie for potential customers. All of these potential customers are men who pay an initial fee of fifty dollars a half hour for the privilege of seeing these girls in their scanties. Of this fifty, the house takes thirty-five and the girls get fifteen. An hour-long session costs ninety-five dollars, of which the house gets sixty-five. The modeling takes place in cubbyhole rooms — two at some locations, more at others — clustered around the main showroom. There are low platforms in these rooms and the girls stand on these platforms while they parade their wares. Nobody ever buys lingerie.

What the men who frequent these shops pay for is a variety of services . . .

"No touching allowed," Clarice says, "supposedly."

. . . ranging from a slow striptease for which every article of clothing dropped costs another ten dollars over the initial entrance fee, to stripping oneself while the girl gyrates, which costs another ten dollars, to masturbating while the girl lies on the platform and spreads her legs to you . . .

"Twenty dollars for that privilege," Clarice explains,

. . . to allowing the girl to take your penis between her breasts . . .

"This is not considered touching," Clarice explains, "since her *hands* never make contact with the organ."

. . . subsequently stroking the client to climax mammillarily, to coin a phrase, which — speaking of coin — costs another fifty dollars. Since this usually occurs after the girl has taken off her bra for ten, this means she earns an additional sixty for a half-hour Tit Job, as it is known on the circuit, a total of seventy-five dollars all told, or ninety for a full hour. The girls prefer negotiating up front for whichever little service they're going to perform, carefully explaining to the client that no one is selling sex here . . .

"Ha!" Clarice says.

. . . and that touching is strictly prohibited by law.

"Some of the men like the slow strip while they jack off," she says, "they like being teased, you know, enjoy tossing the ten-dollar bills on the platform each time they order you to take off another piece of clothing, makes them feel like big financiers. Some of them like you to take off just the panties and spread for them while they do their number. There are girls who tell me they actually *like* the tit jobs, *ick*, because they're not just gyrating while some guy does himself. Maybe they have sensitive breasts, which I don't. Even so. I mean, *ick*. Some weeks, I go home with three, four thousand dollars, it depends on how many hours I want to work, and how far I want to go, because — just between you, me, and the lamppost — if nobody's looking, a hand-job or even a blowjob isn't entirely out of the question provided the guy is nice and the price is right. This doesn't mean you have to do anything you don't want to do. You're hired to model lingerie, and if that's all you want to do, the guy comes in and

sits down in a chair, and you model whichever lingerie he asks you to put on — there's
a screen in the room, you dress and un-
dress behind it and you get your fifteen
bucks for the half, or thirty for the full,
which is a lot better than you get at McDon-
ald's, honey, believe me. What's your shoe
size?"

At first, Lainie is astonished.

She listens to all this while she is putting
on a black garter belt and sheer black
panties and a black Wonderbra, fastening
the garter snaps front and back to black
nylons, listening in amazement to all that
Clarice tells her, wondering what she's supposed to do when she goes back into Mr.
Wilson's office. Chris's office. Chris with
whom Clarice has "a sort of a thing going."
Will she have to do a little dog and pony
act for him, prove to him that she will be
a moneymaker at one of his little sex em-
poriums called Nylon Legs or whatever the
hell?

She has passed these little shops in the
strip malls along the Trail, the discreet
orange neon OPEN sign in the window, but
she actually believed they were legitimately
selling lingerie to women, and that the
"models" advertised in the window were
genuine models in some sort of trunk show
that moved from store to store. Calusa is,
after all, the city where women are arrested

for wearing thong bikinis on the beach. It is also the city where a famous comedian was arrested for masturbating in a pornographic movie theater. So how can these thin disguises for whorehouses be allowed to stay in business? Because, yes, that is what these are. They are whorehouses. And, in effect, she is being asked to become a whore. That is, if she does anything more than merely *pose* for the nice gentlemen callers.

As she takes the size seven, very high-heeled pumps Clarice hands to her, she remembers that this is the nation where Dr. Jocelyn Elders was fired as Surgeon General because she dared to suggest that schoolchildren be taught the meaning of masturbation. Not taught *how* to masturbate, no one even remotely suggested that. And she remembers that right here in Calusa the famous comedian was convicted for the heinous crime he'd committed — whereas the theater was still open and still showing dirty movies. America.

Besides, she needs the money.

The following Monday night, she begins working as Lori Doone in a shop called Silken Secrets, and in six hours, from eight P.M. to two A.M., she earns ninety dollars without once having to take off a single article of clothing and certainly without once touching anyone, which she carefully

288

explains is strictly prohibited by law.

——Then how about touching *yourself?*

——No, we're not allowed to do that.

——Be worth fifty to me if you took off your panties and showed me how you do yourself.

——I'm sorry, we're not permitted to do that.

——Jenny does it for me.

——She'd get fired if anyone found out.

——Come on, who'd ever know?

——They make spot checks.

"How long were you doing this?" Frank asked.

"Only until I did the video."

"What do you mean?"

"A photographer came in one night."

"What's his name?"

"Why do you have to know?"

"We don't, Frank."

"All right, we don't. Tell us what happened."

"He said I could make some very good money if I posed for a video."

"*This* video?"

"Yes. As it turned out."

"Did you know what kind of video it would be?"

"I had an idea."

"When did you learn *precisely* what he had in mind?"

"He made it clear."

"When?"

"That same night. The money was good."

"What did he pay you?"

"A thousand dollars. For what turned out to be a half-hour's work. He edited it down to fifteen minutes later. There were three other girls on the tape. I know them all, one of them is only sixteen."

"When did he shoot the video?"

"That same week."

"Where?"

"He has a studio not far from here. On Wedley."

"Did he pay you the money?"

"In advance."

"What did you think he was going to do with the video?"

"He said there were collectors for this sort of . . . well . . . specialty act, he called it. All of us . . . well . . . you saw the tape."

"Apparently Brett saw it, too."

"I don't know how he got hold of it."

"But he did."

"Apparently."

"And you say he didn't show it to you?"

"No. But he showed me the holder. I knew he had the cassette, too. He wouldn't have tried to blackmail me otherwise."

"Do you know what the prosecution could make of this video? If they knew it existed? If they knew it was on the Toland boat the night you went there? The night he was *killed?*"

"Yes," Lainie said. "I know what they can make of it."

"They'll say you killed him to *get* this damn tape!"

"Yes, but I didn't."

"They'll say . . ."

"And I didn't get the tape, either, did I?"

"She has a point, Frank."

"Why'd you remove this from the boat, Matthew?"

"No reason I shouldn't have."

"No reason?"

"He's right, Frank."

"No *reas*— ?"

"Thank you, Andrew."

"How about tampering with evidence? How about obstruction of . . . ?"

"How do you figure that?" I said. "Lainie's already been indicted, the grand jury's finished, no one told me I *couldn't* remove evidence from the scene. Since when am I not allowed to gather evidence in support of a client's defense?"

"Do you intend to submit this tape to the Court?"

"Come on, Frank. We're under no obligation to turn over any evidence we don't intend to use in our direct case."

"Which doesn't change the fact that you *removed* this from the boat without prior permission and without . . ."

"I was gathering evidence at a crime

scene. Is the S.A. the only one entitled to gather evidence? This is America, Frank."

"Yeah, bullshit," Frank said. "You removed this tape from the boat to make sure Folger wouldn't get his hands on it."

"No, I gathered evidence so I could present it to my client . . ."

"Bullshit."

". . . and question her about it. Which we've now done. Would you have preferred Folger surprising us with it later on?"

"How the hell can he *surprise* us if he doesn't even know it exists?"

Which suddenly worried me.

"Lainie?" I said. "I'm assuming there are other . . ."

"I'm sure there are," she said at once.

"Huh?" Frank said.

"Copies," she said.

"In which case," he said, "what *is* that photographer's name?"

9

The photographer's name was Edison Alva Farley, Jr., and he told Guthrie at once that he had been named after Thomas Alva Edison, the man who'd invented — among other things — the incandescent lightbulb and the motion picture camera.

Farley's great-grandfather — John Winston Farley — was living in West Orange, New Jersey, when the great man moved his laboratory there in 1887. The two men became fast friends, and John Winston's son Arthur — who was twelve at the time, but who would later become Farley's grandfather — had idolized the inventor. At the turn of the century, when Arthur was twenty-five, his young wife Sarah gave birth to a baby boy whom they promptly named Edison Alva, avoiding the more obvious Thomas Alva Edison, which when attached to the family name would have become Thomas Alva Edison Farley, a somewhat cumbersome handle. The first Edison Alva Farley later grew up to be the father of the current Edison Alva Farley, Jr.

"Such are the wonders of naming babies

in America," Farley told Guthrie, "though everybody calls me Junior now."

Guthrie, no stranger to the transmogrification of given names, not to mention surnames, took the photographer's extended hand, and said, "Everybody calls me Guthrie now," which was true.

"So what can I do for you?" Farley asked. "A passport photo? A portrait photo to send to your fiancée in Seoul?" and here he winked. Guthrie winked back, though he didn't get the joke.

"What I need, actually," Guthrie said, "is some information about a video you made back in March sometime."

"Was this a wedding?" Farley asked. "A graduation?"

"No. This was a private session with a woman. Just her and the video camera."

Farley looked at him.

"Would you remember making a video such as that?" Guthrie asked.

Guthrie already knew that last March Farley had shot a video of Lainie Commins, aka Lori Doone, in a half hour interlude that could have been construed as compromising, not to mention dirty. He gave Farley a little time to think things over. It was always best to get the percolator boiling before you started pouring the coffee.

There was, in fact, a percolator bubbling

away on the little hot plate in one corner of Farley's studio, though the photographer had not yet offered Guthrie a cup. The studio was in what was called a "cluster unit" on Wedley and Third, close to the Twin Forks Shopping Mall in "downtown" Calusa, such as it was. The mall had been a disaster. There was talk of turning it into a huge multilevel parking lot that would service the entire "downtown" area, though everyone in Calusa knew there was, in reality, no true "downtown" now that all the shopping had moved further south on the Trail into far more successful malls than Twin Forks.

The studio was somewhat small, as was true of most spaces in these beautifully but sparingly designed cluster buildings that had become the vogue over the past few years. One entire wall was composed of floor-to-ceiling windows that slid open onto an interior courtyard spilling good northern light. Another wall was covered with standing bookshelves that held an array of cameras, boxed film, and a stereo system complete with a tape deck, tuner, CD player, turntables for both 78 and 45 rpms, and a pair of giant speakers. Guthrie had never been in a photographer's studio that didn't have its share of very expensive stereo equipment. Many junkie burglars broke into photography studios not to steal the cameras, which were often etched for identification, but to steal the audio equipment, which was easier to fence. Along a third wall a battery of lights was set up to illuminate a seamless backdrop against which a stool was positioned.

"Does the name Lori Doone ring a familiar note?" Guthrie asked.

"Mr. Lamb, I do hundreds of videos," Farley said impatiently. "I really can't remember the names of all my subjects."

Sounds like a ruling monarch, Guthrie thought, but did not say.

"During the Gulf War," Farley went on, "I must have shot a hundred videos. In January of '91, when things really heated up over there, I couldn't keep count. I don't know how they played them, they must've had VCRs there in the desert, to show them on, don't you think? Otherwise why would all these women be coming to a professional photographer to have videos made? I had girls in here who wanted to talk sexy to their boyfriends on camera, wives who wanted to look glamorous for their men far far away, even mothers who wanted to send something more personal than a letter. I had all kinds coming to me."

"This wasn't the Gulf War," Guthrie said.

"I know. I'm only saying."

"And Lori Doone didn't come to *you*," Guthrie said.

"She didn't? Then why . . . ?"

"*You* went to *her*."

Farley looked at him again. Long and hard this time.

"Are you a policeman?" he asked, sounding suddenly cautious.

"No, I am not," Guthrie said, and took out his wallet to show his private investigator's ID card. "I'm working this privately," he said, and winked as Farley had when he'd mentioned the future bride in Korea. "Anything we say is privileged and confidential."

"Mm," Farley said, not winking back, and managing to convey in that single mutter an iciness as vast as a Norwegian fjord.

"Perhaps I can refresh your memory," Guthrie said.

"I wish you would."

"Lori Doone was modeling lingerie at a place called Silken Secrets on the South Trail?"

Ending his sentence in a question mark. The prod.

"Don't know it," Farley said.

"Last March?"

"Last March or anytime."

"You came in one night . . ."

"I did *not*."

". . . and asked her if she'd care to pose in her lingerie for a video you were making? You said you'd pay her . . ."

"People pay *me* for making videos, not the other way around."

"Pay her a thousand dollars," Guthrie went on, undaunted, "if she'd . . ."

"Ridiculous."

". . . masturbate for the camera for a half hour."

"You have the wrong . . ."

"While you taped her."

"I'm sorry, your information is wrong."

"There are three other girls on the tape, Mr. Farley."

"I don't know anything about such a tape."

"I have their names. They all work for Buttercup Enterprises. I can track them down."

Farley said nothing for several moments. At last, he said, "What are you looking for, Mr. Lamb?"

"I told you. Information."

"Gee, and here I thought it might be money."

"Wrong."

"What kind of information?"

"How many copies of that tape did you make? How many did you sell? And have you still got the master?"

"None of that is any of your business."

"Right, it isn't. Miss Doone says one of the girls on that tape is only sixteen years old."

"Not to my knowledge."

"Oh, you remember the tape now?"

"How much are you looking for, Mr. Lamb?"

"Say that one more time, and I'll find it insulting."

Farley looked at him.

Guthrie nodded encouragingly.

Farley kept looking at him.

At last, he sighed.

Guthrie waited.

"I made and sold fifty copies," he said at last.

"For how much a copy?"

"Twenty bucks. Which was very reasonable for an hour-long video."

"I feel certain."

"Of professional quality."

"Who's complaining?"

"*I* am. I expected to sell five hundred."

"You made only fifty copies, but you expected . . ."

"I made copies as the orders came in. Stupid I may be, but dumb I'm not. I had a four-thousand-dollar initial investment, a thousand to each of the girls who posed. *Plus* the cost of the raw stock. *And* my time. *And* the black vinyl cases. I printed the photo insert for the cover myself. Even so, you add all that up, I was maybe in for five thousand bucks. I figured if I could sell five hundred copies of the tape, that would've been a hundred-percent return. *Espresso* joints make ten times that."

"Who'd you sell the tapes to?"

"Who knows? I took ads in all the girlie mags. That's right, I forgot the cost of the goddamn ads. I was probably in for six, *seven* thousand. Man."

"Sell any of these copies to locals?"

"I don't think so."

"Well, did you or didn't you?"

"I'd have to look at my files. I'm pretty sure most of the responses came from states where there's more livestock than people. You'd be surprised what evil lurks in the heartland."

"How'd you like to cut your losses?" Guthrie asked.

"How so?"

"Sell me the master at cost."

"Nossir."

"How much then?"

"Seven grand."

"Why do I keep thinking of that sixteen-year-old?"

"Nobody on that tape is sixteen."

"Try a girl named Candi Lane."

"Seven sounds reasonable."

"Five sounds even more reasonable."

"Make it six."

"Done."

"Cash."

"Forget it."

"Is she really only sixteen?" Farley asked.

"I didn't know how high I could go," Guthrie told me, "and I didn't want to lose it by having to check with you first."

I was wondering what he'd have done if it had been his own money.

"That's fine," I said. "I told you to get the master, and you got the master."

I still hadn't heard that there were fifty copies out there.

I heard that now.

"Yeah," Guthrie said, and shrugged.

Six thousand dollars, I was thinking. With fifty copies still out there alive and kicking.

"Twenty bucks a throw, he got for them," Guthrie said.

"Should have met us first," I said.

"Huh?"

"Could've sold us the whole batch, plus the Brooklyn Bridge."

"I thought six was a bargain," Guthrie said, somewhat petulantly. "This tape ever showed up in court, Miss Commins would've sizzled."

"What if one of the *copies* shows up in court?"

"That isn't likely."

"It's possible."

"Anything's possible. Genghis *Khan* could show up in court. But it isn't likely. Especially since only *one* of the tapes is in Calusa."

"What are you saying?"

"I'm saying only one of the copies is here in Calusa."

"How do you know that?"

"I got a list from Farley."

"A list of what?"

"The people who ordered the tape from him. Guys from all over the country. Even some women. Only one of the customers was from Calusa."

"May I see the list?"

"Certainly," Guthrie said, and took several stapled and folded sheets of paper from his inside jacket pocket. "I highlighted the one we're interested in."

I looked down the first page of typewritten names and addresses. Some twenty or so. None of them highlighted.

"It's on the third page," Guthrie said.

I flipped to the third page.

"Near the top," he said.

The name was highlighted in yellow.

"Some Spanish guy," Guthrie said.

Robert Ernesto Diaz.

Evensong II was one of the older low-rise condominiums on Sabal Key, built some twenty years ago when restrictions were still in force and before builders began reaching for the sky. Clustered around a man-made cove and canals that afforded entrance to the Intercoastal, the shingled two-story buildings in their wooded setting looked cloistered and serene, an image reinforced by the boats bobbing beside the canal docks and in the cove. A breeze was blowing in off the water. A white heron delicately picked its way along the border of the walk leading to unit 21. It took sudden startled flight as I approached. I had called ahead. Bobby Diaz was expecting me.

He told me at once that he had an early dinner date and he hoped we could make this fast. His urgency gained credibility by the fact that one side of his face was covered with lather, and he was wearing only a towel. He showed me into the living room, told me to make myself a drink if I cared for one, and then said he wouldn't be long.

His apartment overlooked the condo swimming pool. Young girls in thong bikinis lay on poolside lounges or splashed in the water. An old man wearing red boxer trunks sat on the edge of the pool, his legs dangling in the water, watching the girls. I watched them, too. Diaz was back in ten minutes, buttoning a cream-colored sports shirt, tucking it into trousers the color of bran. He had trimmed his black mustache and neatly shaved the rest of his face. His long black hair, still wet from the shower, was combed straight back from his forehead. His dark eyes looked suspicious, but the wary look fled before his welcoming smile.

"No drink?" he said. "Can I make you one?"

"Well, this won't take a minute," I said. "I know you're in a hurry."

"Always time for a drink," he said.

"Are you having one?"

"Sure. What'll it be?"

"Little Scotch on the rocks would be fine," I said.

I would have preferred a Beefeater martini with a couple of olives, but Diaz had a dinner date and I had questions to ask. He poured Johnnie Black over a handful of ice cubes, handed the glass to me, and then mixed himself a gin and tonic.

"Cheers," he said.

"Cheers."

We drank. Outside at the pool, one of the girls trilled a laugh that sounded like a kingfisher running a river. Diaz sat opposite me on a blue sofa against a white wall. The condo was furnished sparingly in severe modern upholstered in varying tones of blue and green. Throw pillows and paintings echoed splashes of complementary colors. Even the wedge of lime floating in his drink seemed part of the overall design.

"What's this all about?" he asked.

"Lainie," I said.

"So you told me on the phone. But what now?"

"A video," I said, and watched him.

Nothing showed on his face.

"Something titled *Idle Hands.*"

Still no sign of recognition.

I opened my briefcase. I removed from it a glossy black-and-white photograph I'd had made by a commercial photographer three blocks from my office. It showed the cover art for the video. Lainie's hands caressing the crotch of the white panties, the Victorian ring, the title.

"Recognize this?" I asked, and handed the photograph to him.

He took it in his right hand.

Studied it.

"Forgive the photo," I said, "but at some point I may have to introduce the actual video in evidence."

Which was bullshit.

"Am I supposed to know something about this?" Diaz asked, looking genuinely puzzled.

"You're supposed to have ordered it from a company named VideoTrends."

"Ordered what?"

"The video."

"*I* ordered a video?"

"Titled *Idle Hands* and starring four women performing respectively as Lori Doone, Candi Lane, Vicki Held, and Dierdre Starr."

"I thought you said this was about Lainie."

"It is. She used the name Lori Doone. It's a porn flick, Mr. Diaz."

"A porn flick, I see."

"Yes."

"And you're saying I ordered this video from . . ."

"Yes, that's what I'm saying."

"Well, I never heard of this video."

"The man who did the photography . . ."

"I'm sorry, but I never heard of it. That's that."

"Then how'd your name get on the list of people who'd ordered the video from him?"

"I have no idea. Anyway, I didn't know it was against the law to buy a pornographic video."

"It isn't."

"Then what the hell . . . excuse me, Mr. Hope, but I still don't know what you're doing here."

"If we can get past . . ."

"There's nothing to get past. You've got the wrong person. I didn't order a video from any magazine, and I don't know how . . ."

"Who mentioned a magazine?"

"What?"

"I didn't say anything about a magazine."

"Well, I . . . I just assumed that someone advertising a pornographic video would . . ."

"I didn't say anything about anyone advertising it, either."

We looked at each other.

"Okay?" I said. "Can we at least get past *this* part of it?"

"Depends on which part we go to next."

"Did you at any time own a video titled *Idle Hands*?"

"I did."

"Okay."

"So?"

"Did you ever watch it?"

"I did."

"Did you recognize Lainie Commins as one of the performers in that video?"

"I did."

"When was this?"

"When I first received it. A week or so ago."

"Would you remember the exact date?"

"Well, yes. But only because it got here on my birthday."

"Nice present."

"Better than a tie."

"When was that, Mr. Diaz? Your birthday?"

"The eleventh."

"Of September?"

"Yes. September eleventh."

"The day before Brett Toland got killed."

"Well . . . yes. I suppose it was. I recognized the ring the minute I looked at the

307

cover. Lainie wore it all the time. I thought, Hey, what's this?"

"So you knew it was Lainie even before . . ."

"Well, let's say I suspected it. Then when I watched it, of course . . ."

"When was that?"

"That night."

"The night of the eleventh."

"Yes. UPS delivered it that afternoon, it was waiting in the manager's office when I got home from work."

"So you watched it that night."

"Yes."

"The eleventh of September . . ."

"I'm sure it was."

"And recognized Lainie Commins that same night."

"Yes."

"What did you do then?"

"I went to sleep."

"What I mean, Mr. Diaz, is when did you tell Brett Toland you'd seen Lainie Commins performing in a porn flick?"

"I don't know what you mean."

"I think you know what I mean."

"I *never* told Brett about it."

"Then how'd the tape get in his possession?"

"I have no idea."

"You didn't give it to him?"

"Never even mentioned it to him."

"Do you still have the tape?"

"I'm sure I do."

"May I see it?"

"I'm not sure I know where it is."

"Could you look for it?"

"I'd be happy to. But as I told you . . ."

"I know. An early dinner date."

"Yes."

"Mr. Diaz," I said, rising and putting my empty glass down on the coffee table, "here's what I think. I think you called Brett Toland the minute you spotted Lainie on that tape . . ."

"No, I'm sorry, I didn't."

"I think you told him he had nothing to worry about anymore because . . ."

"He had nothing to worry about, anyway. The bear was ours. Lainie stole it."

"How'd *that* happen to come to mind just now, Mr. Diaz?"

"What?"

"How'd you happen to make *that* connection?"

"Because the only thing Brett had to worry about was Lainie's false claim."

"So now he didn't have to worry about *that* anymore, did he? Because you had a tape of Lainie Commins masturbating."

"Please."

"Well, isn't that what she was doing, Mr. Diaz?"

"Well, sure, but . . ."

"What's the matter? Does the word bother you?"

"No, but . . ."

"Does the act bother you?"

"No, but . . ."

"*You're* the one who ordered that tape, you know?"

"I realize that. But what an adult does privately . . ."

"Ah."

". . . isn't always a suitable matter for discussion."

"Do you think Mr. and Mrs. America would buy a teddy bear from someone who'd masturbated in a porn flick?"

"I don't know what Mr. and Mrs. America would buy."

"Well, you design toys for Mr. and Mrs. America, don't you?"

"I design toys for children."

"The children of Mr. and Mrs. America."

"I'm telling you I never once discussed this with Brett Toland."

"Never told him you'd watched Lainie Commins masturbating on your birthday?"

"My birthday was a coincidence."

"Never called and said, 'Hey, Brett, guess *what*'?"

"Never."

"Never gave him that tape."

"Never."

"Never told him he now had a bargaining tool . . ."

"Never! He didn't *need* a bargaining tool. Lainie stole my design for that bear, the bear was *ours!*"

"What?"

"I said . . ."

"No, no, just a minute, Mr. Diaz. The last time we . . ."

"Look, this is ridiculous, Mr. Hope. Truly. I never gave that tape to Brett, I never discussed . . ."

"Forget the tape! The last time we spoke, you told me Lainie delivered working drawings of the bear . . ."

"No, you must have misunder—"

"I didn't misunderstand *you,* and I didn't misunderstand *Brett,* and I didn't misunderstand *Etta,* either. All of you said the idea for the bear was Brett's and that he'd assigned its design to Lainie while she was still working for Toyland. Isn't that what all of you said? You were there at the meeting, Mr. Diaz, isn't that what you told me? You were there when Brett gave Lainie his brilliant idea and asked her to design the cross-eyed bear and its corrective eyeglasses. You were *there,* Mr. Diaz. You told me you were *there!*"

"Yes, I was."

"Okay. And you also told me she delivered working drawings of the bear by the end of last September . . ."

"That's where you've got it wrong."

"Oh? What have I got wrong?"

"I told you I saw some drawings . . ."

"Yes?"

". . . but I didn't know if they were Lainie's."

"Then whose drawings . . . ?"

"Sketches, actually."

"Sketches?"

"Yes. Of a bear with glasses."

"Well, who did you think *made* these drawings, these sketches, whatever the hell they were?"

"I thought maybe Brett did."

"I see, you thought maybe Brett did. So the bear was Brett's idea, and these sketches you saw were maybe Brett's, so Lainie's out of the picture altogether, right? She never *did* design the bear while she was working for Toyland, is that what you're saying now?"

"I'm saying . . ."

"No, no, Mr. Diaz, you're saying *now* what you didn't say *earlier.* You told me you saw working drawings before you . . ."

"I told you I didn't know if they were working drawings."

"Then what the hell were they?"

"Sketches."

"When *did* you see working drawings?"

"I told you I didn't remember *when* I

312

saw working drawings."

"Okay, Mr. Diaz, flat out. A few minutes ago you said Lainie stole *your* design for that bear." I looked him dead in the eye. "*What* design?"

"I said she stole *our* bear. The bear she designed for Toyland."

"No, that's not what you said."

"Are you telling me what I said?"

"Yes."

"You're wrong. Mr. Hope, I have a date at the Plum Garden at six-thirty. It will take me half an hour to get there, and it's now five to six. If you'll excuse me . . ."

"Sure," I said, and gingerly picked up the photograph and dropped it into my brief-case.

Dr. Abner Gaines was sitting on a high stool drawn up to a counter upon which were microscopes, test tubes, pipettes, Bunsen burners and a dozen other scientific measuring tools and instruments I could not have named if you pulled me apart on a rack or burned me at the stake. As sole proprietor and principal analyst at Forensics Plus, the private lab with which I had worked on several other cases, Ab was a scientist with exacting standards and meticulous work habits, a faultless professionalism belied by his uncombed hair, his nicotine-stained fingers, his rumpled trousers and unshined shoes, and an allegedly white lab smock stained with the residue of God knew how many previous tests here at this very same counter.

He was expecting me, and so he greeted me with his customary gruffness and the impatient air of a very busy professor who had very little time to spend with inquisitive students. Actually, he *was* a very busy professor at the University of South Florida.

I tented a handkerchief over my hand, and showed him the black-and-white glossy of the dancing fingers on the white silken crotch of the Victorian-ringed lady on the *Idle Hands* cassette box. I showed him the actual black vinyl cassette box, with the original color photograph on its front cover, and then I opened the case to reveal the cassette within.

"There should be one set of fingerprints on the photograph," I told him. "I'm looking for a match with anything on the cassette or its case."

"When?" Ab asked me.

"Yesterday," I said.

"Tomorrow," he said.

I went back to the boat again that night.

The yellow CRIME SCENE tapes were down, there was nothing to prevent me from going up the gangway and onto the boat itself, but I simply stood there on the dock, looking at her. If I'd ever known the lines that follow "I must down to the seas again, to the lonely sea and the sky," I've forgotten them since the coma. I've forgotten a lot of things since the coma. I was dressed in the colors of the night. Black denims and black loafers and a black T-shirt and a black windbreaker. A mild breeze blew in off the water, riffling my hair. Sniffing the salt air that spanked in off the Gulf, I think I realized something of what John Masefield must have felt when he wrote his poem. *Toy Boat*'s outline was sharp against a moonlit, midnight sky. A man had been killed aboard this boat. And my client had been with him on the night he'd died.

I wished she hadn't posed for a pornographic tape.

But she had.

I wished Brett Toland hadn't tried to use that tape in a blatant blackmail attempt.

But according to my client, he had.

Two bullets in the head.

But she kept insisting she wasn't the one who'd killed him.

I kept staring at the boat, perhaps willing it to yield its secrets. As I listened to the high clinking sound of halyards striking metal masts, the lines came to me. "And all I ask is a tall ship, and a star to steer her by." Progress.

"Help you, sir?"

The voice startled me. I wheeled away from the dock, my fists clenched, the hair at the back of my neck bristling. I was expecting my cowboys, the twin horrors that come in the dead of night and strike terror to the heart, my nightmare apparitions. But I was looking instead at a rotund little man wearing gray polyester slacks and a blue T-shirt bearing a logo, in white, that read SILVER CREEK YACHT CLUB. He was carrying a flashlight in his left hand, its beam casting a small circle at his feet. In the moonlight, I could make out a round face and a white mustache. Blue cap with a long bill. Nothing menacing about the face. Nothing even mildly challenging.

"I'm the defense attorney on the Toland murder case," I said. "I just wanted to see the boat again."

"We get lots of sightseers," he said.

"Matthew Hope," I said, and extended my hand.

"Henry Karp," he said.

We shook hands.

A cloud scudded past the moon, darkening the dockside area. It passed in an instant. We stood looking out over the water. A Florida night. Silver wavelets dancing in the moonlight. Boat sounds all around us. Insects in the tall grass. September sounds.

"Almost didn't see you," Karp said. "The black."

"Sorry," I said.

"Quiet night, ain't it?"

"Very."

"Almost always like this. I don't mind it. Quiet like now, you can hear the sounds. I like nighttime sounds."

"So do I."

"You think she done it?"

"No," I said.

"Me, neither," he said. "Did they ever find The Shadow?"

"I'm sorry?"

"The man I told them about."

"What man?"

"The one I saw going aboard the boat here. I told them all about it."

"Told who?"

"The detectives from the State Attorney's Office."

There is nothing that compels a state attorney to follow a lead that will not support his version of events and take his case where he does not wish it to go. On the other hand, it is his constitutional obligation to disclose any evidence that might support the innocence of the accused. If what Henry Karp was telling me was true, I could very well argue during trial that the police had been sitting on exculpatory evidence that was not turned over to me during disclosure and that this, Your Honor, warranted immediate dismissal of the case. The judge would undoubtedly give a variation of the "Now, now, counselor" speech, advising me that he would admonish the prosecutor for his oversight, and if I needed further time to find a witness, he would give me, oh, "What would you say is fair, Mr. Hope? Two weeks? Three weeks? Would that be a sufficient amount of time?"

I would not, of course, argue for dismissal unless I had already attempted, and *failed,* to find the man Henry Karp was now describing to me, in which case an additional two or three weeks would be redundant. I intended to put Guthrie Lamb on this immediately, or at least as soon as Karp finished his description, which was turning out to be sketchy at best.

What he saw was a man who looked like the pulp magazine hero called The Shadow, wearing black trousers and a black cape and a black slouch hat pulled down over his eyes, moving out of the shadows and onto the Toland boat.

"That's why I call him The Shadow," Karp said. "Cause he *looked* like The Shadow and he came *out* of the shadows."

"From where?"

"The parking lot. Moved across the lot and went straight to the boat. Cape flying behind him. Hat pulled low."

"Did you see his face?"

"No, I was down the other end of the lot. He went up the gangway, was out of sight by the time I came abreast of the boat."

"What time was this?"

"Around a quarter past eleven. I'm supposed to relieve at eleven-thirty, but I got there a little early that night."

A quarter past eleven. Twenty-five minutes before the Bannermans heard shots coming from the Toland boat.

"Before you spotted him, did you happen to see a car pulling into the parking lot?"

"No, I didn't."

"Did you hear a car door opening and closing?"

"No."

"You just saw this man . . ."

"The Shadow."

"On foot, coming across the parking lot . . ."

"And going on the boat, yes."

"Did you see him *leaving* the boat at any time?"

"No, I didn't. I move all over the grounds, you see. I don't cover just the marina. I have regular rounds I make all around the club."

"Were you still in the parking lot at eleven-forty?"

"No, I wasn't. I was back behind the main

clubhouse by then."

"Did you hear any shots coming from the marina?"

"No, I didn't."

"And you say you told all this to some detectives from the State Attorney's Office?"

"Yes, I did."

"When was this? When they talked to you?"

"Day after the murder. I figured I was giving them a good lead, you know? Seeing a man go aboard the boat."

"Did they think so?"

"They said they'd look into it."

"Ever get back to you?"

"No."

"You wouldn't happen to remember their names, would you?"

"No, I'm sorry. But one of them had a knife scar on his right cheek."

The lights were on in Lainie's studio when I got there at ten minutes to one that morning. I had called ahead from the car phone, and I knew she was expecting me, and so I was surprised to find her in a robe and slippers. She told me she'd been getting ready for bed when I called, and apologized for looking so "casual." We went into the main section of the house, where she turned on a living room lamp, offered me a drink, which I declined, and then poured herself a glass of white wine. I sat on a sofa upholstered in a nubby white fabric. She sat opposite me in a matching armchair. When she crossed her legs, the lacy hem of a short blue nightgown showed momentarily.

"Lainie," I said, "when you left the parking lot at ten-thirty that night . . ."

"Or thereabouts," she said.

"You saw a car parked just outside the entrance pillars, is that right?"

"Yes."

"But you didn't see anyone in the car."

"No, I didn't."

"And you're sure you didn't see anyone walking around in the parking lot?"

"Positive. Well, just the people coming out of the restaurant."

"Yes, but aside from them."

"No one."

"No one lurking in the shadows? Someone who might have been watching the boat? Waiting for you to leave?"

"I wish I could tell you I had."

"Someone who looked like The Shadow?"

"Who's The Shadow?"

"A magazine character. *And* radio. *And* a bad movie."

"I never heard of him."

"A man wearing a black cape. And a black slouch hat."

"No. A black *cape?* No. I didn't see anyone like that."

"Lainie, there's a gap of about an hour and a half between the time you left the boat and the time Etta Toland found the body. If we can place someone else on that boat *after* you left . . ."

"I understand the importance. But I didn't see anyone."

He had allowed her to use the bathroom again, and now they stood topside, the boat drifting on a mild chop, its running lights showing its position to nothing but a starlit night, not another vessel in sight for as far as the eye could see. They were silent for a very long time.

At last she said, "I'm sorry."

He said nothing.

"I don't know how it happened, Warr, I really don't. I hate myself for letting it happen again."

He still said nothing, grateful that she was at last admitting she *was* hooked again, but knowing this was only the beginning, and the hard part lay ahead. Back in St. Louis, Warren had seen too many of them lose the battle, over and over again. Relapse was the technical term for it. Again and again and again. And kicking the habit seemed so very *simple* at first because what the dealers told you was partially true, cocaine *wasn't* addictive. Hey, man, this ain't heroin, this ain't morphine, this ain't no downer like Seconal or Tuinal, this ain't no tranq like Valium or Xanax, this ain't even a Miller *Lite*, man, ain't *no* way you gonna get hooked on *this* shit, man.

True.

Cocaine wasn't physically addicting.

The lie was in the claim that there was no way this shit could harm you, man, nothing to fear, man, quit anytime you want, man, no pain, no strain. And even *this* was partially true because when you quit cocaine — when you *tried* to quit cocaine — you didn't experience any of the physical symptoms that accompanied withdrawal from the opoids or the tranquilizers or even alcohol. There was no shaking, no sweating, no vomiting, no muscle twitching . . .

"Did you know . . . ?" he started, and then shook his head and cut himself off.

"What?" she asked.

The night black and silent around them.

"Never mind."

"Say," she said.

"Did you know where the expression 'kicking the habit' comes from?"

"No. Where?"

"When you're quitting the opoids, you lie there in your own sweat, and your legs start twitching involuntarily, like they're kicking out. So it became *kicking* the habit."

"I didn't know that."

"Yeah," he said, and the night enveloped them again.

No muscle twitching when you quit — *tried* to quit cocaine — no gooseflesh either, no appearance of a plucked turkey, which is where the expression "cold turkey" came from, such a weird and wonderful vocabulary for the horrors of hell, did she know the origin of *that* one? He didn't ask.

Thing the man selling poison in a vial forgot to mention was that cocaine was psychologically and emotionally addicting, concepts too lofty for anyone to comprehend, anyway, when what we are selling here is a substance that will make you feel like *God.*

Oh yes.

So when you quit cocaine — *tried* to quit cocaine — you were trying to forget that for the last little while, or the last longer while, you were God. No physical symptoms of withdrawal. Just madness.

He was here to see her through the early madness.

Keep her here on this fucking boat while her depression was keenest and the desire to kill herself was strongest. Nobody ever kicked cocaine on a boat. Nobody ever kicked it on the street, either. Later there would be choices for her to make. For now . . .

"I'm sorry," she said again.

And he believed she was.

10

The scar-faced detective to whom Guthrie Lamb spoke early on Thursday morning, the twenty-first of September, was named Benjamin Hagstrom. He told Guthrie at once that the scar was a memento of a little knife duel he'd had with a burglar when he was still a uniformed police officer twelve years ago. The duel had been somewhat one-sided in that the burglar had the knife and Hagstrom had nothing but his underwear. That was because the burglary was taking place in Hagstrom's own condo unit, which he shared with a then stripper named Sherry Lamonte, later to become his wife, subsequently his ex. All of this in the three minutes after the men had shaken hands and introduced themselves.

In the *next* three minutes, Hagstrom explained that on the night of the attempted burglary Sherry was downtown stripping while Hagstrom himself was doing a little stripping of his own. That was because he'd just got home from a four-to-midnight shift on a very hot Calusa summer night, and had begun undressing the minute he stepped into the apartment, peeling off clothes and dropping them on the floor behind him as he made his way toward the bathroom shower. He was down to his underwear shorts when he stepped into the bedroom and found himself face-to-face with a kid of nineteen, twenty — *eighteen,* as it later turned out — going through his dresser. Hagstrom had left his holstered gun on the seat of an upholstered living room chair alongside which he'd dropped his uniform pants. Now the teenybopper burglar had a surprised look on his face which matched the one on Hagstrom's. One thing else the burglar had was a knife, which appeared magically in his right hand. Before Hagstrom could say anything like "Stop, police!" or "Put down the knife, son, before you get yourself in trouble," or any such warning or admonition that might have detained the burglar from slashing out in panic at Hagstrom, the knife came at him. He put up his hands in self-defense and got cut across both palms, and he backed away in terror and got cut again down the right-hand side of his face . . .

"This scar you see here now," he explained, "a beaut, huh?"

Backing away from the flailing knife, he banged up against the dresser, glimpsed a heavy glass ashtray on its top . . .

"I used to smoke back then . . ."

. . . spread his hand wide over it, picked it up, and hit the kid across the bridge of the nose with it and then again on the cheek and again on the right temple, by which time the kid had dropped the knife and there was blood all over the place, from Hagstrom's hands and face and also from the kid's bleeding nose and cheek.

"He drew twenty years and was out in seven. I drew twelve stitches and a lifetime souvenir. So what can I do for you, Mr. Lamb?"

"Call me Guthrie."

"Fine, call me Benny. What can I do for you?"

"September thirteenth?" Guthrie said.

Question mark at the end of it. His little trick. Sometimes it worked. Sometimes the prod was all they needed. Not this time.

"What about it?" Hagstrom asked.

"Day after the Toland murder?"

"Yeah?"

"Down at the Silver Creek Yacht Club?"

"Uh-huh?"

"Understand you talked to a night watchman named Henry Karp, who told you . . ."

"I talked to a lot of people the day after the murder."

"This one told you he'd seen someone boarding the Toland yacht shortly before the shots were fired."

"He did, huh?"

"Didn't he?"

"What if he did?"

"Somebody dressed all in black. Like The Shadow."

"You're asking did the S.A.'s Office Squad follow up on it, is that what you're asking?"

"That would be a reasonable question," Guthrie said.

"The reasonable answer is that we follow *all* leads in an ongoing murder investigation."

"Yes, but did you follow *this* lead?"

"I believe I said *all* leads."

"So you tried to locate this person described as 'The Shadow,' is that correct?"

"First, Mr. Lamb . . ."

"Call me Guthrie."

"*First*, Mr. Lamb, we tried to determine whether Karp was a man *accustomed* to seeing comic-book characters materializing out of the night. The Shadow tonight, maybe Batman or The Joker tomorrow night, hmm?"

"Maybe," Guthrie agreed.

"We checked. All the way back to when he was a private in the Vietnam War. Bad war, that one. Left a lot of people *still* seeing things in the night. But we didn't find any record of a mental problem," Hagstrom said, "so maybe Karp really *did* see The Shadow on the night of the murder. Or someone who looked like The Shadow."

"Maybe he did," Guthrie agreed, and waited.

"We tried to corroborate the sighting. Questioned anyone who was still around the club at the time Karp says the person went aboard . . ."

"Which was around eleven-fifteen."

"Give or take. Nobody saw anybody dressed all in black."

"How about the Bannermans? Who said they heard shots from the boat twenty-five minutes later."

"Went all the way to West Palm to talk to them," Hagstrom said, and nodded. "Nothing."

"So that was the end of it."

"That was the end of it."

"And if he exists?"

"*You* go find him," Hagstrom said.

Instead, Guthrie went to find Nick Alston over at the Calusa P.D. facility.

"How you doing on my tire track?" he asked.

"I called Gracie last night," Alston said.

"Oh, yeah? How'd it work out?"

"You didn't tell me she was still hooking," Alston said.

"I really didn't know."

"I asked her would she like to go to a movie or something, she laughed in my face."

"I'm sorry about that."

"I just wanted her to see me sober," Alston said.

"I'm sorry."

"Yeah. Well."

Both men were silent for several moments.

At last, Guthrie asked, "Does this mean you won't run down the tire track for me?"

"I just haven't got to it yet," Alston said.

Warren was standing outside the closed and locked door to the head, listening to Toots taking her morning pee inside there, when he heard the boat approaching. He looked up curiously, and then, as the sound of the motor got closer and closer, he realized the boat was pulling alongside, and he was starting topside when he heard a voice shouting in a Spanish accent, "Allo, anybody aboar?"

He went up the ladder to the cockpit.

A bearded man who looked like one of the banditos in *Treasure of the Sierra Madre* was already aboard. Big toothy smile in his scraggly beard. Wearing chinos, thong sandals, and a loose white fisherman's shirt bloused over the trousers. Another man was standing at the rail of a shitty little fishing boat bobbing alongside Amberjack's rig. He, too, was smiling. No beard on this one. Leaner and taller than the squat

331

bearded guy. More muscular. Wearing jeans and a faded blue T-shirt. Both of them smiling. Which meant trouble. Smiling men meant trouble.

"What can I do for you?" Warren asked.

"You alone here?"

Still smiling. Accent you could slice with a machete. Warren debated which way to play this, seemingly pleasant or obviously annoyed? Man came aboard without a by-your-leave, sailor had a right to be pissed, no? Sí. On the other hand, there were two of them.

"Nice bo you have here," the lean one said, and climbed onto the rail of the fishing boat and leaped down to where the bearded one was standing near the dash. Warren noticed the fishing knife in a sheath at his belt.

"You alone?" the first one asked again, smiling.

"Yes," Warren said, and hoped Toots wouldn't suddenly come out of the head and wander topside. "What do you want?"

Sharply this time, bracing himself, letting them know they had boarded his vessel without permission and he wasn't happy about it.

"He wanns to know wah we wann, Luis," the husky one said.

"So tell him, Juan," the lean one said.

"We wann dee bo," Juan said, still smiling in his beard.

"Fat Chance Department," Warren said.

"*Qué dices?*" Luis asked.

"I said I'm a private detective and you're making a big mis—"

"So arress us," Juan said, smiling, and reached under the blousy fisherman's shirt and yanked what looked like a nine-millimeter Glock from his belt. At the same moment, Luis pulled the fishing knife from its sheath. It was rather large.

"Fellas . . ." Warren said.

Juan hit him with the butt of the gun.

Toots knew she shouldn't come out of that bathroom.

She had heard enough through the door to know that two Spanish-speaking men were aboard and that they had done something to Warren. She'd picked up a lot of Spanish because her previous fandango with cocaine had necessitated buying dope *from,* and selling herself *to,* all sorts of people, white, black, Hispanic, you name it, men, women, gays, lesbians, who gave a shit? Knew enough to ask "*Cuento el kilo, amigo?*" knew enough to explain "*Por cinco dólares con mi mano. Con la boca, le cuesta diez. Y mas de veinte por mi concha pristina, señor,*" fine little lady Tootsie Cokehead had been back then. Or was now, for that matter, though this time around she hadn't yet run out of her life savings, hadn't yet had to degrade herself, not yet, not quite yet.

The engines had started half an hour ago, and she knew they were now under way, but she couldn't tell in which direction they were moving. There was a sliding glass window in the bathroom, but all she could see through it was grayish-green water rolling away to an empty, featureless horizon far in the distance.

She kept wondering when either of the two men would want to use the toilet.

The door was locked from the inside.

She kept listening, waiting.

And then there was the BAER, which was not a misspelling of BEAR, but was instead an acronym for Brainstem Auditory Evoked Response testing, wherein sound is applied to the ear's eighth cranial nerve (the CNVIII, as it was known to Spinaldo and others in the trade) in order to assess how long it took for the waveform to travel from the ear stimulus to the brainstem and back again. Spinaldo assured me that my responses were fast enough, which was good.

Everything looked good, they kept telling me.

But . . .

I still had trouble with short-term memory. I would store something for immediate recall and hours or sometimes minutes later could not remember what it was.

This will improve, Spinaldo kept telling me.

But . . .

I still had trouble finding words. I would know the word I was searching for, but I simply could not bring it to my tongue. Spinaldo called this aphasia. I called it a pain in the ass. He said it would pass. I tried to tell him I was hopeful it would, but I couldn't think of the word "hopeful." He told me not to worry.

But . . .

One day they asked me to draw a clock face, and to set the hands at five o'clock. When I did this task successfully, they asked me what time it was, and I replied "Happy hour." I was being nasty, yes. But I really *didn't* know what time it was. They were targeting motor, sensory, memory and cognitive functions, you see. The goal was to identify any problems I might have with the activities of daily living. (ADLs in the jargon, go ask Spinaldo.) Things like dressing, bathing, shaving, eating, and writing legal briefs, ha! I made hourly calendars reminding me of what I was to do when. But I became easily fatigued, and I found myself distracted and edgy — "You're like yourself, only more so," Patricia said — and increasingly more impatient with all the tests and their goddamn *initials* in caps, the SSEP and the MRI and the SPECT and the VEP and the *SHIT!* — my chest still hurt!

I'd been shot, you see. Twice. That was the start of all my troubles. Getting shot. And I was recovering from a pair of serious wounds that had taken me to the very brink of oblivion. While I was on the operating table, the surgeons had performed a thoracotomy, which — translated from Spinaldo's medicalese — meant they had cracked open my chest, some fun. And whereas I hadn't felt a thing while they were opening me up, or while they were reaching in there to massage my heart and whatnot, I was now in excruciating pain, which the good staff at Good Sam tried to alleviate by administering epidural morphine and anti-inflammatories and Tegretol. Controlling the pain helped me to cough, which Spinaldo said was one of the body's most important protective reflexes. Controlling the pain meant increased activity and mobility. Controlling the pain meant I could tie my own shoelaces.

But I was a lawyer.

And I wanted to get back to *work!*

I caught Bobby Diaz coming out of the Toyland offices at ten past twelve that Thursday afternoon. He told me he was on his way to a luncheon meeting and I told him this wouldn't take a minute, and he said, "You always keep saying this won't take a minute, but it always takes half an hour."

"Shows how the time flies when you're enjoying yourself," I said.

"What is it *now?*" he asked, and looked impatiently at his watch. Behind us was the low yellow-brick building with its boy-girl logo on the roof. Employees were coming out of the building now, heading toward the Cyclone-fenced parking lot. We stood in brilliant sunshine. I was wearing my seersucker suit with a white shirt and a tie the color of sand. I felt I looked like a lawyer. Bobby was wearing gray tropical slacks, a pale blue sports shirt, and a white linen jacket with the sleeves shoved up on his forearms. He looked the way the cops on *Miami Vice* used to look.

"Bobby," I said, "I sent your fingerprints to a forensics lab . . ."

"My *what?*"

"I'm sorry. That's why I handed you the photograph."

"The *what?*"

"The black-and-white glossy. I'm sorry."

Diaz shook his head.

"What a cheap private-eye trick," he said.

"I agree. But your prints match prints on both the videocassette *and* its case. So now there's a chain of custody from you to Brett Toland."

337

"So what?" he said.

"So now maybe you'd like to tell me when you gave him that cassette."

"Why should I?"

"Because I'll be calling you for a deposition, anyway . . ."

"You're going to introduce as evidence a cassette that shows your client . . ."

"What I choose to introduce in evidence is my business. Whether the cassette is relevant to the murder of Brett Toland is another matter."

"How could it be?"

"I have no idea," I said. "That's why I want to talk. What do you say? Now, informally. Or in my office at a later date, with a tape recorder and witnesses."

"Let me make a call first," he said.

"Sure," I said.

The phone was in his car, a metallic-gray BMW, with black leather upholstery. He called a restaurant named Manny's Manor on Flamingo Key, to leave word that he would not be joining Joan Lensky Robert for lunch, and then he drove us west on Weaver Road and south on the Trail to a Chinese restaurant called Ah Fong, which several Italian-speaking friends of mine have nicknamed Ah Fong *Gool.* I ordered one of the six-ninety-five luncheon specials, which consisted of the egg roll, the chicken chow mein, the white rice, and a pot of tea. Bobby ordered the wonton soup, the pepper steak, the fried rice, and his own pot of tea for the same six ninety-five. We both asked for chopsticks.

Clicking and munching away, we began discussing how Bobby's hot little tape had landed in Brett's hot little hands. Bobby seemed more interested in his pepper steak than in his recitation. Almost offhandedly, he told me that he had called Brett the moment he recognized Lainie on the tape . . .

"This would have been on the night of September eleventh . . ."

"Yes, but I didn't get him."

"You called him . . ."

"Yes, and kept getting his answering machine."

"So when *did* you reach him?"

"Not until the next day."

The next day would have been the twelfth of September. Brett Toland had appeared in Judge Santos's courtroom at nine that morning, in the company of his wife and his attorney. I had been there with my client and my sole witness. We had all left the courtroom at about one o'clock, when Santos adjourned.

"What time did you finally reach him?" I asked.

"Not until later in the afternoon."

"You phoned him again?"

"No, I saw him in person. At the office."

"What time was that?"

"After lunch sometime. Two, two-thirty?"

"Did you give him the cassette at that time?"

"I did."

"How did you present it to him?"

"I said I thought it might be of interest to him."

"In what way?"

"I said I knew he was involved in this lawsuit with Lainie, and I thought the tape might be of importance to him."

"Did you suggest *how* it might be of importance?"

"Well, I told him it might be useful to him."

"In what way?"

"Well, as leverage. I told him to take a look at it, he'd see what I meant."

"Did you describe the contents of the tape?"

"More or less."

"How did you describe it?"

"I said the graphic on the cover pretty much said what the tape was about. And the title."

"Did you mention that Lainie was on the tape?"

"No, I wanted him to discover that for himself. I *did* say the ring looked like the one Lainie wore all the time."

"The ring in the cover photo?"

"Yeah. On the case."

"So in other words, you suggested that the tape was about a woman masturbating, and that Lainie Commins was the woman depicted on the . . ."

"Well, her ring, anyway."

"The *ring* was Lainie's."

"I said the ring looked familiar."

"So Brett pretty much knew what you were talking about."

"I guess so."

"He pretty much knew what to expect when he looked at that tape."

"Well, I think he knew what I was getting at."

"What was his reaction?"

"He seemed pleased."

"Did you suggest he might be able to use the tape as a means of settling the lawsuit?"

"Well, I told him a designer of children's toys might not want to have such a tape gain circulation in the trade."

"You said this to him."

"Yes, I said it to him."

"And you also said he'd know what you meant after he looked at the tape."

"Well, yes."

Chopsticks moving in a rhythmic flow from platter to mouth, grains of fried rice falling back onto the pepper steak. A gulp of tea. Food was of prime importance here, never mind the incriminating tape he had turned over to his boss. Never mind that, technically, he was an accomplice in the crime of extortion in that he had suggested how the tape might be used.

"Did Brett look at the tape then and there?"

"No."

"When *did* he look at it, would you know?"

"I have no idea."

According to Lainie, Brett had called her at nine that night, to invite her to the boat to discuss a settlement. The so-called settlement had later turned into a blackmail attempt . . .

——And warned me that unless I dropped the infringement suit, all of kiddieland would learn about that tape.

——And out the window goes your teddy bear.

——No. Out the window goes my *life.*

. . . which was good enough reason to commit murder.

"By the way . . ."

Shoveling pepper steak into his mouth.

". . . I didn't see Brett again after I left his office."

"What time was that?"

"Three o'clock. And I can tell you exactly where I was that night. In case that's of interest to you."

"Just as a matter of curiosity," I said.

"Just as a matter of curiosity, I was in bed with a woman named Sheila Lockhart in her condo on Whisper Key. She's free, white, and twenty-one, and she has nothing to hide. We were together all night long, ask her. I left the condo at eight the next morning."

"What were you wearing?"

"What?"

"What were you wearing, Mr. Diaz."

"Just what I'm wearing now, with a different shirt."

"I suppose she'll confirm that, too."

"Ask her," Bobby said, and shrugged. "Waitress," he said, and signaled to a pretty little Chinese girl in a green silk Suzie Wong dress slit to her thigh. "Could I get some more hot tea, please?"

The waitress scurried off.

We sat silently for a moment.

"What deal did you make, Bobby?"

"Deal? *What* deal?"

"That's *my* question."

"I didn't make any deal."

"You told me yesterday that the bear design was *yours* . . ."

"You keep getting that mixed up."

"Was that the deal? You show Brett how to solve all his problems . . ."

"Hey, all I did was hand him a tape."

". . . and in return, he gives you credit for the bear's design? Was that it?"

The waitress was back with his tea.

Bobby poured himself a fresh cup.

Drank.

Peered at me over the cup he was holding in both hands.

"I don't need credit for anything anybody else designed," he said. "I have enough credits of my own."

"Then what were you looking for? Money?"

"I've been working for Toyland for almost fifteen years," he said. "If I could help the Tolands in any way . . ."

"Including extortion?"

"Come on, *what* extortion? Besides, I didn't even know what his reaction was going to be, you want the truth."

"What do you mean?"

"When I told him Lainie was on that tape. For all I know, he might have been offended."

"I still don't know what . . ."

"I didn't know how he'd take it. I didn't know whether something was still going on between them."

I looked at him.

"Whether they still had a thing going, you know?" he said.

One of the men was talking in English now, just outside the bathroom door. She guessed Warren was sitting on the lounge diagonally across from the bathroom. She knew it was just a matter of time before someone had to pee. She had no idea what they would do when they discovered the bathroom door was locked.

"Where are we headed?"

Warren's voice.

"Well, *señor,* you don nee to know that, do you?"

"Well, yes, as a matter of fact, I do, *señor.* Because people will be contacting me, and I'll have to give them my location. This isn't my boat. The owner will be calling. On the radio."

"Then we will ha to *break* the radio."

"Then the owner will call the Coast Guard. He loves this boat."

"Then you will juss ha to lie to him."

They argued back and forth, Warren trying to find out where they were taking the boat, the man stating over and over again that if the owner of the boat happened to radio, Warren would just have to tell him he was sitting in the water, drifting, the way he'd been when they boarded an hour or so ago. She gathered they had tied Warren's hands and feet — he asked the man once to at least untie his feet, he wasn't about to go jumping overboard — and then dragged him down below here and tossed him on the lounge. Well, she guessed the lounge. That was where his voice seemed to be coming from. The other man's voice came and went, back and forth, fading, rising, as if he were alternately pacing and then either leaning against the sink or sitting momentarily on one of the banquettes opposite the lounge, or even leaning against the bathroom door as he had not a moment ago, the door creaking against his weight, she'd backed away startled.

She kept wondering if she should slide open the window above the sink, remove the screen, and climb out onto the narrow deck that ran the full length of the boat, fore and aft. The deck outside the bathroom window was what, a foot wide? Broadening to some three feet or so up front. She could step out the window and move toward the rear of the boat, get to the steering wheel, clobber him with her high-heeled shoe, whatever. But the second man had to be up there, didn't he? Driving the boat? This wasn't the fucking *Queen Mary*, this was a little thirty-foot boat you could see from front to back of it in a single glance. The wheel was immediately aft of the bathroom. He'd hear her sliding open the window. Hear her taking off the screen. Be watching for her the minute she climbed through onto the deck.

But what if someone wanted to use the bathroom first?

Only in books and movies did nobody ever have to pee.

She came walking up North Apple with her head bent, studying the leaf-covered sidewalk ahead of her. She was wearing a short white beach coat over a green tank top swimsuit and white sandals. A white tote was slung over her shoulder. It jostled her right hip as she came steadily toward where I was waiting outside her house. I had not called ahead. I wanted to surprise her.

Still not seeing me, she stopped on the sidewalk and dug into the tote for her keys, and then, raising her head as she started toward the house again, spotted me standing at the curb in my seersucker suit. She hesitated only a moment, and then came toward me.

"Hello, Matthew," she said.

"Lainie."

"I was at the beach."

"Your neighbor told me."

"Such a lovely day."

As she unlocked the door, I noticed that she hadn't worn the Victorian ring to the beach. We went into the house where first she put down the tote and took off the beach coat, and then checked her answering machine for messages.

"Lainie," I said, "we have to talk."

"My, so serious," she said. "I'm all sandy. May I shower first?"

"I'd rather we . . ."

But she was already sliding open one of the glass doors that led to the back of the house where a small patio gathered dappled sunlight in a clearing under the dense overhead growth. An outdoor shower was set up at one end of the patio. It consisted of a simple wooden stall with a plastic curtain hanging from a rod. The curtain was translucent, patterned with great big white daisies, pulled back now to reveal shower head and knobs on one wall, soap dish below them. A white bath towel rested on a painted blue stool just to the left of the stall. Lainie reached in, turned on the cold water, fiddled with the hot water knob till the mix suited her, and then kicked off her sandals, stepped into the stall, and pulled the plastic curtain closed behind her. I could see her feet below the bottom of the curtain. The green bathing suit dropped to the floor of the stall. Everything behind the daisy-splashed curtain was a blur of flesh-colored movement.

"Lainie," I said, "were you having an affair with Brett Toland?"

Not a word from behind the curtain. Blurred flesh tones moving among the big daisies. Water splashing. I waited. At last:

"Yes."

"Want to tell me about it?"

"I didn't kill him."

"That's not the topic under discussion."

The topic under discussion, or rather the topic under recitation because I merely listened and said nothing, was a two-year-long love affair that had started shortly after Lainie moved from Birmingham, Alabama, to Calusa and began working at Toyland. The affair had ended just before Christmas of last year. According to Lainie, both she and Brett had been inordinately circumspect, limiting their torrid romance to after-hours trysts, never publicly revealing by the slightest glance or touch that there was anything untoward happening between employer and employee.

Which made me wonder how Bobby Diaz had known they "had a thing going," but I said nothing.

"Did you ever notice," she asked, "that married men tend to end affairs during the holiday season, when the tug of home and family is strongest? On Christmas Eve, right after Brett handed out the Christmas bonuses, he told me he wanted to end it. Merry Christmas, Lainie, it's over. I gave my two weeks' notice at the beginning of January." She turned off the water. A wet arm slithered from behind the curtain. "Could you hand me the towel, please?" I picked it up from the stool, put it in her hand. Behind the curtain, she began drying herself.

I was silently piecing together a timetable.

Christmas Eve of last year: Brett ends the affair.

Middle of January *this* year: Lainie leaves the company.

Beginning of April: She comes up with the idea for Gladly.

Twelfth day of September: Brett is mur—

The curtain rattled back on its rod. Lainie was wearing the towel now, wrapped around her, its loose end tucked between her breasts. She stepped out, sat on the stool, began putting on her sandals again. Long wet blond hair cascaded over her face.

"Ever see him again?" I asked.

"Around town now and then. But we didn't travel in the same social . . ."

"I meant was it *really* over?"

"Yes, it was really over."

"Never called you again . . ."

"Never."

"Never asked to see you."

"Never."

"Until he phoned on the night of the twelfth."

"Well, that was strictly business," she said.

"Was it?" I asked.

"Yes," she said at once, and sat erect, tossing the wet hair in what I took to be a gesture of annoyance. Rising, she reached into the stall for the wet bathing suit, picked it up, and started walking back to the house, the suit swinging in her right hand. I followed her.

The living room was cool and dim.

A clock somewhere chimed three times.

The afternoon was rushing by.

"If you haven't any other questions," she said, "I'd like to get dressed."

"I have other questions," I said.

"Really, Matthew, can't they wait?"

"I'm afraid not."

Exasperated, she let her body go limp, her shoulders slumping on an exhalation of breath, her wandering right eye seemingly more vexatious than usual.

"Okay, what?" she said.

"Did you go to bed with Brett Toland on the night he was killed?"

"Yes, damn it!"

11

So there we were."
This is Lainie talking.

This is what she is now telling me about the time she spent on the Toland yacht on the night of September twelfth, a revised version, to be sure. I sometimes think all of life is *Rashomon*. If you have not seen the Akira Kurosawa film, too bad. It is almost as good as his *High and Low*, which was based on an American mystery novel the title of which I have now forgotten. *Rashomon* is about variations of the truth. It is about reality and the different ways in which reality can be perceived. It is about the nature of verity and falsehood. It is almost as good as the five-finger exercise Lainie Commins now performs as she sits in a towel in a white wicker chair in the living room of her small studio-house. Her suntanned legs are stretched out in front of her. She is relaxed in the chair. It is as if the truth — if this is, at last, the truth — has made her free.

I listen.

So there they were.

Lainie Commins and Brett Toland, lovers

352

until December of last year, at which time Brett simultaneously handed her a Christmas bonus and her walking papers. There they were. Sitting on a sultry September night in the cockpit of a sailboat that has been described as "romantic" in the various magazines devoted to great yachts of the sailing world. Alternately described as "opulent" or "luxurious." Asking her if she'd like a drink. Why, yes, she says, that might be nice. This is now some five minutes after she gets to the boat. She has taken off her white-laced blue Top-Siders and her blue scarf with its tiny red-anchor print . . .

It occurs to me that this is now the *third* version of Lainie's story, her own personal *Rashomon* — "but I didn't kill him," she has told me over and over again.

. . . and she hands these to Brett as he goes below to mix their drinks. Perrier and lime for her, at least the *first* time around. Vodka-tonic in the second telling, bit more than one, she says, Brett freshened the drink for her, right? It is perhaps five minutes past ten or thereabouts. In this telling — the third and final one, I hope — she has drunk two rather *strong* vodka-tonics, which may explain why she is now amenable to his invitation to revisit old times and renew old acquaintances.

In her first version, Brett offered her a licensing agreement. In a second version of the tale (though admittedly not hers) Brett offered her a flat settlement of five thousand dollars to drop the infringement suit — thus spaketh Etta Toland. In Lainie's *own* second version, Brett tried to blackmail her by threatening to disclose the nature of *Idle Hands* to the kiddie world at large. But now . . .

Enfin . . .

The truth.

I hoped.

In this version, Lainie does *not,* in fact, leave the boat at ten-thirty. Instead, she is drinking her *second* vodka-tonic in the cockpit when a sloop comes in under power, its spotlight guiding the way to a slip further down the marina dock. This is Charles Nicholas Werner, though she does not know the man's name at the time, or that he will later testify to having seen her and Brett sitting there *tête-à-tête,* drinking, at ten forty-five. Understandably, and considering the fact that someone later thoughtlessly pumped two bullets into Brett's head, Lainie afterward felt it expedient not to mention that Brett at that very moment was inviting her belowdecks to see his etchings. Or rather, to show her the videocassette case with its cover photo insert of two busy hands, one of which is wearing a heart-shaped Victorian ring Brett himself gave her one Valentine's Day, back when their affair was running as swift and as torrid as the waters of Babylon.

A ring she still wears, by the way.

The very ring that captured my attention when first I discovered the cassette.

Which he shows her now in the master bedroom of the yawl called *Toy Boat*.

Shows her *Idle Hands*.

Her hands.

On the cover of the cassette case.

Undeniably *her* hands wearing *his* ring.

The case is empty.

——I'd have been stupid to bring it here to the boat, wouldn't I? It's safe at home.

He makes no mention of blackmail just yet, merely shows her the cover photo of her hands working her crotch, and mentions that he watched the tape that afternoon and that it aroused old memories and isn't it foolish of them to be battling in court over something as nonsensical as a fucking *teddy* bear, you should pardon the expression, when not too very long ago they'd meant everything in the world to each other?

At which point he kisses her.

So there they were.

In what was unmistakably a bedroom (albeit on a boat it is called a stateroom) standing beside a bed, which is what a bed is called even on a boat (although on naval vessels it is frequently called a sack or a bunk), their lips together again for the first time (at least since December), his fingers spread on what is called an ass, hers, even on a boat, his cock growing what is called tumescent in certain novels or tumid in others, a palpably steamy urgency rising between them as they stand clinging to each other, hoo boy!

So what was a fun-loving couple to do under such circumstances, even if in court they were adversaries? Well, it could reasonably be assumed that they might fall together onto the bed, locked in each other's arms, and it could further be assumed that his hands might slide down into the back of the blue silk slacks she's wearing to find the cheeks of her aforementioned ass, and then inadvertently to find, from behind, the lips of her swollen pudendum although only grazingly. They are expert at this. For two years they were doing this before Brett called a halt to it on Christmas Eve, some present, sweetie. Doing it in motels hither and yon, in and around the environs of Calusa, Bradenton and Sarasota, the so-called Calbrasa Triangle, even doing it two or three times in this very stateroom on *Toy Boat* when the unsuspecting Etta Toland was in Atlanta, Georgia, visiting her mother in a nursing home there.

They know just what they're doing, these two.

They've done it again and again until they are rather knowledgeable about the heres and theres, the goings and comings, so to speak, practice makes perfect. In fact, they are *sooo* good at what they're doing that the time just *flies* by, honeylamb, and it is close to eleven-thirty when Brett withdraws physically *and* emotionally, and mentions casually that unless Lainie drops the infringement suit . . .

——all of kiddieland will learn about that tape. I'll send copies to every company in the field . . .

. . . although he did very much enjoy fucking her again, for which his heartfelt thanks.

Lainie tells him he's a no-good son of a bitch and leaves the boat in high dudgeon, putting on her Top-Siders first, but forgetting the blue scarf in her haste to get away.

It's *eleven*-thirty, not *ten*-thirty as she'd claimed in her initial telling of the tale now retitled *Babes in Toyland Redux.*

A car is parked on the road outside the pillars at the club's entrance.

This has not changed from her second telling.

Ten minutes later, Jerry and Brenda Bannerman hear shots coming from the Toland boat.

I was thinking about time.

I was thinking about ten crucial minutes.

Because if Lainie had previously lied about an hour, why not now lie about a critical ten-minute period when she could *still* have been on that boat, shooting and killing the man who'd fucked her and later tried to blackmail her?

If she told me one more time that she didn't kill him, I would scream.

"Believe me, Matthew," she said.

Toots had slid open the bathroom window just a crack. She could hear the two of them topside, talking in Spanish. One of them driving the boat, the other one standing alongside him, both of them yelling over the sound of the boat's motor. She guessed Warren was still trussed on the lounge down here, but she didn't hear a word from him. All she heard was the sound of the motor and the two men yelling. What they were yelling about was cocaine. Getting the cocaine down to Miami on the east coast.

They could yell as loud as they wanted out here in the middle of the Gulf, nobody was going to hear them. Except Toots, who was all ears, Spanish coming back to her in a welcome rush, courtesy of all those Hispanic dealers past and present, near and far. Mother is the necessity of invention, dears, and when you are hooked, the dealer *is* Mother, and don't you ever forget it. Enough cocaine on this boat to keep her high for a year and a half, from what she could gather. Problem was their people in Miami were expecting some *other* boat, their *own* boat, the one they'd had to ditch because of something wrong with the carburetor, whatever, she couldn't make out all the technical language, fumes in the engine compartment, a flash fire, burned wiring — the Spanish she heard was *"carburador defectuoso"* and *"gases dentro del motor"* and *"auto combustión"* and *"cables quemados."* Transferred the shit to Warren's boat when they realized they weren't going to make it to Miami in their *own* vessel. But now they were afraid their people wouldn't recognize *this* boat coming in, so they were trying to figure how they could make contact so they could get the stuff ashore. Eight kilos, she was hearing. *Ochos kilos.* Worth a hundred and thirty-two thousand dollars, she was hearing. *Ciento treinta y dos mil dólares.*

Tengo que orinar, she was hearing.

Which in English meant "I have to take a piss."

At lunch earlier today, Bobby Diaz told me that on the night of the murder he was in bed with a woman in her condo on Whisper Key.

——She's free, white, and twenty-one, and she has nothing to hide. We were together all night long, ask her. I left the condo at eight the next morning.

It was now precisely four o'clock on Thursday afternoon, some eight days, sixteen hours and twenty minutes after the Bannermans heard someone firing three shots aboard the Toland boat. I was driving over the Whisper Key bridge on my way to see a woman named Sheila Lockhart because a long-ago law professor once told me, "Matthew, an alibi isn't an alibi till a second party swears to it."

Whisper is a bad marriage between Florida as it used to be and Florida as the big real estate interests would wish it to be. It is less developed than Sabal Key, for example, which has been thoroughly exploited to its legal and environmental limits — albeit tastefully, to be sure. Taste is the middle name of SunShore Development, which bought up most of this northernmost barrier island when it was worth less than two cents and a collar button and turned it into a vast overlapping retirement theme park of high-rise condos, golf courses, swimming pools, cluster homes, tennis courts, white sand beaches, and private homes in gated enclaves. Flamingo Key is fully developed as well, but only with private homes, some of them quite luxurious, most of them looking pink and Floridian on the outside and brown and Middle Western on the inside, meaning that all that heavy dark furniture inherited from Grandma Hattie in Lansing or Indianapolis or Grand Rapids has been bodily transported down here where it wages staid and stuffy battle with clear blue skies and bright green water.

There's a lot of old Florida still extant on Whisper Key, but it's inexorably losing the battle against the developers. You'll drive past a long stretch of impenetrable vegetation behind which you know is a low, rambling house on shallow brackish water leading nowhere, a ramshackle dock jutting out to where a flaking rowboat sits in mottled sunshine, and suddenly the wall of green is gone and there is a white tower jutting up into the sky, a fountain splashing water in the center of a landscaped oasis, parking sheds over shaded spaces, the sound of children shouting and giggling in a cool blue swimming pool hidden somewhere behind the building's steep facade, voices rising and falling on the sullen hot September air. And several hundred yards beyond that, the road will amble past half a mile of lopsided overgrown wooden fence, and you know that behind this fence there is yet another residential relic of what this area used to be. And your heart breaks.

Sheila Lockhart lived in a new sixteen-story condo called Sandalwind, at the southern end of Whisper Key, adjacent to the public beach. The day was humid and hot, the Gulf surging in restlessly against the shore, whitecaps cresting on the dark waters beyond. I would not have liked to be on a boat in a chop like today's.

I parked the Acura in a row of spaces reserved for VISITORS and then found my way to a building called the Sundowner, and took the elevator up to the fourteenth floor. Sheila lived in apartment 14C. I had called ahead, and she was expecting me. I rang the doorbell and waited. I rang again. Waited. The door opened at last.

She was not twenty-one, as Diaz had claimed, nor was she even any longer close to that age, but perhaps he'd merely meant she was *over* twenty-one. But he'd also said she was free and white, and whereas I had no quarrel with her apparent liberty, she could not have been considered white under any circumstances. Then again, Diaz merely may have been using a figure of speech. Nonetheless, Sheila Lockhart appeared to be in her late thirties or early forties, a very good-looking barefooted black woman wearing white cutoff shorts and a white halter top, her long black dreadlocks strung with tiny bright-colored beads. A rush of cold air swept out of the apartment.

"Come in," she said, "before the heat does."

White she wasn't, but neither was black a proper classification. Her skin was the color of dark amber, her eyes the sort of grayish-green one finds a lot in the Caribbean, the end result of centuries-old admixtures of black, white and *Indian* Indian. I followed her into a longish living room that ran from the entrance door to a screened terrace overlooking the Gulf. Sliding glass doors closed now because the air-conditioning was on. Kitchen off to one side of the room. Closed door adjacent to it. The bedroom, I supposed. A choice apartment in that it was on an upper floor and facing the water.

"So what kind of trouble is Bobby in now?" she asked.

"None that I know of," I said.

"Then why's he looking for an alibi?"

She had gone briefly into the kitchen as she spoke, and now she returned with a tray bearing a pitcher of iced tea and two tall glasses brimming with ice cubes. Our eyes met. I hadn't mentioned anything on the phone about wanting to verify Bobby's story of where he'd been on the night of the twelfth. I could only assume that she'd called him to say I'd be visiting her, and that he'd asked her to confirm his whereabouts that night.

"Tea?" she asked.

"Please," I said.

She broke eye contact.

Poured over the ice in each glass. Cubes crackled and popped. She put down the pitcher. Sat opposite me in a white leather sling chair. I was sitting on a platform sofa with a foam rubber cushion covered in pale blue linen. We lifted our glasses. Drank.

"What makes you think he needs an alibi?" I asked.

"I got the feeling," she said, and smiled.

"*Would* you alibi him?"

"Depends on what for?"

"How about murder?"

"I wouldn't alibi *anybody* for murder. No matter how well I knew him."

"How well do you know Bobby?"

She shrugged.

"Meaning?"

"We've been seeing each other on and off for four, five months now."

"On and off?"

"He comes here, I go to his place. Like that. We're not living together, if that's what you're asking."

"He told me he was here with you on the night Brett Toland was killed. Was he?"

"Yes, he was."

"Do you remember what he was wearing?"

"When he arrived, do you mean?"

"Yes."

"Something black. Or very dark blue. Slacks and a shirt. Long-sleeved shirt. Silk,

364

from the feel of it."

"Was he wearing a hat?"

"No."

"Or a cape?"

"A *cape?* No."

"What time did he get here?"

"Seven. We went out to dinner, then came back."

"How long did he stay?"

"All night."

"Left the next morning?"

"Yes."

"Wearing the same clothes?"

"Well, yes. He doesn't keep anything here."

"What time was this? When he left?"

"About eight-thirty. We both had to get to work."

"What sort of work do you do, Ms. Lockhart?"

"I'm an R.N."

"Oh? Where?"

"Good Sam."

"My alma mater."

"I know. You were a celebrity there. We all wanted to carry in your bedpan. Big hero lawyer got himself shot."

"Not a hero, I'm afraid."

"*We* all thought so. All that fan mail! Like a movie star."

"Sure," I said.

The room was silent except for the hum

of the air conditioner. Out on the water, lightning flashed.

"Well," I said, "I don't suppose there's anything else I have to know. If Mr. Diaz really *was* here that night . . ."

"He was."

"Then that's that."

I put down my glass. More lightning flashed over the Gulf. There was the sense of a tight, enclosed space, cool and dry and protected, while outside a storm was gathering.

"Did you *really* think he killed that man?" she asked.

"I was wondering why he volunteered an alibi, that's all. Then again, he'd been talking to Brett earlier, so perhaps he felt . . ."

"Yes," she said, and nodded.

I looked at her.

Lightning flashed again.

"He called from here," she said.

I kept looking at her. Now there was the sound of thunder, close by, on the left.

"Isn't that what you meant?" she asked. "About talking to Mr. Toland earlier?"

"No," I said. "That's not what I meant."

From where Warren lay bound hand and foot on the lounge, he first saw the door to the head fly open and then Toots coming out with a fiercely determined look on her face. He almost said something to her but the warning look in her eyes shut him up at once. She moved swiftly and silently across the cabin to the starboard side opposite the head, into the small recessed cooking area, partially hidden from above by a bulkhead adjacent to the ladder. She was reaching down to take the high-heeled pump from her left foot when Warren saw a man's shoes and trouser legs moving down the ladder. He almost yelled a warning this time, but he realized at once that Toots *knew* the man would be coming down those steps, which was why she was backing away against the sink, squeezing herself into the tiny galley, trying to flatten herself out of his sight line as he came below, the shoe gripped in her right hand like a hammer now — she had done this before, she knew how to do this, he was confident she knew how to do this.

The man moved directly toward the bathroom door on his left, Toots's right hand coming up alongside her head as he reached for the doorknob, still unaware of her presence. Her knuckles were white where she gripped the shoe, her eyes focused on the back of his head as he opened the door. She stepped into the swing, her right arm uncoiling, the heel of the shoe moving out and sideward to catch him just behind the right ear. Stunned, he fell against the opening door, and she hit him again as he turned toward her, catching his breath when the narrow end of the heel went deep into his forehead, opening a hole, spurting blood. He reached for the knife sheathed at his belt, yanked it free, and took a stumbling step toward her.

Take him out! Warren thought but dared not yell.

Toots brought her arm back again like a pitcher about to hurl a fastball, unleashed it with a snap, the heel of the shoe colliding with his right temple this time, opening another deep wound there, staggering him. She hit him yet another time because this wasn't fun and games here, girls, this wasn't a coy maiden with an ardent suitor, this was a man with a knife, and a woman who would kill him if she had to. Her next blow did almost that, ripping into his face and tearing his right eyeball from its socket. The knife clattered to the deck. He fell unconscious beside it.

There's still the other one, Warren thought.

With a gun.

Toots tried to catch her breath.

Far out on the water, there was sudden lightning.

The storm had swept out to sea.

Sunshine was breaking through in patches.

We sat in Sheila's living room, the clouds tearing away in tatters beyond the sliding glass doors. She was telling me they'd got back to the apartment at about eight-thirty on the night of the murder. She was saying that Bobby seemed anxious and upset, constantly checking his watch, finally going to the phone to call Brett Toland.

"What time was this?"

"About nine."

"Did you overhear the conversation?"

"Bobby's end of it."

"What did he say? Can you tell me?"

"I don't want to get him in trouble."

"You told me you wouldn't alibi anybody for murder. No matter how well you knew him."

"I don't think he killed anyone."

"Then he has nothing to worry about."

She nibbled at her lower lip. Her hands were clasped in her lap. Blue sky was beginning to show close to shore now. Dark angry clouds were racing out over the water.

She took a deep breath.

I waited.

"He asked Mr. Toland if he'd looked at the tape."

"And?"

"Then he said, 'So? Do we have a deal?'"

I nodded.

"He got angry then. 'What do you mean,

no? You're telling me *no?* Like that. Very angry. 'It's of no *use* to you? It's only your whole fucking *case!* You're *sorry?* Oh, you don't *know* sorry, Brett! You'll find *out* sorry!' And he hung up."

"Then what?"

"He began pacing, back and forth, like a wild animal, cursing, telling me he'd offered the man something that would solve all his problems and he turned it down, 'I should have made my deal *first,* I was stupid, *stupid,* I thought I was dealing with a gentleman. But I'll show him, oh, he'll be *sorry,* all right, he'll be sorrier than he's ever been in his whole fucking *life!*' "

The room went silent.

"Were those his exact words?"

"No, not exactly. But that was the gist. Mr. Toland would be sorry for turning down Bobby's deal, whatever it was."

"Okay."

"That doesn't mean he killed him."

"Not if he was here all night," I said.

Something flitted across her eyes.

"He *was* here all night, wasn't he?" I asked.

She shook her head.

In a very small voice, she said, "Well, no. Not exactly."

Toots put on her shoes, picked up the knife, and went immediately to where Warren sat tied up. Neither of them said a word. Over her shoulder, Warren was watching the ladder behind her. The blade was exceedingly sharp. She cut through the lines in an instant. Warren massaged his wrists. Still, they said nothing. He nodded toward the ladder. She nodded back. He made a pistol with his hand, cocked it with his thumb. She nodded again.

And suddenly, there was the sound of rain sweeping across the topside decks.

It was a good half-hour drive from Sheila's condo on the end of Whisper to Diaz's condo on Sabal. Sandalwind to Evensong II, door to door. Well, to be precise, thirty-two minutes by my car clock. I got there at a little past six that evening. Rain from the swift recent storm lay in huge black puddles on the parking lot asphalt, reflecting a clear blue sky and fast-moving puffy white clouds. I parked the car and walked to unit 21. The same white heron picked its way along the path's border of Blue Daze. This time, he did not take wing at my approach. The same teenyboppers in thong bikinis were splashing in the pool behind the condo. The same old man in red boxer trunks was sitting watching them, his legs dangling in the water. There is sometimes, in Florida, the feeling that nothing ever changes, everything remains ever and always the same, smothered by sunshine.

Diaz had just got home from work. He was still dressed for the office except for his bare feet. His shoes and socks were on the living room floor in front of the couch, where he'd left them when he took them off. He'd been at the bar mixing a vodka-tonic when I arrived. He finished doing that now, asked me if I wanted one . . .

"No, thanks," I said, though I was exceptionally thirsty.

. . . dropped a wedge of lime into the glass, and then stood with drink in hand, waiting.

"This won't take a minute," I said, and smiled.

He did not smile back.

"Bobby," I said, "I hate to assume these confrontational stances with you, but . . ."

"Then *don't*," he snapped. "Because I find them frankly irritating."

"Me, too."

"Good. We agree on something."

"But," I said, "there *are* some . . ."

"No buts," he said. "You said a minute. You've already had thirty seconds."

"Then I'll make it fast. Where'd you go when you left Sheila Lockhart at a little past nine on the night Brett Toland was killed?"

"You're *already* wrong," he said. "I was with Sheila all night long. I didn't leave her till eight the next morning."

"No, I'm sorry. You made a call to Brett

372

Toland at nine . . ."

"No, I didn't make any call to . . ."

"I can subpoena Ms. Lockhart's phone bills."

Diaz sipped at his drink.

"Do we always have to pull teeth?" I asked.

"All right, I called him."

"What about?"

"I wanted to know if he'd had a chance to look at that video."

"And had he?"

"Yeah, he said he'd watched it."

"Did you ask him what he'd thought of it?"

"I'm sure I did."

"In fact, didn't you ask him if you had a deal?"

"No, I don't remember asking him any-thing like that."

"And didn't he say no, you *didn't* have a deal? Didn't he tell you the tape was of no *use* to him?"

"No, we never had that conversation."

"Well, *gee*, Bobby, didn't you tell him the tape was only his whole fucking *case?*"

"I'm sure I never . . ."

"And when he said he was sorry, didn't you say, 'Oh, you don't *know* sorry, Brett! You'll find *out* sorry!' Isn't that what you said?"

"No."

"You told Sheila he'd be sorrier than he'd

ever been in his whole fucking *life!* Those were your words, Bobby."

"She's wrong."

"Then she's also wrong about you leaving the condo a few minutes later."

"I told you she was."

"To go down for a pack of cigarettes."

"Oh, that. Sure. I thought you meant *leave* her. I didn't actually leave *her* till eight the next . . ."

"Yes, that's what she thought, too."

"Good. Then . . ."

"She thought leaving for the *night.* Not just running down to pick up a pack of cigarettes. Which is where you said you were going."

"That's exactly right."

"So what took you two and a half hours, Bobby?"

He did not answer.

"Sheila says you didn't get back till almost midnight. Where were you?"

He still said nothing.

"Where'd you go for those cigarettes, Bobby?"

"I sure as hell didn't go to the Silver Creek Yacht Club, if that's what . . ."

"Well, now, who said you did?"

"If that's what you're sugg—"

"But where *did* you go?"

He turned back to me. Mixed himself another drink. Dropped a wedge of lime into

374

the glass. Turned to me again.

"What deal did you offer, Bobby?"

"Ten percent of the bear's gross, okay?"

"For handing over that video to Brett?"

"Yes. I didn't kill him."

"Even though he turned you down cold?"

"That only made him a son of a bitch. It doesn't mean I killed him."

"What'd you mean when you said you'd make him sorrier than . . ."

"I meant I'd get even."

"How?"

"By making him sorry."

"By killing him? By going to the boat . . ."

"I *didn't* go to the fucking . . ."

". . . and shooting him twice in the head . . ."

"No!"

". . . with his own gun? Weren't you the man in black who parked your car outside . . ."

"Man in black? What man in . . . ?"

". . . the club and then walked to the boat . . ."

"I was nowhere *near* the boat, nowhere near the cl—"

"Didn't you board the Toland boat at eleven-fifteen that night?"

"No, I didn't!"

"Didn't you shoot Brett Toland at eleven-forty?"

"No!"

"Then where were you at that time, Bobby?"

"In my car! On the way back to Sheila's condo."

"From where? Where the hell were you for two and a half . . . ?"

"I went to see Brett. But not on the boat. I didn't know he was on the boat. He was home when I called him, I thought that was where I'd find him."

"You went to the Toland house?"

"Yes. I wanted that tape back. If Brett . . ."

"Why?"

"Because I didn't want him to use it unless he fucking well *paid* for it!"

"There are other copies out there, you know. He could easily have . . ."

"Good, let him go find them! Meanwhile, a judge was making his decision and Brett knew he'd stolen the bear! If he wouldn't deal with me, then I wanted that fucking *tape* back!"

He nodded angrily, took a long swallow of the drink.

"That's why I went there that night."

"What time did you get there?"

"Around ten. He wasn't home. Etta told me . . ."

Etta tells him her husband has gone to the boat.

Bobby figures he'll catch him there. It's only ten, fifteen minutes from their house to the club. But then she tells him he's gone there to meet *Lainie*. So he asks Etta if Brett happened to mention a videotape to her. No, he hadn't. What videotape? Well, did he happen to be *carrying* a videotape when he left the house? No, she doesn't know anything about a videotape. What videotape?

He tells her what it is.

Idle Hands.

Lainie Commins's busy little hands.

He tells her about the deal he offered Brett, a lousy ten percent of the gross, is that a lot? As a finder's fee? People get more than that for finder's fees, Etta. But now Brett was going to bypass him and use the tape, anyway. That isn't fair, is it, Etta?

Etta tells him she's sure he's mistaken.

Brett is going to offer Lainie a flat five thousand dollars in settlement.

That's why he's meeting her on the boat.

That's what he plans to propose to her.

She doesn't know anything about a videotape.

"So it suddenly occurred to me," Diaz said, "that maybe he *didn't* take the tape with him, after all, maybe it was still there in the house someplace. Maybe he really *didn't* think he could use it, the shmuck, or maybe he was saving it as an ace in the hole in case Lainie turned down the flat five, who knew? So I asked her did she know where he might *keep* such a tape if

377

there was such a tape?"

Diaz drained his glass.

"We went into the den, where their television set is, and their VCR, and all their stereo equipment. This is now maybe twenty to eleven, I'd been there forty minutes already. We searched through all their videos, but we couldn't find *Idle Hands* — though there were some other porn flicks there, which Etta knew about, and which she didn't find embarrassing, by the way. I asked her if they had a safe. I figured if Brett planned to use the tape later, then maybe he'd put it away someplace secure. I wanted to get out of there already, it was at least a forty-five-minute drive back to Sheila's, but I didn't want to leave if there was a possibility the tape was still there. I wanted that *tape*."

"*Did* they have a safe?"

"Oh yes. Upstairs. Etta went up to check, and five minutes later . . . this is now a quarter to eleven, around then . . . she comes down with a videotape, but no case. The cassette is there, but it's not in the little black vinyl case. She tells me this is the way she found it, at the back of their safe, and I say Well, that must be it, don't you think? and she says There's only one way to find out. So we played it. Just enough to confirm it was Lainie doing her thing."

"Then what?"

"I told Etta I wanted the tape, please. She said she was sorry but she would first have to ask Brett if he'd already paid me anything for it. So I thought Oh yeah? Well, fuck *you*, lady. And I told her."

"Told her what?"

Diaz nodded.

A small satisfied smile crossed his handsome face.

"That until last Christmas her husband was having an affair with Lainie Commins."

12

Warren was telling her the guy upstairs had a gun. Toots was translating what the guy upstairs was yelling. He wanted a poncho. He was getting soaked up there, bring him a fucking poncho. She was thinking if they took the guy out, she'd have a gun and eight kilos of coke.

The rain was one of those hard hasty squalls that came on you suddenly and made you think you were going to drown. They seemed worse when you were on a boat because suddenly the entire world was overwhelmed by water. Thing about them was that they didn't last long. Even so, the guy upstairs kept yelling for a poncho. Bring me a fucking poncho, Luis!

Warren whispered the plan to her.

Fatback Key is in Calusa County, but it is not within the city limits of Calusa itself. Instead, it falls within the boundaries of Manakawa to the south. It is the wildest and narrowest of the county's several keys, flanked on east and west by the Gulf and the bay, two bodies of water that during the hurricane season sometimes join over Westview Road, the two-lane blacktop that skewers Fatback north to south. The bridge connecting Fatback to the mainland is a humpback that can accommodate only one car at a time. Directly over the bridge is a large wooden signpost with two dozen arrows pointing off either left or right, the names of the key's residents carved into the wooden arrows and then painted in with white. The name DEMMING was on one of those arrows; Patricia lived on Fatback. The name TOLAND was on another arrow.

Bobby Diaz had estimated that it was a forty-five-minute drive from Sheila's condo on Whisper to the Toland house on Fatback. Driving fast, in light off-season traffic, I made it from Diaz's condo on Sabal in an hour and ten. I had not called ahead. I was hoping Etta Toland, a recent widow, would be home and not out dancing. There were lights on in the house, a sumptuous, architecturally pristine bayside mansion that opened westward past gulfside dunes to yet another glorious Calusa sunset. A greenish-black Infiniti was parked on the driveway's white gravel. I parked the Acura alongside it. It was twenty minutes past seven.

I walked through the evengloam stillness of a lush tropical garden flanking the path to the front door. Somewhere a cardinal called. The light was fading fast. I rang a doorbell over the discreet brass escutcheon with the name *Toland* etched upon it in black script lettering. The cardinal fell silent. The sky over the Gulf turned purple and deep blue and blue-black and black. A single star appeared.

"Who is it?"

Etta's voice behind the door.

"Matthew Hope. May I come in?"

There was a moment's hesitation. Then: "Is this allowed?"

"I believe so."

"Just a minute."

Silence.

At last the door opened.

Etta Toland was wearing a clay-spattered blue smock over jeans and sandals. Her sleek black hair was pulled to the back of her head, tied there with a short red ribbon. She had a towel in her hands, and she was still wiping the left hand clean when she opened the door. Rumor had it that she was a sculptor. Then again, in Calusa every other person you tripped over either sculpted or painted or wrote plays or . . .

"What is it, Mr. Hope?"

"I'm sorry if I'm inter—"

"You are."

"*May* I come in?"

"Why?"

"There are some things we need to discuss."

"I'm sure this isn't permitted."

Dark eyes angry and suspicious. Standing there in the doorway, head erect, shoulders back, barring entrance.

"I can come back with a subpoena for a deposition," I said.

"Then maybe you ought to do that."

"I'd prefer we talked informally."

"All right," she said, "come in."

I stepped into the foyer. She closed and locked the door behind me. I was in a tiled entry that seemed an extension of the lush garden outside, tubbed flowering plants and trees everywhere, many of them taller than I was, some of them squatting low on the earth-colored floor. I followed her past a shallow pool in which golden carp swam, moved with her through wide windowed corridors toward where a light showed in the otherwise dim interior of the house.

Her studio — a huge room skylighted and windowed to show a star-drenched sky — faced eastward toward the bay. There were clay models of female nudes of various heights on stands and tables and platforms. The one she'd apparently been working on when I arrived was a life-size nude captured in midstride, arms swinging, left leg stepping out, right leg back. She began draping it with wet cloths. I had the sudden image of someone covering a birdcage at nightfall.

"Mrs. Toland," I said, "Bobby Diaz told me he was here on the night Brett was killed. Is that correct?"

"Is it correct that he told you? Or is it correct that he was here?"

"Etta," I said, "let's not play games. I think you killed your husband."

"Do you?"

One eyebrow arching over a dark, almond-shaped eye. The Dragon Lady. Calm and cool and spattered with clay, her hands deftly draping rags over the clay figure that stood almost as tall as she did.

"Diaz came here looking for a videocassette, didn't he?"

"Did he?"

Same cool look. Hands working as busily as Lainie's had on the tape in question.

"Which you found in an upstairs safe."

"Did I?"

Infuriatingly cool. Hands wrapping the clay in the wet cloths. Wrapping the arms of the nascent torso, and the legs, and the breasts, and the head. Wrapping. Studiously wrapping. Studiously ignoring me. Icily ignoring me.

"You watched the tape together," I said.

No answer now. Her entire attention focused on the clay model, wrapping it like a mummy, wet cloths enveloping it, enclosing it, smothering it.

"You confirmed that one of the women on the tape was Lainie Commins."

Still no answer. Still working. She dipped her hands into a basin of muddy clay water on a table beside the platform. Rinsed them. Dried them on a clay-smeared towel. Folded the towel neatly. Placed it on the table beside the platform bearing the mummy-wrapped woman in full stride. Turned away from basin and towel and mummy and me. Began walking out of the studio.

"Etta," I said.

"I think we're finished here, Mr. Hope."

"It was Matthew once."

"When we were friends."

"Etta, what did you do after Diaz left here that night?"

No answer. Still walking toward the studio's open entrance frame, a woman in full stride, like the piece she'd been sculpting.

"Etta, he left here at about ten to eleven. What did you do then?"

"I went to sleep."

"I don't think so."

"It doesn't matter what you think."

"It does if I can prove you were on that boat the night your husband was killed."

"I *was* on the boat that night. *After* he

385

was killed. I found his body, remember, Mr. Hope?"

"Did you go back to the boat after that night?"

"No."

"Never?"

"Never."

"Then how did the cassette get there?"

She stopped just inside the doorless frame. Thought it over for a moment or two. Turned to me.

"Bobby took it with him," she said.

"No, he didn't."

"That's his word against mine."

"Not if he wasn't on the boat that night."

"Then he must have been."

"I don't think so."

"Still his word against mine," she said again, and shrugged airily, and was turning toward the open door frame again when I said, "The cassette holder was empty at eleven-thirty."

She hesitated again.

Stopped in midmotion, partially turned toward me, partially turned toward the door frame and the immense house beyond.

"So?" she said.

"Bobby was on his way back to Whisper Key at that time. He got there shortly before midnight. I have a witness to that effect. He couldn't have been on the boat after Lainie left it. And the cassette holder

386

was *empty* at that time."

"Who says?"

"Lainie says."

"Lainie killed him."

"No."

"Yes."

"No. The cassette was here in this house at ten minutes to eleven. Lainie never had it in her possession. Eight days after the murder, I found it on the boat. You just told me you never went back to the boat. So how . . . ?"

"I also told you Bobby took the cassette with him when he left here that night."

"I don't think so, Etta. I think *you* carried that cassette to the boat. I don't know why you did that. Maybe you'd like to tell me."

"Please, this is absurd."

"No, Etta. I think you went to the boat to confront your husband. I think you . . ."

"*I* think you should leave."

"I have a witness who saw you," I said.

She looked at me.

"Going aboard at a quarter past eleven."

She kept looking at me.

"Do I have to get a court order for a lineup?" I asked.

And suddenly she was weeping.

The first thing Juan saw was her blond hair.

Squinting through the torrential rain,

barely able to see the boat's running lights, he clung fiercely to the wheel and yelled again for Luis to bring him a fucking poncho. White fisherman's shirt plastered to his big barrel chest now, pistol tucked into the waistband of his soaking-wet chinos, he yelled "Luis!" again, and saw the blond head coming up from below.

Warren was sliding open the bathroom window.

Juan's mouth fell open.

Truly fell open.

He watched her coming up from below, slow languid glide up the ladder, tight black skirt and black high-heeled shoes, wrinkled yellow blouse, where the hell *had* she come from?

Warren was crawling out onto the narrow deck outside the window. Rain beating down everywhere around him. Gripping the stainless-steel grab rail as he ducked low and crawled back toward the wheel.

"How you doin, man?" Toots said in the sultriest voice she could muster, considering that she could see the outline of the nine-millimeter gun where the guy's shirt was plastered to his belly. Big Glock on a big bearded guy who could tear her in half even without the piece. She wanted that gun. She wanted the eight keys of cocaine. That was the only thing on her mind right now. Take the guy out, get hold of the gun, find the coke.

He was turned toward her now, away from the wheel. Never mind the wheel, never mind the boat, or the storm or anything but the beautiful blonde slithering toward him through the rain like some kind of wet sea serpent, Come to me, baby.

Warren was coming to him, too, baby.

But Toots kept her eye on Juanito here, sidling toward him, not giving him the slightest hint that Warren was about to drop in uninvited, licking her lips instead, narrowing her eyes like some kind of screen siren of the thirties, *Sí, come to me, querido,* Warren almost in place, lust and greed and sheer joyous amazement at his good fortune all shining together in Juanito's eyes as he lurched toward her through the driving rain. A moment too late, he realized that someone had dropped into the cockpit behind him. He was starting to turn when Warren's clenched fist smashed a hammer-blow to the base of his skull. Stunned, stumbling forward, belatedly realizing he'd been tricked, he grabbed for Toots and she said, "Sí, *muchacho,*" and took him into her embrace and brought her knee up into his groin.

He went for the nine.

Doubled over in pain, yelping in Spanish, he fumbled under the wet shirt for the stock of the gun, but Warren was on him now, grabbing him in a choke hold he'd learned on the St. Louis P.D., dragging him down to the deck, and then releasing him suddenly, kicking him unceremoniously in the head, and then kicking him once again for good measure. Juan was out of it.

Toots knelt and yanked the nine from his belt.

"Good," Warren said.

"Where'd they stash the shit?" Toots asked, and leveled the gun at him.

Skye Bannister himself, the elected state attorney for the Twelfth Judicial District of the State of Florida, was present at the deposition I took at ten o'clock that Thursday night in my office on Heron Street. Also there were Assistant State Attorney Peter Folger, my partner Frank Summerville, and Sidney Brackett, the very same copyright attorney who was defending the infringement case for the Tolands. Why she had called *him,* rather than a criminal lawyer, was beyond me. But she was here to confess — or so she'd led me to believe — so perhaps she just wanted to get it over and done with.

Skye Bannister does not like me, nor does he like the fact that I am romantically involved with one of his best prosecutors. What Skye *does* like is the governor's mansion in Tallahassee, and there are frequent recurring rumors that he will run for that office in the next election, or the one after that, or the one after that. Meanwhile, he is still here, and he is still a blond blue-eyed pain in the ass who looks a lot like Dan Quayle. Given that Brackett looked like a pudgier Newt Gingrich and Folger a skinnier Phil Gramm, all we needed was a video technician who looked like Bob Dole, but unfortunately the technician was a woman, and she looked like a beautiful redhead in her twenties who was pissed off because she'd been called at home while she was watching television.

Etta Toland kept weeping intermittently as she was sworn in. I led her swiftly through the preliminaries of identifying herself, asked her to tell me where she lived, asked if she and I hadn't had a lengthy conversation at that same address earlier tonight, and then asked if she'd be willing to repeat for me and for the camera — in the presence of her attorney and the gentlemen from the State Attorney's Office — essentially what she'd told me earlier. She said she had no objections.

Brackett sighed.

Etta dabbed at her eyes.

She had changed her clothes before we'd left the house on Fatback, and was wearing now a pair of simple tailored slacks, a beige blouse to match, and low-heeled pumps.

Her black hair was combed sleek and straight to her shoulders. Her eyes, wet with tears, looked luminous and large. The redhead looked at her watch. We began.

Q: To begin with, can you tell me whether or not you were present when your husband called Lainie Commins and asked her to meet him on your boat?

A: I was.

Q: What time was it that he called her?

A: At about nine o'clock.

Q: Did he call from the house?

A: Yes.

Q: In an earlier deposition, you said that he'd called her from the boat. Are you revising that now?

A: He called her from the house.

Q: Did you have opportunity to overhear that conversation?

A: I heard what he said to her.

Q: And what was that?

A: He told her he wanted to discuss a settlement. Said he didn't want to drag lawyers in just yet. Wanted to discuss this face-to-face, just the two of them. But not on the phone. He said he wasn't going to compromise her case at all, this wasn't a trick.

Q: Did he say he was already on the boat?

A: Yes.

Q: Then he was lying.

A: Yes. He wanted to lend urgency to it. Wanted to make it seem he was already there waiting, eager to make a deal. She agreed to meet him, said it would take her an hour or so to get there.

Q: You didn't hear her say that, did you?

A: No. Brett repeated it to me. Before he left the house.

Q: What time did he leave the house?

A: A few minutes after the phone call. Nine-fifteen? Thereabouts.

Q: How long does it take from your house on Fatback to the Silver Creek Yacht Club?

A: Ten, fifteen minutes. Depending on traffic.

Q: So he would have been there no later than . . . well . . . say, nine-thirty?

A: I would say so.

Q: Mrs. Toland, you told me earlier tonight, did you not, that a man named Bobby Diaz came to your house on the night of the murder . . .

A: Yes.

Q: Sometime after your husband left for the boat.

A: Yes.

Q: At around ten that night, isn't that so?

A: Yes.

Q: Can you tell me who Bobby Diaz is?

A: Design chief for Toyland.

Q: Was he aware of the infringement suit Lainie Commins had brought against the firm?

A: He was.

Q: Did the matter of this suit come up at all while he was in your house that night?

A: It did.

Q: Can you tell us what was said about it?

A: He said he'd given Brett a videotape.

Q: What sort of video?

A: A pornographic tape.

Q: Did it have a title?

A: *Idle Hands*. It's four women masturbating. Lainie Commins is one of the women on the tape.

Q: How did Bobby happen to give this tape to your husband?

A: He said it would help him win his case. He wanted a finder's fee for it. Ten percent of whatever we grossed on the teddy bear.

Q: By the teddy bear . . .

A: Gladys. *Our* bear. The one Lainie claims we stole from her.

Q: Had your husband agreed to give Bobby this ten percent?

A: No. That's why he was there. He wanted the tape back.

Q: Did you know anything about this tape before he mentioned it to you?

A: Nothing.

Q: Had you ever seen it?

A: Never.

Q: Ever watched it?

A: Never.

Q: Did you even know of its existence?

A: No, I did not know of its existence.

She began crying again. The Republican look-alikes looked patient and supportive. The angry redhead looked bored. I offered Etta a box of Kleenex. She blew her nose, dabbed at her eyes, wiped her cheeks. She brushed a strand of hair back from her face. She raised her chin. Her eyes met mine. They were clear and intent and alert. We resumed.

Q: Did Bobby Diaz ask you to look for that tape?

A: He did.

Q: And did you conduct a search for it?

A: Yes, I did.

Q: Did you eventually find it?

A: Yes. In our bedroom safe. Just the cassette. The case was gone.

Q: What time was it when you found the tape?

A: About a quarter to eleven.

Q: Then what?

A: We watched a little of it. To make sure it was the right one. Because the case was missing, you see. The black vinyl case they come in. There was no way of identifying it.

Q: *Was* it the correct tape?

A: Yes. Lainie was on it.

Q: You watched it for how long?

A: Oh, no more than a minute.

Q: Then what happened?

A: Bobby wanted it back. I told him I wouldn't give it to him. Because I thought maybe Brett had paid him for it, after all, and this was just some kind of trick.

Q: What did he say to that?

A: Nothing. He just left.

I looked at her.

The room was silent except for the whirring of the video camera. I glanced at Frank. His nod was almost imperceptible.

"Mrs. Toland," I said, "excuse me, but didn't you tell me earlier tonight that your refusal to give Diaz . . . ?"

"I told you earlier tonight exactly what I'm telling you now."

"Didn't you tell me that he . . . ?"

"I told you that he left the house."

"Didn't he say something to you *before* he left the house?"

"Yes, he said good night."

"What else did he say?"

"Nothing."

"Didn't he tell you that until this past Christmas, your husband was having an affair with Lainie Commins?"

"No, he did not."

"And wasn't it this that caused you to . . . ?"

"Do I have to answer any more questions?" she asked, and turned to Brackett.

"Not if you don't choose to," he said.

"I don't choose to," she said.

"Where?" Toots said. "Where'd they put it?"

"I don't know what you're talking about," Warren said.

"The eight keys, Warren. Where?"

"I don't know anything about . . ."

"I was in the john when they came aboard with it. Where'd they put it?"

"I never saw it."

"Warren, I'm going to shoot you."

"Go ahead."

"You know where that coke is, Warren."

"This is the first I'm hearing of it."

"Tell me, or I'll shoot you."

"You see this man here?" Warren said, and jerked his head toward where Juan lay motionless and silent on the deck. "Three minutes after they came aboard, he hit me with that gun you're holding in your hand there. I never saw anybody bringing any dope onto this boat."

"You're lying."

"I'm not."

"Fuck you, then, I'll find it myself."

"Go right ahead."

She went down the ladder. The rain kept pouring down. He shook his head, sighed, and went to the wheel. He could hear her storming around belowdecks, banging cabinet doors, tossing around pots and pans, whatever. He sighed again. Some ten minutes later, she came topside again.

"Where is it?" she asked.

"I don't know."

She began searching through the storage bins on either side of the boat, tossing aside life jackets and lines, rags, a billed cap. Lifted the lid to the bait locker. Felt around under the ice and the beer cans. Warren held the boat steady. The rain kept slashing the deck. She came to where he was sitting, gestured with the gun toward the closed compartment under the dash, just above his knees.

"Move," she said.

"It won't drive itself," he said.

"Then open that."

He thumbed the button in the drop-front lid. The lid fell open. He saw at once a yellow oilskin-wrapped package wedged inside the compartment among the charts and a flashlight and a cigar box and a whistle.

Eight keys, she'd said. Two point two pounds to a kilo, ask any schoolboy. Seventeen and a half pounds of the white lady, give or take.

"Give it to me," she said.

"No," he said, and slammed the compartment shut, and raised his knee against it as if to tell her it was going to *stay* shut. Right knee wedged against the drop-front lid. Rain sweeping in over the boat, slicing back to where they stood side by side, the gun steady in Toots's hand, and the wheel steady in his.

"Warren," she said, "this isn't a joke here."

"I know that, Toots."

"Then move away."

"No."

"Warren, I need that."

"No, you don't."

"Don't tell me what I fucking *need* or *don't* need!"

"Toots . . ."

"Don't force me to *hurt* you, Warren!"

She peered at him through the fiercely falling rain, her eyes squinted, her hair plastered to her head, her clothes drenched, water streaming down her face. He wasn't sure whether that was just rain on her face or whether she was also crying. He didn't think she would shoot him, but he wasn't sure of that, either. The gun was trembling in her fist.

"Warren . . ." she said, "please."

"Toots . . ."

"Please, Warren . . ."

"Toots . . ."

"Please."

He sighed heavily.

He thumbed open the compartment. Reached in. Took out the package wrapped in yellow oilskin. Slammed the compartment shut. She realized what he was about to do even as he started doing it. She reached for him as he turned, reached for the package in his hands, was still reaching for it as it left his hands, reaching across him to rescue it, salvage it, snatch it from the rain and the night as he hurled it over the side of the boat into the sea.

Her shoulders slumped. She stared disconsolately into the rain and suddenly began crying. He rose and put his arm around her. Still holding the wheel with his free hand, he pulled her gently close to him.

"Toots," he said, "let's go home now, okay?"

She could not stop sobbing.

"Toots? Can we go home now?" he said.

Deep wracking sobs that broke his heart.

"Okay, Toots? Can we please go home?"

She nodded weakly.

"Toots? Okay?"

She nodded again.

He held her close in the rain.

13

"Well," Bannister said, "that was one hell of a confession, Matthew."

"Look," I said, "you know me well enough to . . ."

"Oh, I know you well enough," he said.

He was impeccably dressed in a hand-tailored blue tropical suit with a faint green shadow stripe. Blue shirt. Green tie. Highly polished black shoes. He and his wife had been having dinner with a state senator when he took my call. I'd told him I had a confession in the Toland murder case. I'd told him I wanted to do a videotaped Q and A in my office.

So here we were.

And Etta Toland had recanted.

Pete Folger, who looked like Phil Gramm and sounded like Phil Donahue, looked at his watch. His expression said this had been a waste of time and he wanted to go home to his wife and kiddies in time to catch the eleven o'clock news. Skye Bannister, who looked like Dan Quayle and who, in fact, sounded like him, was wearing an expression that said he knew me well enough to realize I was smart enough not to have dragged him down here if I didn't have what is known in the trade as "real meat," in which case why the hell *was* he here?

"Matthew," he said, "I'm going to assume she told you something you wanted us to hear . . ."

"Didn't sound that way to me," Folger said.

"Pete," I said, "she *recanted*. What the hell's wrong with you?"

"What's wrong with me is we've got your lady cold and you're dragging in somebody you *claim* . . ."

"He's not stupid," Bannister said sharply.

"What?" Folger said.

"I said he's not *stupid*. Make that mistake, and you're in trouble. What'd she tell you, Matthew? And what do you want us to *do* about it now that she's turned her back?"

"He told her just what I said he told her."

"Who? And what?"

"Bobby Diaz. Said her husband broke off his affair with Lainie Commins this past Christmas."

"And?"

"You want it exactly the way she told it?"

"I'd be much obliged," Bannister said.

She doesn't know quite how to answer Bobby's accusation.

It's not something that hasn't crossed her

402

mind before, the hours Brett and Lainie spend together late at night, poring over designs at the office, the possibility has occurred to her. She supposes Lainie is an attractive woman, in a lost-waifish sort of way, if that kind of thing appeals to you. Brett has always had a roving eye, but his taste runs more to sleek, sophisticated women. Still, it's entirely possible that what Bobby is telling her is true, though she won't reveal this to him by even the faintest flicker of recognition on her face, the tiniest glimmer of suspicion in her eyes. Instead, she tells him to get the hell out of her house, and the moment he's gone she calls the boat.

"This was now about ten to eleven," I said. "In her earlier deposition, she told me she called the boat at eleven forty-five. That was to cover her tracks."

Calls the boat at ten to eleven and gets no answer.

Wonders why he isn't answering the phone.

Wonders if he's already on the way home.

In which case, why hasn't he called to say how the meeting went?

Wonders then why he asked Lainie to meet him on the boat in the *first* place. Instead of here at the house.

Wonders why he didn't even *mention* this hot little tape in his possession, his hot little bimbo doing herself for all the world to see, wide open.

Has he been watching his hot little tape in private?

Does it recall memories of his hot cross-eyed little bimbo, wantonly spread and energetically enticing?

Does she excite him to tumescence?

Incite him to action?

Meet me on the boat again, hmmm?

Wonders, in fact, if his cockeyed little bitch isn't doing herself right there on *Toy Boat* right this very *minute*, doing *him* in the bargain, shouldn't be a total loss, no wonder no one's answering the phone.

She decides that if this is true . . .

If he really *did* have an affair with Lainie . . .

If he is *still* having an affair with her . . .

She will kill him.

It is a decision she makes in the snap of an instant.

She will kill him.

As simple as that.

In the state of Florida, you do not need a license to purchase and own a gun. Or guns. There is a Colt .45 automatic aboard *Toy Boat* and there are two guns in the Toland household, one of them a Walther P-38, which Brett keeps in the nightstand on his side of the bed, and the other a .22-caliber Colt Cobra, which Etta keeps in the nightstand on her side. Her gun is fully loaded. Six-shot capacity. She plans to shoot her husband with it, if what Bobby Diaz told her is true.

There is no question about this.

It is a firm decision.

If he is cheating on her, she will kill him.

Toward that end, she dresses for the part before leaving the house. Pulls on a pair of black tights and a black leotard. No bra. Black Nike running shoes. Takes from her closet a black silk cape she wore over a long black gown to the Snowflake Ball last Christmas. *Until last Christmas, your husband was having an affair with Lainie Commins.* Finds a sassy black slouch hat she bought at Things Amiss on St. Lucy's Circle not a month ago. Pins her hair up. Puts on the cape and the hat and looks at herself in the mirror-lined wall of the bedroom she may now be sharing with a philanderer. She looks like the Phantom of the Opera. The walnut stock of the Cobra feels cool to her touch. The fifteen-ounce gun is light in her hand. She drops it into a black tote, drops the cassette into it as well, and slings the bag over her shoulder. Gloves. Remembers gloves. Basic black needs basic black gloves. She finds a pair she bought in Milan last September, soft black leather, slips into them. Looks at herself in the mirror again. Yes, she thinks.

Her greenish-black Infiniti J30 is parked in the driveway outside. She loves the name Nissan has given the color: Black Emerald. She fires up the engine.

The time on the dashboard clock is 11:10 P.M.

This time of night, with no traffic on the road, she makes it to the club in ten minutes flat.

Her car is known here. She cannot have it recognized and later remembered, not if what Bobby Diaz told her is true, not if she is going to kill her husband. She plans to confront him with the tape. Ask him why he kept the tape from her. Ask him if it's true that . . .

Is it *true?*

Is it?

Ask him.

She parks the car on the shoulder of the road outside the club. Moves in the shadow of the trees inside the stone wall, black as the night, her hands beginning to sweat inside the buttery-soft silk-lined gloves. The black leather tote bangs against her hip as she works her way toward the parking lot. She is starting across it, out of the shadows, when . . .

A white Geo.

Parked under the single lamppost at the far end of the lot.

Lainie's car.

The time is eleven-twenty.

Etta nods bitterly.

Strides determinedly across the lot to the boat. The dock is silent. The boat is silent. As she moves swiftly up the gangway, past the empty cockpit, she hears cries from below, the unmistakable sounds of a woman moaning in ecstasy, hears a woman's *voice* now, Give it to me, yes, Lainie's voice, yes, do it, *do* it, and there is no longer any need to ask her husband anything at all.

She will kill him.

She is starting down the ladder leading to the saloon when she hears their voices again. He is reminding her of the tape he now has in his possession. He is telling her the tape can be very damaging to her career. He is suggesting that she might care to drop her infringement suit before all of kiddieland learns about that tape.

——What are you saying, Brett?

——I'm saying drop the suit or I'll send copies to every company in the field.

——What?

——I think you're hearing me, Lainie.

——Five minutes ago . . .

——Yes, but . . .

——You told me you still *loved* me!

——I know, but drop the suit.

——You son of a bitch!

——Drop the suit, Lainie.

Etta almost loses her resolve. If he lured Lainie to the boat only to threaten her with exposure if she didn't . . .

In which case, why did he make love to her?

In which case, why did he tell her he still loved her?

——You told me you still *loved* me!

——I know, but drop the suit.

She hears more angry words from Lainie, hears her shouting she'll *never* drop the suit now, go to Ideal, go to Mattel, go to *hell,* you rotten bastard, and realizes she's about to leave the stateroom, her voice is at the stateroom *door,* she is hurling these last words at him as she storms out. Etta knows this boat, knows every corner of it, every curve. There is a head adjacent to the saloon, and she slips into that now, closes the door swiftly behind her, and listens, waiting.

Her wristwatch reads eleven-thirty.

There are footfalls rushing past in the passageway outside, hurried footfalls moving through the saloon and onto the ladder leading above. The gangway creaks under Lainie's weight as she goes ashore. Etta stands still and silent behind the bathroom door, listening for the sound of a car starting, but she hears nothing. Has she gone? Has she really gone? She waits.

Her watch reads eleven thirty-five.

At last, she opens the door.

From the stateroom at the far end of the passageway, she can hear the sound of the shower running. Good, she'll do a *Psycho* on him, kill him in the fucking shower. Her hand dips into the shoulder bag. Her fingers find the Cobra. Tighten around the walnut stock. She comes down the passageway. The stateroom door is open. The shower is still running. She comes stealthily into the room. Kill him in the shower, she is thinking. And sees several things on the bedside table. Brett's side of the bed. Sees all these things in the very next instant.

Sees the time on the digital bedside clock. 11:38.

Sees an empty black vinyl cassette holder. *Idle Hands.*

Sees a woman's scarf lying on one of the upholstered stateroom chairs.

Blue scarf, red-anchor design.

And sees Brett's pistol.

Everything suddenly comes into clear, sharp focus.

She smiles.

Actually smiles.

And drops the Cobra back into the tote.

The digital clock reads 11:39.

The shower stops.

She moves swiftly to the side of the bed, picks up the forty-five in her gloved right hand. The bathroom door opens. She turns toward it. Brett is wearing only a towel. His eyes open wide in surprise.

"Etta?" he said. "What . . . ?"

Her first shot misses him.

The next two take him in the face.

The digital clock on the bedside table reads 11:40.

Before she leaves the boat, she slips the cassette into its holder, carries it across the room to the bookshelves holding similar cassettes and places it there in plain view. Let them find it, she thinks. Let them link it to Lainie's scarf and conclude she was here to get the tape from him. Let them link it with *this*, she thinks, and tosses the forty-five onto the bed. She looks down at Brett where he lies bleeding on the carpet, the towel open now, his penis looking shriveled and shrunken and small.

Good, she thinks, and leaves the boat.

She drives home in twelve minutes.

Gets there at eleven fifty-five.

Changes her clothes.

Leaves the house again at midnight.

Is back at the club again by twelve-sixteen.

Which is when she discovers her husband's body.

"She told you all this, huh?" Folger asked.

"Yes," I said. "I wouldn't have brought her here otherwise."

"Too bad she wouldn't repeat it," Skye said.

"Too bad," I said.

"What do you want from us, Matthew?"

"Drop the charges against my client . . ."

"No way."

". . . pending full investigation of Etta Toland."

"Can't do that," Folger said, shaking his head.

"Why not?"

"Make us a laughingstock," Skye said.

"And suppose we come up empty?" Folger said.

"How can you?" I said. "Get a warrant to search her closets. The night watchman saw someone dressed in black . . ."

"She may have burned the clothes by now," Skye said.

"Subpoena her phone bills. In her deposition, she told me she called the boat at eleven forty-five, and got to the club at twelve-sixteen. Instead, she *really* placed the call . . ."

"How does that prove she killed him?" Folger asked.

"It proves she's a liar."

"So? You never lie?"

"Pete, I've got her calling the boat at ten to eleven, and leaving the house ten minutes later. Dressed to kill, I might . . ."

"No," Skye said. "The phone bills may

411

show when she called the boat, but they won't show when she left the house. That's all in your head so far."

"It's in *her* head, too, Skye."

"If it is, she's not letting anybody else in there."

"How do you see the timetable?" Folger said.

"Full cast?"

"A to Z."

"From the top?"

"From minute one."

I took a lined yellow legal-sized pad from the top drawer of my desk. I picked up a pencil and began writing.

9:00 PM: Bobby Diaz calls Toland.

"Toland tells him to buzz off," I said. "Says he doesn't need the tape."

9:05 PM: Toland calls Lainie to invite her to the boat.

"He called her from *home*," I said. "Not from the boat as Etta later claimed."

"Why would she lie about *that?*"

"She lied about *everything*, Skye. She *killed* him."

"So far, I have no evidence of that. Let's see the rest of the timetable."

I began writing again.

9:10 PM:	Diaz leaves for Fatback Key.
9:15 PM:	Toland leaves for the boat.
9:30 PM:	Toland arrives at the boat. Lainie leaves for the boat.
10:00 PM:	Lainie arrives at the boat. Diaz arrives at the Toland house.
10:45 PM:	Werner spots Lainie and Toland on the boat. Etta finds the videocassette in the Toland safe. Lainie and Brett move to the boat's bedroom.
10:50 PM:	Diaz leaves the Toland house. Etta calls the boat, gets no answer.
11:00 PM:	Etta leaves for the boat.

"Here's where it begins to get speculative," Skye said.

"Bear with me," I said.

"None of this jibes with the deposition you took on the eighteenth," Folger said.

"She was lying under oath, Pete."

11:10 PM:	Etta arrives at the club, parks on roadside shoulder.
11:15 PM:	Etta spots Lainie's parked Geo. Night watchman sees Etta boarding the boat.
11:20 PM:	Etta discovers Brett and Lainie in bed together.
11:30 PM:	Lainie leaves the boat. Witnesses report seeing car parked on road.

11:35 PM:	Etta starts for stateroom.
11:38 PM:	Etta enters stateroom.
11:39 PM:	Brett comes out of shower.
11:40 PM:	Etta shoots him.
	Bannermans hear shots on Toland boat.
11:43 PM:	Etta heads home.
11:55 PM:	Etta arrives home, changes clothes.
12:00 AM:	Etta leaves for boat again.
12:16 AM:	Etta arrives at boat, "discovers" body.
12:20 AM:	Etta calls the police.

"The rest of her story is true," I said.

"I ask you again, Matthew. What do you want us to do?"

"You know what he wants," Frank said. "He wants you to stay all proceedings until you further investigate Etta Toland. That's what he wants."

"Show me a way out," Skye said.

"You've got the black clothes . . ."

"Maybe."

". . . and a witness who saw her going aboard twenty-five minutes before the murder," Frank said. "You've got her lying about Brett calling Lainie from the boat instead of the house, where she overheard the call. You've also got her lying about when she *herself* called the boat. You've got witnesses who saw a dark, expensive car parked on Silver Creek Road, which is where she herself told Matthew she . . ."

"What she told Matthew doesn't interest me!"

"She says she didn't get to the club till twelve-sixteen. Witnesses saw this dark, expensive car between eleven-thirty and midnight. Etta drives a dark green Infiniti. That puts her at the club while the murders . . ."

"You call that reliable?" Folger asked. "A half-hour time span?"

"Gentlemen, I need proof," Skye said. "You can't expect me to . . ."

"Will tire tracks do?" I asked.

"What do you mean?"

"Matching tire tracks?"

"Do you *have* matching tire tracks?"

"I have a cast of the track found where the witnesses say they saw the car."

"Does the track match the tires on Etta Toland's car?"

"I don't know yet."

"Well, when you *do* know . . ."

"You can find out quicker than I can, Skye."

"Oh? How can . . . ?"

"The police department's been sitting on the cast since Wednesday."

"Who's got it?"

"Nick Alston."

"Find him," Skye snapped.

Folger went to the phone.

"If we get a match . . ." I said.

"You get a stay," Skye said.

We got a match.

Nick Alston reported that he'd heard from the FBI late that afternoon, and that the tire in question was a Toyo A05 all-season, steel-belted radial tire in size P215/60R15 manufactured by Toyo Tire and Rubber Company Ltd. as standard factory-issued equipment on Nissan's Infiniti J30 luxury sedan — the car Etta Toland drove.

Pete Folger merely asked for a court order to seize the car.

The rest was a piece of cake.

Patricia, I said, there are things we have to talk about. I know I have a reputation for being a sensitive, understanding, violin-playing, macho-loathing male, but I have to tell you I learned a great many things about myself after my accident — if you can call getting shot an accident — and I'm not sure the person who got out of that hospital bed is the same person who . . . no, please let me finish.

To begin with, I no longer have any patience with stupidity. I cannot abide stupid people. Nor can I abide amateurs. I'm not saying you're a dumb amateur, don't misunderstand me. In fact, I respect and admire you as a highly intelligent professional, which is really the only sort of woman I've ever been involved with . . . well, that's not entirely true, I *have* known some pretty dumb broads, to tell the truth, and if you take exception to the use of that word, I can tell you here and now I don't give a damn. Anyway, that was in another country, and the wench is dead, so to speak. That was then and this is now, and what we're talking about, Patricia, is *now.*

So if I seem impatient with the *trivia* of life and living, it's because I was in that valley, Patricia, I was walking in the valley of the shadow of death, and there was no one walking beside me, no one who'd gladly bear the cross of extinction for me. I wandered all alone in that valley with the clouds gathering black on the horizon, I came *this* close, Patricia, and I don't ever want to come that close again. Ever.

So, yes, I may be cranky and grouchy these days, I may be a fucking *grizzly,* I may be short-tempered with all the ignorant, insolent, intolerant, self-centered, self-righteous, abusive, oblivious, suspicious, distrustful, blithely unaware people who would enjoy nothing better than to impose *their* narrow views and beliefs upon *me,* who would love to limit *my* right to choose a path appropriate to *my* needs and *my* wishes — which are very strong these days, my needs and wishes, I can tell you that, Patricia, very strong. I see things a lot more clearly now, Patricia. Getting shot did that to me. Coming close did that. I don't care *who* marches in the St. Patrick's Day parade. I just don't want to march in any parade but my *own.*

Which brings me to what I've been trying to express for the past four months now, ever since I got out of the hospital, but which for a lawyer who's been called glib at times, I've had a difficult time putting into words. I have to tell you I've been noticing other women, Patricia . . . no, please, no objections, counselor, let me finish, please. I've been noticing their legs and their thighs and their breasts, I sound like someone ordering a bucket of fried chicken, I know. And I know it's politically incorrect and possibly sexist to take notice of a woman's parts, but I really don't care about political correctness anymore, I don't care about *any* labels anymore. In fact, I find them boring. In fact, they piss me off.

A lot of things piss me off these days.

My own mortality pisses me off.

Patricia . . .

What I'm trying to say . . .

I'm okay now.

I've been okay for the past four months.

I want to make love to you.

I want you to stop feeling I'm not quite whole, I want you to stop thinking of me as an invalid. I was there, Patricia, but I'm back.

I'm here now.

I'm alive.

Can we start again?

Please?

"Okay," she said.

On Monday, the twenty-fifth of September, a hot, sunny, sticky Rosh Hashanah morning, Judge Anthony Santos handed down his decision in the *Commins v. Toyland, Toyland* copyright, trademark, and trade dress infringement action. It read in part:

> Since the early 1900s, millions of teddy bears have been sold worldwide by thousands of different manufacturers. Teddy bears trace their name to Theodore "Teddy" Roosevelt, the 26th president of the United States.
>
> Shortly before Christmas in the year 1902, the President took his family away from Washington on a four-day bear-hunting trip in the state of Mississippi. Although he was a skilled hunter, his fortunes ran against him, and the only bear he had an opportunity to shoot was a

cub trapped in a tree. He chose not to take advantage of the poor frightened creature.

This episode was widely reported and became the basis of a cartoon by Clifford K. Berryman, which appeared in the *Washington Post*. Berryman later drew the bear in many other cartoons, utilizing the cuddly little cub as a symbol for the President. It was not long before an enterprising toy manufacturer brought out a stuffed toy in the cub's image. Dubbed the "Teddy" bear, after the President, it immediately captured the public imagination.

Elaine Commins moves for preliminary injunction, alleging that Toyland, Toyland's *Gladys* the Cross-Eyed Bear ("the Toyland bear") infringes her company's *Gladly* the Cross-Eyed Bear ("the Commins bear"). Commins's complaint contains three counts. Count I is a copyright infringement claim under the United States Copyright Act. Count II is a trademark infringement claim under §32(1)(a) of the Federal trademark law. Count III is an unfair competition or trade dress infringement claim under §43(a) of the same statute.

Toyland moves for summary judgment on all three counts.

Impatiently, I began scanning the document.

. . . after examining the Commins and Toyland bears, the Court makes the following findings regarding Commins's assertions of substantial similarity:

(1) Commins contends that both bears are identical in size, shape, color and fur length. The bears are roughly the same size, approximately nineteen inches in height, although the Toyland bear is noticeably fatter and heavier. There is nothing unusual about this. In fact, teddy bears of this size are the most popular among consumers, and thus are produced . . .

I kept turning pages . . .

. . . asserts that both bears are cross-eyed and both wear corrective eyeglasses. This is true, but the button eyes on the bears are very different, as are the eyeglasses themselves. On the Toyland bear, the eyes are almost completely hidden by fur. On the Commins bear, the eyes are larger, more visible and better defined, with dark irises and white pupils. The Toyland eyeglasses are simple plano lenses behind which straightened eyes have been painted. The Commins eyeglasses make use of mirrors to . . .

And turned yet more pages . . .

. . . are the very same features that are so inherent in the abstract idea of a teddy bear that they are not subject to copyright protection. Based upon these findings, the Court concludes that the Toyland bear's "total concept and feel" is significantly different from that of the Commins bear, and no reasonable juror would find the Toyland bear substantially similar to the Commins bear. Accordingly, Toyland's motion for summary judgment on Count I is granted.

My heart sank.

Count II alleges trademark infringement . . .

I kept searching ahead.
And once again . . .

. . . upon these findings, the
Court concludes that no reasonable
juror would determine that there is
any likelihood of consumer confusion
between the trademarks Gladys and
Gladly. Accordingly, Toyland's motion for summary judgment on Count
II is granted.

I took a deep breath.

Count III alleges unfair competition,
or more specifically, trade dress
infringement. Here again, and despite
the superficial similarities of
crossed eyes and corrective eyeglasses, the Court finds that no
reasonable juror would conclude that
there is any likelihood that an
appreciable number of ordinarily pru-
dent purchasers are likely to be
misled, or indeed simply confused, as
to the origin of the two bears.
Accordingly, Toyland's motion for summary judgment on Count III is granted.

And finally . . .

Plaintiff's motion for preliminary

injunction is denied.

Defendant is entitled to judgment as a matter of law.

Judgment is entered *for* the defendant Toyland, Toyland and *against* plaintiff Elaine Commins.

Some you win, some you lose.

NOV 1 5 1996